The Col Rancher's Doorstep Bride

STAND-ALONE NOVEL

A Western Historical Romance Book

by

Nora J. Callaway

Disclaimer & Copyright

Table of Contents

The Colorado Rancher's Doorstep Bride 1

    Disclaimer & Copyright...2

    Table of Contents 3

    Letter from Nora J. Callaway................................5

Prologue 6

Chapter One...14

Chapter Two...23

Chapter Three...34

Chapter Four...46

Chapter Five...57

Chapter Six 65

Chapter Seven 77

Chapter Eight 84

Chapter Nine 91

Chapter Ten...100

Chapter Eleven 111

Chapter Twelve 117

Chapter Thirteen 124

Chapter Fourteen 134

Chapter Fifteen...140

Chapter Sixteen 148

Chapter Seventeen....................................153

Chapter Eighteen.......................................159

Chapter Nineteen......................................166

Chapter Twenty 173

Chapter Twenty-One 188

Chapter Twenty-Two 195

Chapter Twenty-Three 200

Chapter Twenty-Four...207

Chapter Twenty-Five 211

Chapter Twenty-Six 219

Chapter Twenty-Seven 227

Chapter Twenty-Eight 235

Chapter Twenty-Nine 243

Chapter Thirty 251

Chapter Thirty-One..259

Chapter Thirty-Two...267

Chapter Thirty-Three 277

Epilogue 284

Also by Nora J. Callaway......................................291

Letter from Nora J. Callaway

"How vain it is to sit down to write, when you have not stood up to live." —*Henry David Thoreau*

I'm a lover of nature in the mornings and a writing soul at nights. My name is Nora J. Callaway, and I come from Nevada, the beautiful Silver State.

I hold a BA in English Literature and an MA in Creative Writing. For years, I've wanted to get my stories out there, my own 'babies' as I like to call them, inspired by my own experience leaving out West and my research of 19th-century American history.

All my life, I have been breeding horses, cows, and sheep, and I've been tending to the land. It's time to tend now to my inner need to grow my stories, my heart-warming Western romance stories, and share them with the rest of you!

I'm here to learn and connect with others who enjoy a cup of black coffee, a humble sunset, and a ride with a horse! Bless your hearts, as my nana used to say! Come on, hop in!

Until next time,

Nora J. Callaway

Prologue

Crested Butte, CO

April 1897

Rough planks scoured his sunburned back, stinging it with splinters. He was sliding... no, he was flying, free-falling through pine-scented air. His skin scraped clear of the coarse wood as the wagon plummeted out from under him. His heart gave a great lunge of terror.

Leon woke, flailing, surrounded by screams. His mother's, his father's, his sister's... Even the horses were screaming. His own scream was cut off abruptly as he crashed through the canvas wagon top into cold, cutting rain and slammed into a tree. His body bent like a ragdoll and he bounced off, slamming into the stony ground.

The wagon loomed over him, tipping toward him. He could neither move nor breathe as it fell. It crashed down on his outstretched leg and continued to slide down the mountainside, twisting and dragging him with it.

Pain such as he had never known ripped through him as the ligaments in his leg stretched and tore. Leon screamed through gritted teeth, the sound almost inhuman in his own ears. Blinded with rain, pain, and terror, he threw his hands out to both sides, feeling them scrape through mud and stone.

One hand closed around a sapling, sticky with sap. Or was it blood? His body yanked to a halt. The wagon continued on, releasing his leg with a final, cruel wrench. Another wordless scream of pain tore from his throat as he felt flesh and bone separate. Sobs heaved through his chest, and hot tears joined the cold rain in pouring down his face.

It's a dream. Somehow, the thought pierced the pain and chaos and terror.

But it felt real. It all felt terribly, terribly real.

Leon's fingers slipped on the sapling. Desperately, he rolled onto his stomach, grabbing with his other hand to keep himself from following the wagon. Behind him, he could still hear it crashing and tumbling on down the mountain to the boulders far below, carrying the bugling horses with it. Carrying his family...

"No!"

Leon twisted, still dangling from the sapling, still battered by the rain. Thunder rumbled, drowning out the echo of his family's cries. He watched in helpless horror as the wagon toppled end over end, crashing through the evergreens.

It hit the bouldered valley floor and shattered. He closed his eyes, ducking his head against his chest. Fresh, painful sobs billowed through him, shaking his body like a bough in the wind. The rain sluiced into his face, and his fingers slipped once more on the sapling.

"Pa!" he screamed through his tears. "Ma! Ruby!"

His heartbeat became nothing more than a throb of pain and grief. He could feel the will to hold on draining from his body with each one. His grip gave way, and he fell after his family, through the dark...

Leon's eyes flew open. He threw himself upright with a gasp.

The pain was real, clawing at his leg and heart like an angry badger. The tears streaming down his cheeks and the sound of his own ragged sobs were real.

It was all real.

But it was also a dream.

The walls of his room slowly came into focus, gray smudges in the early morning darkness. Outside, thunder rumbled distantly, barely louder than the rain pattering on the roof and plinking into the bucket under the leak in the corner.

Leon unclenched his hands from the bedclothes twisted around him. Leaning forward, he buried his face in his palms. The sobs continued to come. He still felt ten years old, still felt the horror of what had happened as if he was in the midst of it.

He rocked forward, groaning at the bone-deep pain that shot up his leg like a spear.

Then, he felt the tremor.

His bed was moving slightly, rumbling under him like a wagon bumping over a mountain path.

He lifted his head, still struggling to be sure what was real and what was imagined. The house shuddered around him. Dust from the ceiling beams brushed his cheeks and nose, settling on his eyelashes.

"Leon?"

The tremulous call was followed by a tap on Leon's bedroom door.

"Leon, are you awake?"

Leon blinked away the dust.

"Yeah!" he choked out through the emotion that still clogged his throat. He threw away the blankets, swinging his legs over the side of the bed.

"Yeah, just a minute."

Grabbing the trousers he'd left on the floor when he'd gone to bed, Leon stepped into them. He grimaced, easing them over his knees and hips and buttoning them. Then he limped as quickly as he could to the bedroom door and tugged it open.

Ruby's face was ashen in the light of the oil lamp she clutched. Her hand trembled as she lifted it and looked up at him, wide-eyed.

"Did you feel that?" she asked breathlessly. "The shaking? What was it, Leon?"

Her brown eyes glimmered with frightened tears. Leon reached up, dashing any remnants of the same from his own eyes before reaching for her.

"It's okay," he said. "I think it was just—"

The plank floor trembled once again beneath their feet and the roof creaked above them. Ruby yelped and nearly dropped the lamp. Leon took it from her. His heart pounded as he put an arm around her and turned her toward the end of the hallway.

"I think it's an earthquake," he finished. "We should get out of the house."

Ruby wrapped a thin arm around his waist, cowering into his side.

"An earthquake?" she whimpered. "Is the house going to fall? Leon?" Her voice quavered upward at the end, culminating in a little shriek as another tremor made both of them stumble.

Leon didn't answer. He just clutched the lamp with whitening fingers and hurried both of them down the shuddering stairs as quickly as his stiff leg could handle.

The dogs were already at the door, whining and pacing. Piper was cocking her head from one side to the other as a low rumble sounded. Her ears were perked, and her expression was puzzled. Shell flattened her ears when she saw Leon and Ruby, wagging her tail anxiously. Crocket scratched at the door, growling low in his throat.

"All right, pups," Leon mumbled, wading through them to open the latch. "Just get out of the way."

He opened the front door. The dogs clustered about them as he and Ruby hurried across the front porch and into the wet grass of the front yard. Thankfully, the storm seemed to be at an end. The rain had slowed to a drizzle, and the horizon was faintly gray with the coming dawn.

Beneath Leon's bare feet, the ground felt solid, as it always did.

A rooster crowed from the henhouse, and a sheep answered with a low baa from the barn. The world stood still and peaceful, as if it had never shaken. But Ruby was still trembling in Leon's arms. And he still felt unsteady on his legs. Piper trotted across the yard, her nose to the ground, her tail waving slowly above her haunches. Crocket followed her while Shell stayed close to Leon's side, watching.

The lamp sputtered in the slight rain.

"Is that it?" Ruby whispered. "Is it over?"

She tilted her face upward to look at him, her brows still scrunched with anxiety.

"I think so." He tilted his head, indicating the cluster of oaks around the porch. "Listen, the birds have started singing again. They always stop during a quake."

A robin trilled from the branches, joined halfway through his song by another. From the aspens along the pasture fence, a mourning dove cooed its own solemn tune.

Once he really started listening, the thick chorus of morning chirping and trilling and cooing was almost overwhelming.

"Damn, we have a lot of birds around here," he muttered.

Ruby gave a faint, hiccupping laugh. She twisted out of his arm and turned to face him. Leon resisted the urge to pull her safely back to his side. He studied her familiar, half-annoyed face as she stared up at him. Her eyes, the same chocolate shade as his own, flashed up at him. She reached up to tuck a stray tendril of matching brown hair behind her ear, her eyebrows crinkling.

I came so close to losing her, he thought. The dream was still vivid in the back of his mind, like a disaster just out of sight around some corner. He could feel his heartbeat quickening again just at the memory of it, and a lump rose in his throat.

"How are you so calm?" Ruby demanded. "We just had an *earthquake.* You're acting like that's something that happens every day!"

"Not every day," Leon agreed. "But we've had them before. Don't you remember?"

Focusing on a slightly more recent memory helped him push the dream further back into the dusty corners of his mind. Where it belonged. He managed a crooked half-smile as Ruby scowled up at him, unconvinced.

"There was that one time at dinner... when we still lived with the Harringtons. You must have been at least eight. That quake shook the dishes in the cupboard," he reminded her. "Mr. Harrington told us it was because this part of Colorado is over a fault line."

He paused, trying to remember the details.

His sister continued to scowl up at him, looking unconvinced.

"It's something about... titanic plates or something."

Finally, Ruby shrugged.

"I don't remember much from our childhood," she said. "You know that."

She reached up and tapped a finger to the scar that ran from her temple up into her hairline.

Leon suppressed a shudder. That kind of thing was exactly what he *didn't* need to be reminded of this morning.

Realizing it was light enough now for him to make out her features without the sputtering lamp, he cupped a hand around the glass chimney and blew it out.

Ruby turned toward the house. She had her arms wrapped around her waist, hugging herself in a way that was familiar. It hurt Leon a little to see the gesture; Ruby had done it ever since she was little when she felt unsettled. Even if she didn't remember.

"Is it okay to go back in now?" she asked. "You're sure it's over?"

She twisted back to give him a worried glance over her shoulder.

"Yeah. You should be fine," he said gently.

"Good. Because it's about time I got ready and headed to work anyway."

As if determined to put her fright behind her, she hurried away from him, up the steps and into the house.

Leon watched her go. A cool breeze blew across his shoulders, reminding him that he hadn't taken time to pull on a shirt before rushing outside. His bare feet were also growing cold against the rain-wet earth. But before he followed his sister in, he turned back toward the eastern horizon.

It was blushing pink. The rain had stopped completely now, and the breeze was sweeping the sky clear of the lingering traces of gray cloud cover. It was going to be a beautiful day.

The peaceful scene was completely at odds with the heavy feeling that still sat in his stomach.

Almost as if the dream was an omen.

The thought crossed his mind and firmly lodged before he had a chance to avoid it. Grudgingly, he let it complete itself.

We're about due for something bad to happen.

He shook his head, hating the pessimism that had become a permanent part of his character since he was only ten years old. Mrs. Harrington had always assured him that eventually he would grow out of it, but fifteen years had only served to embed it deeper into his personality— and he knew why.

It was because he was always right.

Turning back to the house, he took the steps purposefully, as quickly as his leg would allow. He tapped on Ruby's closed bedroom door as he passed it.

"I'll drive you into town today," he raised his voice to say. "Just give me a minute to get ready and hitch the horses."

He heard the beginnings of a muffled protest through the thick wood, but he hurried on before Ruby could burst out and question him about it.

Better safe than sorry. That was all he could think right now.

13

Chapter One

Kansas City, Missouri

April 1897

It was good. The best she'd ever done.

At least, she thought it was.

Myra bit her lip, tilting her head to get a better look at the painting propped on the easel before her. Murky sunlight spilled through her bedroom window and lit the stern, gray eyes of the woman on the canvas.

The likeness was accurate enough that Myra felt her heart skitter a bit in trepidation. Although she'd done her best to capture her adoptive mother in her warmest expression, she still found herself quailing beneath the piercing gaze and running through the list in her mind to be sure she hadn't forgotten any of her chores.

No, she'd done them all. She'd purposefully left wiping all of the floors 'til last so she could leave the bucket in her room and touch up after her painting session.

Myra let a slight, nervous laugh huff from between her lips.

Stupid, she thought. *That's what I am. Just like Mother is always saying. I'm sitting here being afraid of a portrait I just finished painting.*

Still, it took a moment for her to gather the courage to wipe her fingers on her smock and stand up to remove the canvas from the easel. She turned toward the bedroom door, her emotions a confusing mixture of anticipation and dread.

She hoped that her mother would love the portrait. That she would accept it as the token of respect it was intended to be. But there was always the possibility that Edith Barnes would resent something about it. Whatever it was, she would, of course, think Myra had done it on purpose. Which would lead to further unpleasantness.

Myra's step faltered just outside the kitchen door as she mentally calculated the probability of things going either way. Was it worth risking her mother's anger for a chance at a few moments of her attention and praise?

She had nearly made up her mind to turn around and carry the portrait straight back to her room when she heard a swift, heavy step behind her. She spun around. Her adoptive mother was directly behind her. Her thin lips were pursed, her eyebrows lifted above her gray eyes.

"Myra, dear, what have I *told* you about lurking outside of doorways?" she said sternly. "It makes you seem all kinds of shiftless. And we've taken such pains to raise you out of that."

Myra felt her face flushing, something her fair skin did easily . She tucked the painting behind her back, feeling not only foolish now, but guilty.

"I'm sorry, Mother," she said. "I was just coming to speak with you."

"Well, I was just coming to speak with *you*," Edith said. "Come into the kitchen and take a seat, please."

Despite her adoptive mother's even tone, Myra felt her stomach flip. Was she in trouble? Once again, she racked her brain for anything she had done or failed to do in recent days. Once again, she came up empty. She and her parents had been existing rather peacefully for quite a while now. Perhaps that should have made her wary of something coming up soon, but most of the time, Myra tended toward optimism.

She tried to feel optimistic now as she followed her mother into the kitchen and took a seat at the table. She kept the portrait on her lap, hidden under the edge of the table. Since her mother had expressed no interest in seeing it, she decided against showing it to her until she did.

"Myra, your father and I have been talking some things over ever since you celebrated your twenty-first birthday last month," Edith began, folding her hands on the table.

Myra focused on her mother's perfectly manicured nails to avoid spouting the thought that immediately sprang into her head. "Celebrated" was an interesting word for how she had spent the day of her twenty-first birthday. Edith had decided it was a perfect day for spring cleaning; Myra had spent most of it washing windows, scrubbing out corners, and beating rugs.

She shook the disgruntled thought from her head, doing her best to concentrate as her mother continued.

"We believe it is high time for you to be married, and we have chosen a suitable match."

Edith said the words in the same calm, even tone she always used. For a moment, Myra thought she had misheard her. She blinked, listening uncomprehendingly as her mother continued.

"Mr. Walshman and your father have come to an agreement. You are to be married next month."

Once again, the word "married". It dawned on Myra that her mother meant every word she was saying. Heat flooded her body, followed by a strange chill.

"*I* am to be married?" she whispered. Her lips felt numb. They barely moved. "To whom?"

"Myra, darling, how many times have I told you to listen when I'm speaking to you?" Edith scolded. The lines of her face hardened as she frowned across the table at Myra. "*Yes*, you are to be married. To *Mr. Walshman.*"

She emphasized the words in an irritated cadence, but Myra was past feeling the fear she would have usually felt at her mother's tone. Her shock was now liberally mingled with horror.

"But Mr. Walshman is... old!" she exclaimed. She realized her mistake too late as she watched Edith's face blanch with anger.

"Myra," the woman snapped. "Of all the rude, ungrateful, insensitive things to say! I can't believe what I am hearing right now."

She rose to her feet and pushed back her chair with a forceful movement that made Myra wince.

"Mr. Walshman is a respected member of our community, and he is *very* well-off. The fact that your father was able to arrange this marriage for you is an honor and a blessing. You should be in his study right now, hugging and kissing and thanking him for what he's done."

"Why should I be?"

Myra couldn't seem to stop the words from flying off her tongue. All her childhood training, and all the punishments she'd received over the years for sassing her mother seemed to have been swept entirely out of her brain by the sick dread that the thought of marrying their elderly neighbor brought to her.

"I don't want to be married!" she exclaimed. "And I especially don't want to be married to... someone I don't even care for."

"Who you do or don't care for has nothing to do with this," Edith rapped out. "Why do you think we raised you so carefully, girl, with all of the accoutrements of the most coddled of children? Why do you think we saw to it that you received an exemplary education, drilled into you manners and obedience, paid for your piano lessons and painting lessons?"

The horror of it all kept getting worse. Myra felt she was in a nightmare as she rose to meet her mother. Edith swept around the table and stood in front of her, hands on her narrow hips.

"You sound like... you're listing the traits of a carriage horse you want to sell," Myra gasped finally. Her voice sounded thin and shrill with stress in her ears.

Slowly, raggedly, her thoughts and her mother's words were falling into place.

"Is Mr. Walshman *paying* you to marry me?"

She saw the answer on her mother's face. In that moment, Myra's already fragile world came tumbling down around her. She didn't even notice as the portrait slid from her fingers and crashed to the floor at her feet. She didn't hear the words that Edith was spitting at her as she shook her finger in her face. She was deaf, blind, frozen in place.

"I'm not going to do it." The words came out clear and firm despite the chaos whirling through her brain. As her vision cleared, she saw the shock register on Edith's face.

"You are our daughter, Myra," the woman snapped, "living under the protection and care of our household. You will do it if we say so."

"I'll leave," Myra breathed. "I don't know where I'll go, but I'll live in the streets before I marry a man twice my age who's buying me like some unwanted animal!"

She only realized that the hot, surging emotion filling her body was anger as it poured out in those fierce words. Now that she'd acknowledged it, she realized she was shaking with fury.

How could her parents —the people she had trusted and honored as best as she knew how for all of her remembered life— do this to her?

Under the anger was a hollow, deep and black and cold, that told her the answer.

What she had always suspected was true. The Barnes had never loved her. And they never would. To them, she had been a duty, perhaps even a trophy of their kindness and ability to shape a human being into who they thought she should be.

Would it have been different if she'd actually been their own child, by flesh and blood? She would never know. All she knew was that she had been lying to herself every time she had convinced herself that if she was obedient enough, talented enough, pretty enough, polite enough... they would love her.

Hot tears flooded her eyes and trickled down her cheeks. She barely noticed as Edith grabbed her arm just above the elbow, squeezing it hard enough to bruise, and whirled her around. She dragged her down the hall just as she had countless times when Myra was a girl. Her hard, angry voice pelted down like hail.

"...will be here for dinner, and you *will* be polite to him, and you *will* accept his marriage proposal."

"I'm leaving," Myra murmured again. She felt light-headed, almost as if she was floating outside of her own body.

"You're not leaving this house until the wedding," her adoptive mother countered harshly. "Even if we have to keep you locked in your room until then!"

As she said it, she pushed her daughter through the door of her room, hard enough that Myra stumbled. She tripped on the hem of her skirt and fell in a heap, catching herself with her hand. Her wrist twisted and burned. Her tears fell harder and faster as she looked up at her mother.

Edith stomped a couple of steps into the room, bent forward, and slapped Myra hard across the cheek.

Myra gasped through her sobs. Her hand flew to cover the wet, stinging skin as the woman straightened up.

"You are acting like a complete brat!" her adoptive mother railed. "And I won't have it. This is not who I raised you to be, Myra Barnes. Now, if you don't straighten up and pull yourself together before dinner, you won't have any dinner at all. We'll tell Mr. Walshman that you are ill but that you are very grateful for his proposal and will be there at the wedding. A week from today, girl. Wrap your head around it and get used to it. Your father and I have given our word. There's no changing it now."

With that, her mother turned and swept out of the room. She pulled the door firmly shut behind her, and Myra heard the familiar sound of the key turning in the lock.

A sob catching in her throat, Myra's gaze dropped to her own reflection in a mirror leaning against the wall next to the door. The mirror had been a birthday present from the girls in the catechism class she taught— a delightful surprise that had left her in happy tears when they presented it to her. Her father had not yet gotten around to hanging it for her, and now she knew why. Because he did not plan on her living in this house for much longer.

Her reflection appeared to her as someone she didn't know, a girl she immediately pitied. Unruly ginger hair spilled from the lopsided bun on the top of her head, hanging in ringlets against her pale, tear-streaked cheeks. The look in her green eyes was pleading, as if even now, her mother might take pity on her.

But it was too late for that.

Myra was on her feet in an instant. She didn't even wait for her mother's footsteps to fade down the hall as she had in her girlhood days. There was no more time to wait. She turned, searching wildly about the room.

Looking through the eyes of one betrayed, she realized how very few of the things in the room actually felt like her own. She would take clothes, she decided, but only because they were needed and she had sewn most of them herself. She would take the Bible she had been given when she started catechism as a girl, and she would take the little book of poems Alice, the parish priest's sister, had given her soon after they became friends.

She would take her pencils and her paints because she wasn't sure she could live without them. But she would leave the canvases on their wooden frames. She would leave the porcelain dolls with their painted faces her mother had always cautioned her not to soil or break as a girl. She had hardly played with them for fear of doing one or the other. And she would leave all of her other books, and the hair ribbons, and the crystal vase on the dresser where she kept flowers all summer long.

Had any of it ever really belonged to her? Or had it all been on loan until she was old enough and well-trained enough to auction off to the highest bidder? The bitter thought brought fresh tears to her eyes, but she refused to linger over them. She had to get out of here— before her father and Mr. Walshman arrived.

She had no bags or luggage, so she settled for a set of pillowcases from the bed. She flew about the room, stuffing everything she had decided to take into the two linen pouches. Then, she tied them together with a stocking and slung them over her neck, letting one hang down over each shoulder.

Her anger and despair gave her strength, driving her forward with an almost blind momentum. Her tears had dried completely by the time she went to the window and slid it open. Tucking her skirt up over the crook of one elbow, she expertly swung a leg over the sill, feeling with her booted foot for the first limb of the maple that grew just outside the window. The limb was waiting for her, where it always had been, firm beneath her sole.

Myra gave one more glance around the tiny room that had been both her sanctuary and her prison for twenty-one years. Then she set her lips in a firm line and climbed down the tree.

Chapter Two

Crested Butte, CO

Seated stiffly in the prickling hay, Leon gently cupped the newborn lamb's tiny face in his hand.

"Come on, little guy," he murmured. "If you don't figure this out soon, all the good stuff is going to be gone."

The soot black ram lamb bleated as Leon guided his velvet nose toward the ewe's teats. The ram's twin sister, a white lamb, was already suckling greedily, her tail flapping back and forth with vigorous joy. The ewe, an experienced mother, munched nonchalantly on her own dinner, staring into the middle distance with a tired expression Leon fully related to.

Outside, the dogs went into a short flurry of barking. A moment later, there was a quiet rumbling sound as the barn door slid open. The cool night breeze slipped through it, ruffling Leon's hair.

"Hello? Leon, you out here?"

Leon didn't answer, wary of startling the new mother or the suckling lambs. The little ram had finally latched on. Leon could feel the excitement in his little body as warm milk flooded his throat. He released a deep breath, unaware until that moment that he had been holding it.

Footsteps sounded behind him, scuffing the barn floor.

"Ah... there you are."

Leon looked up to see Adam Reid, the town doctor, standing in the lantern light just outside the sheep pen. The brawny man was wearing a pin-striped shirt and brown trousers and suspenders. His chestnut hair was slightly wind-tossed, but his mustache was, as always, impeccably tidy.

"Ruby sent me out here to see why you were late for supper," said the doctor. He nodded toward the new lambs. "I guess they answer that question."

Leon checked once more to make sure the ram lamb was continuing to nurse. Then he grabbed the side of the pen and stood up. He stifled a groan as the anticipated pain spiked through his leg. Adam's shrewd expression showed that he had noticed just the same.

"Yeah. The little black sheep is already causing trouble," Leon joked quickly to avoid the doctor's comment. "He couldn't figure out how to eat, and his little sis was about to get all the first milk."

"First milk is important for all babies," Adam agreed. "You think he's okay now?"

Leon glanced down once more and saw two happily wagging tails. He felt a smile turn up the corners of his mouth.

"Yup. He should be good. I'll check on him again a few times during the night."

Adam huffed out a chuckle, stepping out of the way as Leon swung the gate open and shuffled out of the sheep pen.

"That's something a doctor and farmer have in common," he said ruefully. "Hardly ever a full night's sleep, right?"

"Right," Leon sighed. "At least during lambing." He grabbed the lantern from its nail on the beam beside the pen and started toward the door. "Did you drive Ruby home from the clinic then?" he asked as Adam fell in step beside him.

"I did. We had an emergency just before she was about to head out— the Nobel boy cut his hand oiling a hay machine," the doctor explained. "Ruby insisted on staying to help me sew him up and it was getting dark by the time we finished. I didn't want her out on the road by herself after the sun went down."

Leon nodded. "I appreciate it," he said simply. He led the way out into the chilly darkness of the late evening. Once Adam had stepped out, Leon pushed the door closed behind him, latching it.

"Ruby invited me to stay for dinner," Adam added, sounding half apologetic. "She said you wouldn't mind."

"Ruby does the cooking. She's welcome to invite anyone she wants to partake of it."

Leon was conscious of the doctor slowing his step to not outpace his more halting steps as they headed to the house. He tried not to let it bother him. Instead, he focused on moving forward more quickly.

As the two men entered the lamplit warmth of the house, they were greeted by the savory scent of roasted chicken, potatoes, and carrots. Adam took a deep, appreciative breath. Leon held the door for the dogs before closing it behind them.

"Hmm," Adam mumbled. "That smells amazing." He wandered back into the kitchen as Leon sat on the bench by the door and worked to get his boots off.

"Well?" he heard Ruby say.

"He's here," Adam replied. "He was helping a new lamb figure out how to suckle."

Leon finally managed to get the boot off his left foot, always the harder one since he couldn't really bend that knee, and limped into the kitchen. Ruby was pulling a pan of biscuits from the oven. She wore an apron over her dress, and her face was flushed with the heat. She looked around as he entered and smiled.

"Another lamb?" she asked. "How many is that this season?"

"Twins," he replied. "And that brings us up to twenty-five. They're the last ones."

"Ah, good." She set the biscuits on the table and pointed to the chairs. "Lambing season being over means you'll have time to actually eat and sleep now, right?"

"Hey, I eat everything you cook," Leon protested mildly. He took a seat and Adam sat across from him, leaving the chair at the end of the table for Ruby. "Maybe not always right *when* you cook it, but eventually."

Ruby and Adam exchange a look. It was the briefest moment, and if Leon hadn't looked up when he did, he would have missed it. Something shifted inside of him. Uneasiness. Then, Ruby sat down beside him, and the moment passed. It felt too late to say anything or to ask what the matter was.

A slight awkwardness fell over them as they served their plates and began to eat. For a moment, there was no sound other than the clinking of the silverware and the quiet hiss of the oil lamps.

The quiet would usually not have bothered Leon. The doctor was not a common guest in their home —guests in general were not common— but both Leon and Ruby were on familiar enough terms with him to be comfortably silent together.

Tonight, there was just something about it that made Leon feel tense.

"This is delicious, Ruby," Adam said after a moment. Then, to Leon, he said, "You're lucky you have your sister to cook for you. Most bachelors like us have to make do with our own cooking. And let me tell you, I for one have never developed the knack."

"Well, I don't cook like this every night," Ruby said, smiling. "Especially not on the days I'm working at the clinic. Then on days I'm home, there's so much to catch up on, I tend to just throw something together..."

"Whatever she makes is always good," Leon cut in stoutly.

He was conscious of a lingering strangeness to Ruby's manner. Despite having left the heat of the stove, she was still flushed, and uncharacteristically reserved. Adam, too, kept stealing an occasional anxious glance in her direction.

Leon put down his fork. Before he could ask if something was wrong, though, Ruby spoke quickly.

"We passed the old Harrington place on the way in. It looks like whoever bought it has moved in."

If she had intended to sidetrack Leon, it worked.

"I saw a man out walking around the barn today," she continued, "and there was a horse in the paddock. I didn't see a woman, but it seems likely he's married, right? Buying an entire farm like that."

"I was surprised you didn't put an offer in for the place yourself," Adam said quietly. "What with the Harringtons raising the two of you for all those years, I figured it would still feel a little like home."

"It does," Leon admitted shortly. "And I did put in an offer, but I was outbid. We don't have that much to spend right now."

"I'm sorry," the doctor said.

Leon shrugged. He didn't want anyone's pity now, just as he hadn't wanted anyone's pity all those years ago as a proud, orphaned ten-year-old.

What the Harringtons had offered was not pity. Leon still wasn't sure what to call it. Love? But he could never explain to himself why exactly their elderly neighbors should have loved him and Ruby like they did. They had stepped in like grandparents, taking the two children under their own roof and taking over the running of the Sanders ranch until Leon was old enough to carry on alone.

Leon had no idea where he and Ruby would be now if it hadn't been for them.

"I hope there's a woman," Ruby said. "I would love to have a close neighbor. Even if..."

She stopped abruptly. Once again, the swift look passed between her and Adam.

Leon had had enough.

"What?" he said. "What are you two not telling me?"

Adam immediately looked uncomfortable. Ruby patted her lips with her napkin, avoiding his gaze.

"Oh, it's just something we were talking about on the way out here this evening," she said quietly.

"I want her to start working at the clinic full time," Adam blurted. "Six days a week."

Ruby gave him an exasperated look. He shrugged, his handsome features coloring slightly.

Leon looked from one to the other, processing what such a thing would mean.

"I told him I couldn't," Ruby said. Her gaze finally fluttered upward to meet Leon's. "I already barely have enough of the day left to put a meal on the table when I get back on the three days I do work. If I worked the other three, I'd have time for almost nothing outside of driving to town, working there, and driving back."

"Which is why I offered her the cottage behind the clinic," Adam said. He addressed Leon directly, leaning his forearms eagerly against the table. "It's meant to house the doctor," he explained, "but as you know, I live in the house I inherited from my parents. Ruby wouldn't have to drive at all if she lived there."

Leon looked from Adam to Ruby, unsure of what to say. He felt blindsided by the disclosure that the two had been talking about such a huge change without even consulting him.

"It was just a conversation, Leon," Ruby said gently. "Don't look so worried. I wouldn't just go off and leave you like that."

Her voice was soft, but it struck a strange note of irritation in Leon's stirred emotions.

"I wasn't worrying about me," he said sharply. "I was worrying about you. I wouldn't feel good about you living in town all by yourself."

Ruby lifted her chin, giving him a level look. "It's perfectly safe," she said.

"How do you know that?" he insisted.

"Why would it not be?" Her voice sharpened to match his own. "You're always so paranoid, Leon."

"Well, maybe that's with good reason," he snapped.

Immediately, he regretted it. Ruby's cheeks paled, and her lips tightened.

"I'm not a little girl anymore, Leon," she said after a breath. "I've moved on from that. And you should too."

She stared across the table at him, her deep brown eyes stormy with a collision of care and frustration.

Pierced by her words and gaze, Leon looked away.

In doing so, he caught sight of Adam. The doctor was watching Ruby, caught unaware, and the expression on his face was one of undeniable affection.

Reality crashed over Leon like snowfall off the roof in January. He was buried in it, forced to not only acknowledge it but feel the sting of its harsh truth.

Ruby *was* going to go off and leave him eventually. It was inevitable. She was a beautiful, capable woman with dreams and aspirations. Whether they took the form of single-mindedly pursuing her career —as she had for many years insisted they would— or shifted to include a husband and family of her own someday... as hard as it would be to let go, he would never stand in the way of that.

Lying on the rug a few feet from the dinner table, Piper suddenly lifted her head. She looked toward the door, her tail swishing slowly across the floor. Shell and Crocket, who had been sprawled sleeping nearby, immediately sat up as well. Crocket stood up and trotted across the room. He put her nose to the crack of the door.

A moment later, all three dogs exploded into a cacophony of barks.

"Hey! Hush!" Leon said sharply. The dogs obediently fell silent, but they continued to stare at the door, their bodies stiff and their ears alert. Leon stood up and crossed to the door. He opened it, and all three dogs immediately dashed out, bumping him in their haste.

There was a basket sitting on the top step of the porch, barely lit by the light spilling out around him. Piper and Crocket ran past it and out into the darkness, but Shell stopped and stuck her nose in among the blankets spilling from the basket. Her tail began to wag.

Frowning, Leon grabbed a lamp from the table in the entryway and limped across the porch toward her. He was almost to the basket when the blankets moved. The movement was accompanied by a faint whimper. Leon's stride faltered, and he nearly tripped.

"Whoa, it's something alive," he heard Adam say from behind him. "Puppies maybe?"

"Oh no," Ruby replied. Her tone was a mixture of compassion and distaste. "That's how we got the three dogs we have now. I don't think we can handle any more. Do you, Leon?"

Leon didn't answer. He lifted the lamp, scouring the ring of light that it created. The dogs were already circling back. Apparently, they had been unable to pick up the trail of whoever had left the parcel.

He returned his attention to the basket. Bending with a quiet groan, he grabbed the blanket between two fingers and pulled it back.

Two eyes blinked up at him, huge and blue-green and surrounded by dark lashes. The eyes were set in a tiny, heart-shaped face topped with soft, dark curls. Leon felt his jaw drop slightly as surprise shot through him. The baby's bottom lip popped out and trembled.

"Leon?" Ruby said. She came up beside him. A gasp escaped her lips.

"What is it?" Now Adam was crowding close with the two of them, craning his neck to get a look. "Is that..."

"Do you recognize it?" Leon asked. His mind was racing, completely at odds with the calm, distant sound of his own voice.

"Who, me?" Adam asked.

"Either of you," Leon said shortly. "You're the town doctor and nurse. If any baby has been born around here recently, wouldn't you two know about it?"

"I... yes, I think so."

Ruby knelt down, stroking a gentle finger over the baby's face. The infant squirmed. A little hand pushed its way clear of the knit blanket and latched onto her finger.

"Oh, my goodness. You poor dear," Ruby sighed.

She gathered the baby up, blanket and all, holding her to her chest. Then she straightened and turned to Leon.

"I don't know who she is," she confessed. "Adam?"

He was already shaking his head.

"No. But she looks to be only a month or two old, wouldn't you say?"

Ruby nodded.

He rubbed his chin, his eyes narrowed with thought.

"What about the migrant workers?"

Ruby's eyes widened, and she nodded again.

"We don't hire any migrant workers," Leon said.

"No, but they've been coming through town on their way to summer jobs," Adam replied slowly. "We treated a few with travel-related injuries this week."

"Why would one of them leave a baby on our porch?" Leon scrubbed a hand through his hair, feeling overwhelmed.

"Maybe they couldn't care for it," Ruby said soberly. "Some of these people are very poor."

"And very religious," Adam added. "Maybe it was an unwed mother."

"But why would they drop the baby on *my* farm?" Leon lifted the lamp again, searching the darkness.

"Maybe because they know Ruby is a nurse?" Adam ventured.

"We've got to find whoever it was," Leon said. "They can't have gone far. I'm going to go saddle a horse."

As he set out at a half run for the stable, the baby's innocent little face hovered before his mind. His heart clenched at the fact that she had been abandoned like a puppy on his porch.

He tightened his jaw. What if returning her to whoever had left her only led to her being abandoned somewhere else?

No, he thought. They would offer whoever it was help. Whatever they needed to be able to keep their own baby. They would convince them that a child needed their parents.

Chapter Three

Kansas City, Missouri

It had begun to rain almost the moment Myra climbed out of her window and into the free world. The chilly drizzle still fell heavily on her hair and shoulders as she stood in front of the rectory. Still, she hesitated, her hand hovering an inch from the front door.

What if she knocked and the priest answered rather than his sister?

Father Timothy Walker was a kind man, and she respected him. She just wasn't sure she was ready to face him with a pillowcase of her belongings in her hand and a heart full of rebellion and confusion and pain.

Perhaps it was a priest she needed, but it was a friend she wanted.

Lowering her hand, Myra took a few cautious steps toward the side of the house. Her footsteps quickened as she circled around to the kitchen door.

The back of the manse sheltered a tiny orchard, only four trees in all, but they were Alice Walker's pride and joy. They were in full bloom now. Their creamy petals dropped into the path as the rain pattered against the branches, and their fragrance surrounded Myra with a comforting familiarity.

Alice opened the door almost the moment Myra knocked on it. A puzzled but welcoming smile lit her narrow face.

"Myra!" she exclaimed. "I didn't expect to see you this time of day— and in this weather!"

Her gaze flitted over Myra's bedraggled appearance and landed on the pillowcase clutched in her white knuckles. She stilled.

"I'm sorry," Myra stammered. "I didn't know where else to go."

Then, unable to hold her emotions together any longer, she burst into tears.

Alice's lips, which had been parting in a question, pressed back together. Without asking what she must certainly be wondering, she tugged Myra into the house and closed the door behind her.

"You're soaked through," she murmured. "First thing we've got to do is get you warm and dry. Then you can tell me all about it. Come, you can put on one of my dresses. And I'll fix us both a cup of tea."

Her comforting voice gradually soothed Myra's tears as she chattered on lightly, telling her that Father Timothy was away at a conference. She took Myra to her bedroom and gave her a soft towel and one of her own simple, gray gowns to change into.

When Myra emerged a few moments later, it was with mostly dried eyes and more composure.

The rectory kitchen was a cozy place, if a trifle too small to be convenient. Alice was pouring golden tea into two thick mugs on the table, and two generous cinnamon rolls sat on saucers before the two chairs.

Myra managed a weak smile as she slipped into her seat. Alice pushed the cup of tea across the table to her.

"Thank you," Myra said. "I don't... I don't know if you can help me, but I appreciate you at least hearing me out."

"Of course!" Alice said. She sank down into the chair opposite. Her light brown hair was pulled back into a simple twist. Her face, as always, was full of serenity.

Myra had often envied her friend's ability to remain at peace no matter what life threw at her. And life had thrown a lot at Alice, she knew.

"I'm always here for you, Myra," Alice continued. "And I know my brother would say the same." Her blue eyes searched Myra's face. "Are you alright? Are your parents alright?"

"They've arranged for me to marry Mr. Walshman."

Myra hadn't exactly intended to just blurt it out like that, but she was desperate to get the horrid truth off her chest.

"And I said that I wouldn't," she hurried on, tears springing to her eyes again. She was already tired of crying. She finished in a rush, "My mother threatened to keep me locked up until the wedding day, so I ran away."

Alice's eyes widened as Myra spoke. She blinked, taking her time before responding, as she always did.

"I don't know where to go or what to do now," Myra added tremulously. "If I go back... I'm afraid they'll somehow find a way to force me to marry him."

"And that is absolutely out of the question for you?" Alice said carefully, a question in her voice.

Myra felt the horror of it jolt through her anew.

"He's old enough to be my father!" she exclaimed. "Possibly my grandfather! And he's... he's not a nice man, Alice. I don't know if you know this about him."

"He doesn't frequent the church," Alice said quietly. Myra couldn't tell if she was agreeing with her or simply noting that she didn't know much about the man's character.

"I try to honor and obey my parents," Myra continued, "but this…" She choked down the nausea that rose in her stomach. "I can't do this."

"No. And I don't think you should have to."

It was a relief to hear Alice's confirmation. Myra felt the tight knot in her stomach release just slightly.

"Thank you," she breathed.

Alice looked down at her mug, turning it contemplatively in her slim but workworn hands. Her face contracted with a trace of worry as she continued.

"We have a spare bedroom. You can stay there until my brother returns from the conference two days from now. That's not a long-term solution though."

"No, I wouldn't want to impose. And I don't suppose it would be considered proper for me to live here at the same time as the priest," Myra agreed, her heart sinking slightly.

"And your parents may come for you." Alice fixed her with a sober glance. "I can't guarantee that Timothy won't take their side in this matter." She shook her head slightly. "He thinks very highly of marriage as an institution. And he may see your parents' promise to Mr. Walshman as binding. Unless…"

Myra watched as her friend's face shifted slightly. Alice looked up, a spark in her eye.

"Unless you had already promised yourself to another."

"What do you mean?" Her face flushing, she added softly, "I've never even had a beau."

Alice bit her lip, her gaze searching. Then she rose, reaching for a newspaper on the countertop.

"It's almost like God putting the pieces together," she murmured.

Settling herself across from Myra once more, she opened the paper, scanning the page until her eye lit upon what she was searching for. Placing her finger on the spot, she handed it, crinkling, across the table to Myra.

"Here. Read this," she said softly.

Myra lowered her eyes to the page. In her tumultuous state, it took a moment for the words to make sense.

Wanted, the tiny block of text read: *A kind and capable woman, age 18 to 25, willing to travel to Colorado to marry a farmer of 500 acres. Must be able to cook, keep house, and help with farm chores as necessary. Will be well-provided for and treated kindly. If interested, please write c/o Leon Sanders, Crested Butte, CO.*

It was an ad.

For a *wife.*

Myra blinked, her shock complete. She lifted her gaze to Alice, whose face reflected empathy.

"I know it's not perfect," Alice said, "but hear me out. If you answer the ad and receive an offer, my brother will be obliged to support you in holding off your parents' plans and traveling out there. And it's customary for the men who write these ads to pay all travel expenses, so it will give you a way to get out of town."

She leaned forward, reaching for one of Myra's limp, cold hands. "If you get out there and don't want to marry him, at least you'll be somewhere you can start a new life. Surely there

will be a place you can get a job and live. They say opportunity is endless out west."

When Myra remained speechless, Alice sighed gently.

"If I wasn't thirty-two and practically married to this rectory, I'd have half a mind to answer that ad myself," she said with a hint of humor.

Myra opened her lips, but still, no sound emerged. She looked down at their joined hands. She knew her friend was doing all she could to help Myra feel better and find a solution. And as usual, there was wisdom in what she said.

"I don't know the first thing about farm chores," she managed finally.

"But you're an excellent cook and housekeeper," Alice reminded her. "That's something your mother gave you that will be helpful now. I'm sure your new husband would be happy to teach you all you need to know about living on a farm."

Husband. Living on a farm.

It was too much to fully process in that moment. But Myra had a sudden, vivid glimpse of a wide-open place: endless blue skies and rolling green fields bordered by misty, purple mountains.

There *were* mountains in Colorado, weren't there?

Her heart quickened slightly. She looked up, and her expression must have shown the erratic flicker of hope that had lit within her. Alice nodded.

"We'll need to write a reply right away," she said. She leaned forward, adding in a conspiratorial whisper, "So it will be well on its way before Timothy gets home."

Myra's heart reached an almost frantic pace. She pulled her hand away.

"I don't know," she stammered. "I'm not sure…"

"You don't have to be. Not yet," Alice said comfortingly. "It's just something we can do right now that might prove useful later." She shrugged. "He might not even write back. And if he does and you don't like the sound of it, you don't have to go. It's just a fallback plan. Okay?"

Sitting there at the tiny rectory table, her heart fluttering in her chest, Myra understood what her friend was too kind to say. That this was pretty much the only option she had. At least for now.

***

Crested Butte, CO

May 1897

A backup plan, Alice had called it. Yet three weeks later, Myra stood on a desolate station platform thousands of miles from home. The train she had arrived on had departed for its final destination at least an hour before.

Still she stood waiting on the brink of an unknown future with an unknown man.

Until this hour, everything had happened so quickly, Myra could scarcely wrap her head around it. The reply to her letter had been prompt— so prompt it almost seemed too good to be true. But there had been something about the response that had caught and held her.

In a tidy print, Leon Sanders described himself as a quiet man with simple needs. He described the Crested Butte community as welcoming and full of everything a person could want: a clinic, a grocer's, a millinery.

And he described the ranch: Acres of prime pasture dotted with sheep. Big old shade trees that had been there since his parents settled the place. A comfortable house and as much garden space as she could want.

As she read the words, the vision that had pushed her to give in to Alice's idea in the first place had returned to her mind, clearer and fuller than ever before. She saw herself, living on that farm, having her own little house, her own little family— one that actually wanted her and loved her.

Myra blinked, pulling herself back to the present. The empty station.

She had imagined what her welcome might be like on the way here. Would the man be eager or shy? Handsome or plain? She found she had no preference either way. She had so little experience with men in general, she could not quite imagine interacting with the one who was to be her husband.

But there had been no welcome at all. The train had left and the platform had cleared of all the other travelers. Still, no man with hat in hand or confident stride approached her with the expectant: *"Myra? Myra Barnes? Welcome to Colorado."*

I should not have been so hasty, she thought. *I should have written again, asked more questions.*

But she had felt anxious. Father Timothy was having doubts about allowing her to stay at the rectory in defiance of her parents' plans. And she had felt hopeful. A new beginning stretched before her. She had reached for it with both hands.

It was a little late for regrets now.

Her attention snapped back to the present as a man drove a wagon up to the station hitching post. The sight of him only made her feel more desperate. He had driven away with one of the other train passengers, taking the woman to her destination. Now, he was back, and Myra was still waiting, alone and forgotten.

She straightened her spine, fingers tightening around the suitcase Alice had given her for her few belongings. If no one was coming to meet her, she was just going to have to go to them.

She started toward the man as he clambered down from the wagon. Before she had quite reached him, though, another woman stepped out of the shadow of the station.

Myra had not seen her, and apparently, neither had the wagoneer.

"Lord ha' mercy," he exclaimed, clutching his heart. "You give me quite a fright, miss. What are you hiding there for?"

"Oh— I wasn't hiding," the woman exclaimed. Something in her voice made Myra wonder if she was being entirely truthful. It was breathless, a little desperate, and she glanced nervously from right to left.

She was a pretty woman, with thick, curly, dark hair pinned to the back of her head, a full figure, and a heart-shaped face. There were shadowed hollows beneath her dark eyes, though, and a general lack of luster to her hair and skin, making Myra wonder if she might be ill.

"Please, sir," the woman said, "can I hire you to drive me to the next town over?"

The man pushed his hat back, scrubbing a hand through non-to-clean locks. "And what town exactly would that be, ma'am?"

"I'm... not sure exactly," she said. She attempted a bright smile, but it crumbled at the edges. "Just whichever town is next over from this one."

"Well, ma'am, I generally just ferry folks to places that are local-like. Most people take the train to get outten town," the wagoneer drawled. Myra could see his growing suspicion in the way he put a little space between himself and the woman.

"But the last train of the day has already left, hasn't it?" the woman exclaimed. There was definitely desperation in her voice. Myra found herself stepping forward, propelled by concern.

"There'll be another tomorrow," the wagoneer said in a roughly consoling tone. "Listen, lady. If you're in trouble, we got a right good sheriff in this town. I'll take you over to his office if you like..."

"No, no. That won't be necessary." The woman was stepping back, hurried now. A ragtag group of cowboys had appeared at the other end of the street, and they seemed to be making her nervous. "I... thank you. I'll take the train tomorrow, like you say."

As quickly as she had appeared from the shadows, she seemed to melt back into them. The wagoneer stood, scratching his head and staring after her until Myra stepped closer. He turned and blinked at her.

"You wouldn't be looking for a ride to another town too, would you?" he asked with a wry twist to his mouth. He had a chewed mustache and somewhat watery blue eyes.

"No," Myra said. Her voice came out sounding nearly as hesitant as the woman before her.

She cleared her throat and attempted to stand and speak more confidently.

"I would like to get a ride to Leon Sander's ranch. If you can take me there..." Her confidence faltered toward the end, but she saw that she had the man's attention.

"I know where the Sanders ranch is all right," he said, squinting at her. His eyes dropped to the suitcase she still clutched. "You got any more luggage needs loading?"

"No. I... I also don't have anything to pay you with right now." She decided it was best to be honest up front. "But I'm sure Leon— Mr. Sanders will pay you when we get to the ranch."

"Aw, there'll be no need for that, ma'am," the wagoneer said. He reached up and tipped his hat to her slightly, an odd but apparently respectful gesture. "Leon's done me a fair amount of favors in the past. It's high time I paid him back with one myself. Just climb on up in the wagon, miss. My name is Surely. Surely Mason."

Myra kept herself from showing her surprise, but the wagoneer was apparently used to people's reactions.

"I know, I know, it sounds like a woman's name," he rattled on good-naturedly. He took her suitcase and tossed it into the wagon bed before offering her a hand up onto the seat. "But it's spelled S-u-r-e-l-y. Like in the Psalm, you know?"

"Oh, yes. The twenty-third Psalm," Myra murmured. "'Surely goodness and mercy shall follow me...' That's really a very lovely name."

"Well, that's what my mother thought," Surely chortled. He swung spryly up onto the wagon beside her. "Now, you might as well tell me all about yourself and what such a lovely young lady has got to do with our very own Leon Sanders," he said, settling beside her. "It's a bit of a drive out to his place, so we've got time."

Myra took a deep breath, hoping to settle her flip-flopping stomach.

What awaited her at that farm so far outside of town? Would Leon be surprised to see her?

What Surely had said so far seemed to commend Leon's character, but it somehow only made her more aware of how little she knew about the man she had come out here to marry.

This drive out of the ranch, she decided, would be best spent in telling as little about herself and finding out as much about the man who owned it as possible.

Leon Sanders. Her husband-to-be.

Chapter Four

Crested Butte, CO

May 1897

Leon's leg burned and ached from dismounting too quickly. He grimaced as he walked slowly toward the old Harrington house, leading his horse.

It felt strange to be back here now that it was owned by someone else. He'd come by now and then since the Harringtons had passed away to make sure everything was all right —that the roof wasn't leaking and windows were intact— that type of thing.

There was no arguing the ranch had fallen into disrepair over the years, though. Tall weeds straggled up around the doorstep where Mrs. Harrington had always had hollyhocks and peonies blooming through the summer.

Leon swallowed, emotion clogging his throat at the thought of her. He saw that one of the porch steps had caved in and frowned.

The ranch still seemed deserted. Had the new tenants not moved in yet? But Ruby had said...

Movement at the window interrupted his thoughts. Just the faint shape of someone hovering there for a minute, behind the dust-gray glass.

"Hullo?" he called. "Hullo the house!"

Slowly, the front door creaked open. A man stepped out on the porch.

He looked to be in his mid-thirties and he immediately struck Leon as being *not* a farmer. He was wearing a vest over a white shirt and tooled leather boots. His hair was slicked over with shining pomade, while his face was set in a curious frown.

"Mr. Graham?"

Leon limped a few steps closer to the house.

"Who's asking?" the man demanded.

"Uh... your next-over neighbor, if you're him," Leon said after a hesitation.

He was thrown off by the man's apparent hostility. It was not a characteristic one saw much among the folks of Crested Butte. Perhaps, as a newcomer, the man didn't know what a friendly town it was.

"My name is Leon Sanders," he added.

"Oh, yeah... I heard about you. Sheep farmer, right? You wanted to buy this place too. Sorry I got ahold of it before you could."

The man didn't sound sorry. There was a smug undertone to his voice, and Leon immediately felt his anger rising. He took a minute to bite down on it and count to ten.

"That's right," he said finally. "I suppose you could say it has... sentimental value to me."

"Well, it has financial value to me," the man said, smirking. "I'm fixing to run cattle on the place." He sauntered across the porch and leaned against the railing. "Lots of folks are saying it's a lucky thing I got ahold of it before a sheepman, the way those woolheads tear up the grass."

Was he *trying* to make Leon dislike him?

Leon allowed himself another quick glance around, choosing not to react.

"You living here alone?" he asked.

Immediately, the man's scowl returned. "I don't see as how that's any of your business."

"Hey, I'm just being neighborly," Leon said. He could hear the way his own voice was growing short, matching Graham's in hostility.

He was tired of trying to make nice with the stranger. And he no longer felt comfortable sharing the real reason for his visit.

"If you have a wife or children, my sister was thinking to stop by and introduce herself," he explained stiffly. "And if you've hired any migrant workers—"

"Naw." The man cut him off with a disgusted wave of his hand. "I don't need any of them foreigners to help with a dinky little place like this."

He shoved the hand into his pocket and looked around. Despite his words about the financial value of the place, his lips twisted with obvious distaste at what he saw.

"I'm here alone," he added sourly.

"All right, well..."

Under ordinary circumstances, Leon would have added something about being only a few miles away if the man needed anything, but the words stuck in his throat. A bitter taste filled his mouth as he considered the fact that a place that had once been so dear to him should have fallen into the hands of such an unpleasant person.

"...I guess I'll be heading on my way."

As he turned and stepped around to the side of his horse, the man called after him.

"Hey! Sanders."

Leon turned.

"What happened to your leg?" the man asked, nodding insolently to Leon's limp.

Leon felt his jaw harden.

"Accident," he spat out after a moment. "A long time ago."

Then he turned, mounted his horse, and rode off without looking back.

Back on his own ranch, the dogs ran to meet him as usual. He felt a smile tug at his lips as he saw that the calf he'd been bottle-raising had escaped her pen to join them. The dogs grinned and wagged and she kicked up her heels, frolicking alongside them as they followed his horse until he dismounted.

He stopped to rub each head in turn, his heart lifting slightly. The little band capered around him as he cared for his horse and turned him out to pasture. Then they followed him toward the house.

He could hear the baby crying before he'd even reached the porch. Ruby met him at the door, her usually calm demeanor in disarray. Her hair was disordered, her dress was stained, and her face was flushed. She was cradling the infant in her arms, and appeared near to tears herself.

"I can't get her to stop crying," she said. "No matter what I do. She's been doing this almost since you left this morning. I don't think the formula Adam gave us agrees with her. She really seems to be in pain!"

His sister was talking swiftly, the words pouring out of her in a desperate torrent. The infant's tinny wails filled the entryway. Leon could understand why they had run his sister's nerves ragged. His own nerves were on edge from riding around, questioning people about whether or not they had lost a baby all day. A glance at the child's face, though, showed that what his sister said appeared to be true. The baby's face was scrunched, and she writhed in the blanket Ruby had swaddled around her. Her sobs had a heartbreaking rhythm to them.

Catherine, he reminded himself. Ruby had found the name scribbled on a piece of paper tucked among the baby's blankets the night they found her in the basket. It was an imposing name for such a tiny infant.

"Here," he said gruffly. "Let me try."

The baby felt tiny in his hands as Ruby handed her over with visible relief. Leon was used to handling the lambs, but there was something completely different about a human child. She felt fragile, breakable.

The crying was nearly unbearable. Lifting her awkwardly to lay her against his shoulder, he turned around and stepped back out onto the porch. Perhaps the fresh air would help her too, he thought.

He began to pat her back gently and steadily. He paced along the porch, gazing out at the horizon. It was going to be a beautiful sunset tonight.

He paced back and found that Ruby had followed him out. She leaned against the house, twisting her hands in her apron, her eyes tracking his progress. He continued to walk and thump the baby's back, almost in rhythm with her cries.

"No luck finding who her parents are, I suppose," his sister said softly after a moment.

He grunted, shaking his head.

She sighed.

"I can't say I'm surprised. If her mother did abandon her here on purpose, she's not going to admit that she's hers."

She leaned her head back against the faded wooden slats of the house, looking weary.

"One thing's for sure," she murmured quietly. "I am *not* ready to become a mother myself."

Leon felt something twist inside him at the words and the worn expression on his sister's face.

Ruby had immediately agreed to stay home and help take care of the infant until they found her mother, but he knew she missed her work as a nurse in town. And it was easy to see that all of this was overwhelming her.

Against his shoulder, the baby suddenly burped. Then Leon felt warm goo spill over his neck.

"Oh no, she spit up again." Ruby leaped forward, pulling a cloth from her pocket.

Leon stood still, cringing slightly, as she mopped at the mess on his shoulder. The sour smell of the rag and now his shirt made his eyes sting. But the baby had begun to quiet.

Shifting her down to his chest, Leon found that her eyes were open. She gazed up at him, her lips slightly parted, and her big, dark eyes soulful. Tears still trembled on her surprisingly long lashes.

"Well, at least that made *you* feel better," he said quietly.

"Leon," Ruby said hesitantly, "what are we going to do if we can't find her mother?"

Leon had no idea.

"We'll figure something out," he said. He couldn't seem to look away from the baby's big, dark eyes.

Ruby was quiet. Leon finally lifted his eyes to find her leaning against the house once more, watching him with a melancholy expression.

"All this time," she said softly, "and we haven't had a chance to talk about what Adam brought up when he was here for dinner. I still want to move into town, Leon. I want to get back to the profession I studied to become part of, for years," she added, her words passionate. Then her voice quieted again. "But I don't want to leave you alone. Especially now…"

Leon didn't want to talk about this. Their life already felt topsy-turvy enough, and there was a motherless baby to do something about. But he had already wrestled through to the fact that he was going to have to let Ruby be her own person, no matter how scared it made him.

The baby's blinks were becoming long and slow.

"I can take care of myself, Ruby," he said gently. "I took care of both of us for an awful lot of years, if you'll recall."

She nodded. Then she bit her lip.

"But you can't take care of a baby by yourself," she said. "And I don't want you to be lonely, Leon. I know you. Without me here to make you go into town now and then and get involved with church and festivals, you'll just close in on yourself. You'll live for the ranch and the ranch only… and you won't even realize what you're missing."

Leon could feel his shoulders tensing. They were supposed to be talking about Ruby's plans— not his.

"If you're going to start in on me again about picking a girl and getting married, you can just drop it right now, Ruby," he said, more harshly than he had intended. "You're one to talk, anyway. You've said for years that *you* have no intention of getting married."

"Well, one of us should," Ruby said smartly. "And I think it should be you. That way you can have lots of sons to carry on the family name. It's obvious you'd make a good father." She nodded meaningfully toward the baby on his chest

Leon shook his head. The baby stirred, and he forced himself to relax so as not to disturb her.

"You'd think you'd have enough to do taking care of all your patients and everything to not need someone else's life to meddle in," he muttered.

"I'm not meddling," she retorted. "I care about you, Leon. You're always doing what's best for everyone else. I think it's high time you did what was best for you for once. And now, with me moving away, and this baby—"

"I'm not keeping the baby," Leon interrupted.

Ruby cast another pointed look at the infant sleeping in his arms and raised an eyebrow. Before she could say anything else, the dogs began to bark.

Both siblings turned toward the long drive from the road.

Leon immediately recognized Surely's mismatched team and long-bed wagon. It was halfway down the drive. Surely was slouched in the driver's seat, and next to him sat the slim, upright figure of a woman. The setting sun glinted off her hair, making it gleam a bright, impossible red-gold.

"Do you know who that is?" He glanced at Ruby, who had joined him at the edge of the porch, one hand shading her eyes.

The wagon rattled closer. The dogs continued to bark until Leon called them away.

"Piper, Shell, Crocket. Stop that. Come here."

Surely tugged on the reins and his team stopped.

"Howdy, Sanders!" he called cheerfully. "Special delivery for you all."

Hopping down, he circled around the wagon and held up a hand to help the woman step down.

She was young. About Ruby's age maybe. And her hair really was red with a hint of gold. It was also intensely curly, such that he couldn't exactly tell how it was held in the generous heap on top of her head. Her face was petite and pretty and tense as she turned to face him and Ruby. Her gaze stumbled over the baby, and the careful smile faltered.

She took a few steps closer. The dogs ran up to sniff at the hem of her dress, their tails waving in a welcoming manner. The bottle-fed calf sauntered after them, letting out a cheerful bawl.

The woman stopped abruptly, her shoulders hunching toward her ears with tension.

"Will they bite?" she asked.

"Oh... no. They're being friendly," Leon said.

He wasn't sure after he said it why he had. It wasn't something he would usually confide in a stranger, in case they took it as an invitation to show up unannounced again and make free with his property and belongings. But it was obvious that the animals did like her, which to him was a fairly good character reference.

As he spoke, her eyes met his. They were green. Like a summer lake in the sun. Then, her gaze returned to the baby. Once again, an expression he couldn't quite identify crossed her face.

"Here's your luggage, ma'am," Surely said. He handed the woman a small, battered suitcase before climbing back into the wagon. "See you folk later!" he called.

"Wait," Leon said. "Where is he going?" As the wagon began to roll, he shifted his puzzled attention to the young woman. "Why are you staying?"

It hit him all at once. He felt his arms tighten around the tiny, warm weight in his arms. What should have been pure relief was strangely swirled with a cocktail of emotions he couldn't begin to unmix.

Somehow, with all his asking, word had gotten to the right person after all. He cleared his throat. Swallowed.

"Is she yours?" he asked hoarsely.

The young woman blinked. Then she lifted her chin slightly and straightened her shoulders. Once again, her gaze met his with an unusual mixture of shyness and determination.

"I don't know who or what you're talking about," she said straightforwardly. Then, she added pointedly, "I'm Myra Barnes."

The name meant nothing to him. But beside him, Ruby gasped.

"Oh!" she exclaimed, her voice suddenly breathless. "Oh, you're here so much quicker than I thought you would be."

"You know who she is? You knew she was coming?" Leon turned toward his sister, more confused with each passing moment. He was trying to stay calm, with the baby sleeping on his chest, but he could feel his muscles twitching. When Ruby met his eyes, hers were wide with guilt.

"I…"

"*You* knew I was coming," the young woman —Myra— cut in. "You sent me a train ticket."

Leon twisted back to face her, squinting in the rays of the setting sun.

"What? No, I didn't. Why would I? I have no idea who you are."

Myra's skin was already pale, but it seemed to grow a shade paler at his words. It made the delicate spatter of freckles across her nose and cheeks stand out in stark contrast.

"I told you," she said through tight lips, "I'm Myra Barnes. Are you Leon Sanders?"

How did she know his name?

"Yes," he said.

"Well, then," Myra said. "I'm your mail-order bride."

Chapter Five

Myra stood, surrounded by dogs —and inexplicably, a small cow— and watched as Leon whirled toward the woman standing next to him. They were related, she was pretty sure. Brother and sister. Both had brown hair, brown eyes, and similar features: straight noses, well-defined chins, slightly narrow faces.

Beyond that connection, she had very little idea of what was going on.

The baby sleeping against Leon's chest was a complete shock and made no sense as far as she could tell. Equally strange was the fact that Leon apparently was not expecting her. In fact, he appeared even more shocked than she felt at her announcement.

"You did this, didn't you?" he said to the woman beside him. "You took things into your own hands because you wanted to move into town!"

He looked down at the baby asleep in his arms and his face shifted. Fury and pain warred across his striking features.

"Was this part of your plan too?" he asked, voice rising. "How long have you two been scheming?"

The woman reeled backwards, her face reddening. She was the younger of the two, Myra decided distantly. Her face was softer and more open than her brother's. She looked as if she'd had a hard day. Leon looked as if he'd had a hard life.

Despite her confusion and the distinctly troubling argument happening right in front of her, Myra found herself drawn to the man she had come to marry. His lithe build, the way his hair tumbled over his eyes and curled over his shirt collar, the way his hands cradled that inexplicable baby with such gentleness... everything about him sent strange tingles of excitement through her travel-weary body and brain.

"No!" his sister exclaimed in response to his accusation. "I mean... yes, I wrote the ad for a mail-order bride. And when she answered it, I replied and invited her out..."

The man let out a muffled roar between his teeth. Myra couldn't tell if he was trying to muffle it so as not to wake the baby or simply trying to contain his anger.

"Are you *kidding* me? Ruby, how could you do this?"

As the words his sister had spoken penetrated Myra's own whirling thoughts, she felt a moment of intense lightheadedness. *Ruby* had placed the ad? Written the letter?

Leon not only hadn't known Myra was coming— he had never wanted her in the first place.

I'm going to faint, she thought. The beautiful ranch spun around her. She tightened her fingers around her suitcase, forcing herself to breathe as the siblings' voices continued to rattle around her.

"Catherine has nothing to do with it!" Ruby sounded close to tears. "I swear! And I didn't just do it because I wanted to take the job in town. I did it for you, Leon."

"How is this for me? It's exactly what I told you I didn't want! Multiple times!"

Myra felt sick to her stomach. She wished with fervent intensity that she could simply sink through the ground and disappear. The feuding siblings were growing more and more irate. The baby stirred on Leon's chest, and she thought it would certainly wake at any moment.

"I told you I could take care of myself," Leon sputtered.

Ruby scoffed. "If I left you alone, you would live on coffee and canned beans. Think about it, Leon. Now, with the baby, it makes even more sense to have someone here to help you."

"You couldn't have just put an ad in for a housekeeper?"

"No woman is going to travel all the way out to Colorado for a job as a housekeeper," Ruby said sharply.

"Yet they would travel all the way to Colorado to marry a man they've never met?!"

It was as if they had forgotten Myra was standing right there. By this time, tears were burning her eyes. She fought to keep them back. She had imagined many ways this first meeting could go, but none so horrible as this. She felt as if she were in the middle of a nightmare.

This is not my fault, she reminded herself. But the angry voices slashing the air about her were too reminiscent of her mother, and she couldn't seem to escape the creeping sense that she was the one who had failed.

A large, wet nose bumped her elbow. She looked down to see the cow looking up at her. It was a baby, she was pretty sure. She didn't know that much about cows. Distractedly, she reached out and began to rub the curls between its big ears. Its eyes drooped with what looked like contentment.

"A woman has to have some sense of stability," Ruby was saying. "And she has her reputation to think of. If I do move out once the cottage is ready, a single woman isn't going to be able to just live with you..."

Myra closed her eyes, finally letting the tears squeeze from between her lashes. A feeling was rising in her, one that she had only recently grown familiar with. Anger. She was so tired, she realized. So tired of being bullied and scolded and ignored. It was as if her body was finally learning to resort to the only emotion capable of giving her the strength and boldness to fight back.

"Excuse me."

For the first time since the argument had begun, both Leon and Ruby looked in Myra's direction. She felt a jolt of nerves as Leon's smoldering golden-brown eyes struck her. His jaw was tight, and his chin was thrust forward. The fury in his eyes met the frustration in hers.

She tightened her own jaw and straightened her shoulders.

"I would appreciate it if you would stop discussing me like I'm not standing right here," she said in a low voice. "Obviously, I have been misled. You don't want me here, and therefore, I have no intention of staying. If you would just be so kind as to get someone to take me into town —Surely, or someone else— I'll catch the next train back to Missouri."

Even as the words came out of her mouth, she stumbled, realizing how impossible that was. She had no money. No place to go back home to.

Panic fluttered in her chest, but before it could fully take wing, Ruby hurried toward her.

"Myra, I'm so sorry," she said softly when she was standing right in front of her. "I was wrong to make you think you were exchanging letters with Leon. It... seemed like a good idea at the time, but I realize now how cruel it must seem to you."

Her brown eyes were pleading, and somehow less intense than her brother's.

"I meant to bring up what I had done with Leon before you arrived. I just... got distracted with everything that's been happening here. Please..."

Ruby glanced over her shoulder. Leon had been glowering at them, but the baby had awakened and begun to fuss. He was occupied in trying to soothe it.

As she followed Ruby's glance, something twisted in Myra's gut that wasn't entirely unpleasant. She had never seen a man holding and soothing a baby before. Somehow, Leon looked right doing it. She was afraid to ask exactly how the two of them had ended up with a baby —recently, from the sound of things— or why he seemed so practiced in handling it.

"Please, don't go just yet," Ruby begged. "Once Leon has had some time to get used to the idea, he might change his mind—"

"Not a chance," Leon said.

Ruby had been speaking quietly, but apparently, he was hearing every word. She flushed and turned back to him.

"We need help, Leon," she said quietly but intensely. "At least until we find out who Catherine belongs to."

Was Catherine the baby then? How did they not know who she belonged to?

The situation only kept getting more complicated... but Myra felt a faint stirring of hope as she considered what Ruby had just said.

Perhaps there was a place for her here after all— just not exactly as she had imagined. If she made herself indispensable enough, they might keep her on until she could find another job and place to stay, as Alice had counseled.

She cleared her throat, hardly believing that she had the courage to speak out as she was about to. Her eyes caught Leon's over Ruby's shoulder. He, she realized, was the one she was going to need to convince if this was to work.

"May I say something?" she asked. Ruby turned, her face a puzzle of hope and guilt and desperation. Leon said nothing, but his eyes remained fixed on Myra. It was as if he was measuring her, coming to some conclusion in his own mind.

Myra forced herself to hold his gaze and go on. "As it turns out," she said quietly, "I don't exactly want to get married either. I would be willing to be hired on as a housekeeper— or governess." With a glance at the baby. "If that's what you need."

Leon's eyes narrowed slightly. He was bouncing the baby gently up and down in front of him. Over the course of the conversation, two of the three dogs had sauntered over to lie at his feet. The other one —and the cow— were still with Myra. The dog leaned against her skirt while the cow nudged her hand, urging her to keep petting.

Leon studied her silently for a moment.

"If you didn't want to get married, why did you respond to the ad?" he asked finally.

Myra could feel herself flushing. The situation was uncomfortable enough without going into her entire backstory.

"Circumstances back home," she said haltingly. "I... needed some distance. This was the only way I could get it."

"And you swear," Leon said in a low, almost menacing voice, "that this baby is not yours and you did not drop her on our doorstep with this plan in mind the entire time?"

Myra felt her mouth drop open as shock slammed through her.

"Leon," Ruby gasped, "I told you—"

"I want to hear it from her own mouth," he said stubbornly.

It took Myra a moment to gather herself enough to respond. She shook her head, almost inclined to laugh at how crazy it all seemed. The urge bubbled up in her chest, a gurgle of hysteria, and she had to cough to dislodge it.

"I have no idea how you ended up with that baby," she said finally. "I can assure you, I had absolutely nothing to do with it. Until two days ago, I was in Kansas City, Missouri, and if you don't believe me, you can check with..."

She stopped herself before she could go on. Leon was indeed looking at her as if he didn't believe her, and all of a sudden, she knew it wasn't worth it. She didn't deserve to be standing here getting blamed for these people's problems, just as she had never deserved the false accusations her adoptive mother had so often hurled at her.

She blinked, dizzy with the realization that flooded over her, somehow made clear by this bizarre situation.

Lazy, good-for-nothing airhead, her mother had called her. *You never listen. You never do it the right way.*

It wasn't true, Myra thought. Deep down, she had always known it wasn't true, but it wasn't until that moment that she found herself capable of putting it into words.

Her mother had been wrong. Myra had not been lazy— had never been lazy. And she had not been good for nothing because if she had been, she knew now, her adoptive parents would never have kept her as long as they did.

Hot tears sprang into her eyes at the brutality of the thought, but she forced herself to keep going.

She *had* listened— oh, how she had listened, desperate for some word of commendation, terrified of missing some detail that would lead to a renewed scolding later. And she had done so, so many things the "right way". Her mother had just continually changed the way she wanted them done.

"Myra?" Ruby's voice seemed to intrude from miles away. "Myra? Are you all right?"

She was not going to put herself into another situation like the one she had just escaped. Myra suddenly knew it without a shadow of a doubt. It wasn't worth it. With the realization came a surge of serenity to match Alice's calm confidence.

There will be another way.

Giving the cow's head one last pat, Myra turned around and began walking up the long ranch drive.

"Never mind," she said over her shoulder. "I'm going home."

Chapter Six

"Myra, no! Please wait!"

Heedless of Ruby's cries, Myra Barnes continued to walk calmly away from them. Her back was straight and her head was high. Her fiery hair shone like a crown about her head.

Gazing after her, Leon felt a surge of admiration. The woman had had enough of them— that was quite clear. And with that, it was clear to him that she had been telling the truth. She had come here in good faith, based on a letter Ruby had sent her, only to be met with what he realized now was inexcusably rude and demeaning behavior from both of them.

Shame took the place of the deep fury that had been burning in him since Ruby's scheme had been revealed. Myra had no fault in that, and yet he had treated her boorishly. He was no better than his sister.

With the baby's wails growing louder, he was also conscious, in a faint, unsettled way he wasn't quite ready to explore yet, that Ruby was right. The self-possessed, carefully tidy, excruciatingly polite young woman walking away from them right that moment might actually be exactly what they needed. And he had driven her away.

"Myra, just listen for a moment. Leon—" Ruby twisted to look back at him, still hurrying after the retreating woman. As she did so, the calf and Shell, both of which had been gamboling after Myra, dashed in front of her. Ruby tripped over Shell, who yipped shrilly. Then, as she reached to catch herself, her skirt tangled in the calf's retreating hooves.

All three went down in a bawling, shrieking, yelping heap.

Myra stopped walking and turned. She broke into a run at the same time as Leon and reached Ruby first. Shell and the calf had already both wriggled free and scampered a few steps away, looking back sheepishly. Ruby remained on the ground, clutching her wrist and gasping. Myra dropped to her knees beside her.

"What is it?" she asked. "What hurts?"

"My wrist— oh, I think I broke it." Ruby's face was twisted with pain. She rocked back and forth, whimpers turning to sobs. "It hurts so bad!"

Leon stumbled to a halt beside the two women, the baby in his arms. His heart seized at the sight of his sister in so much pain. Catherine's cries were suddenly overwhelming. He could feel his pulse ratcheting upward.

"We need to get something cold on this right away," Myra said in a steady voice. "Otherwise it will swell so much the doctor won't even be able to tell if it's broken."

Ruby blinked, registering surprise even in the midst of her pain.

"You're right," she croaked.

Myra looked up at Leon, her eyes such a searing bright green that he felt a little stunned by them all over again.

"Do you have an icebox?" she asked.

"N-no," he admitted. "We just put things in a spring in the cellar to keep them cool."

"We'll need water from that spring then," she said. "And then you'd better go get the doctor."

For the first time since rushing back to help Ruby, she faltered. She looked back at his sister.

"You do have a doctor in town, right? Like your letter said?"

Ruby nodded, tears spilling down her cheeks. "Adam Reid," she said. "I truly am so sorry, Myra."

Myra simply nodded. Then she stood up and reached for the baby.

"Here, give her to me," she said, "so you can get the water. All right?"

And he handed the baby over and said, "All right."

Ruby was light-headed with the pain of her injury, but between them, he and Myra managed to get her on her feet and into the house. Then, while Myra settled her on the couch and somehow soothed the baby, Leon thumped down to the cellar as quickly as he could, returning with a bucket of the icy spring water.

Myra tested it by dunking her own hand. Then, with a nod of satisfaction, she helped Ruby submerge her arm halfway to her elbow. Ruby grimaced and sighed.

"The cold will help with the pain too," Myra said. "Just wait a minute."

Ruby nodded, leaning her head back and closing her eyes. Myra glanced up at Leon.

"She's going to be okay. I'll take care of things here," she said, "if you'll go fetch the doctor."

Again, he thought, the excruciating politeness. But there was a quiet strength in the words too. He did not hesitate to do as she suggested. He nodded and turned, hurrying toward the stable.

Half an hour later, Leon stood in the doorway of Adam's clinic, watching with mild surprise as the doctor sped about, gathering the things he thought he'd need.

Aren't doctors supposed to be calm in an emergency? he thought. Adam seemed flustered, dropping everything at least once before finally getting it into his bag. His honest face was lined with anxiety.

"Hey," Leon finally broke in, "she's okay, Adam. No bleeding or head injuries or anything like that. It's her wrist, nothing more."

"Right, yes, of course. I just…" The doctor finally snapped the bag shut and turned, running an unsteady hand through his thick hair. "I'm ready to go now."

Leon nodded. "I saddled your horse for you," he said. "We can ride back together."

It was growing dark as the men stepped out into the cool, spring air. There was a bracing quality to it that made Leon think again of Myra.

He had thought of her nearly the entire ride into town, and he found his mind returning to her again and again on the quiet ride back.

The more distance he got from the shock of her arrival and Ruby's deception, the more he found his mind fastening on the astounding qualities of the woman at the center of it all. He had been so upset in the moment that he had given little thought, he realized, to how mortifying the situation must have been for *her*.

Through it all, she had maintained her composure and presence of mind. Something he had grossly failed to do.

The image of her standing ramrod straight in the center of his drive, a single, small suitcase in one hand and the other rubbing the bottle-fed calf's forehead, flashed through his mind. Stricken and serene— in the short time he had known her, he had seen her in both states of mind. In both, she had been quietly, seriously beautiful. And kind.

And she had come to marry *him*.

Why? That was the question that still troubled him. But it was at the bottom of quite a heap of things that troubled him now that he'd had time to calm down and think.

He shifted uneasily in the saddle, thinking of how he had accused her of being the mother of the baby and scheming to force him into something by dropping her on his doorstep. He realized now how foolish a conclusion it was.

For one thing, Myra and baby Catherine looked nothing alike. The infant had wispy dark curls, dark eyes, and a gently rounded face. Myra's hair was undeniably red, the ringlets barely contained. Her piercing green eyes looked out of a face that was almost aristocratic with its even features, serious chin, and winsome brow.

Leon was so deep in his thoughts, he was surprised to realize they had reached the farm. Adam swung from his horse and rushed inside, hardly taking time to fasten him to the hitching post. Apparently, Leon's assurance that his nurse was all right had not been enough to quell his concern, and he needed to see for himself.

In contrast, Leon took his time returning to the house. Ruby was in good hands.

Hands that would be spending at least one night on the farm. The darkness was thickening, and the frogs were singing in full chorus from the creekbank. The doctor had left a note on the clinic door. If he was needed for a nighttime emergency, people would know where to find him. And Myra Barnes…

He wasn't ready yet to think about what to do about Myra. If she had anything else to do with *him*.

Leading both his and Adam's horses to the barn, he brushed them down and settled them in stalls with hay and water for the night. Then he moved on to the rest of his evening chores, checking on all the ewes and their lambs last of all.

Finally, there was nothing left to do. The stars were bright in the sky and his leg was screaming for the relief of his bed as he limped to the house.

It was surprisingly quiet when he opened the door and stepped inside. Even more surprising was the savory fragrance that filled the entryway. Leon hadn't even realized how hungry he was until he smelled it. His stomach gave an eager gurgle as he drew in another deep, appreciative breath. The dogs crowded in around him, sniffing the air with equal appreciation.

Ruby must have had something nearly ready when the accident happened, he thought. She'd simply had to finish heating it. He felt a surge of relief that her injury truly hadn't been too severe and she was able to carry on as usual.

But when he stepped into the kitchen, it wasn't his sister who stood at the stove.

Myra looked up. Her cheeks were flushed from the heat of the fire. She was wearing one of his mother's old aprons; it wrapped around her slender form nearly twice, and she had tied it in front instead of in the back.

She didn't smile at the sight of him, but her expression was carefully pleasant.

"With all that's gone on, I thought you all might not have had supper," she said. "So, I just made something simple. Ruby said it was all right."

There was a hint of question in her tone. Or perhaps apology. Was she apologizing for making dinner for them? Something she absolutely didn't have to do?

"Of course it's all right," he said gruffly. He hadn't meant to be gruff, but he felt awkward, standing in the doorway of his own kitchen, unsure of what to say or do. "Where is Ruby?" he added. His self-consciousness dissipated as anxiety took its place. "Is Adam still with her? Is she hurt worse than we thought?"

"They're in the sitting room," Myra said diffidently. "The doctor just took her dinner in to her and said he would eat in there with her. She invited him to stay the night."

Again, that apologetic tone. She seemed to assume he was just looking for a way to find fault in what she did. He supposed he could hardly blame her after the welcome he'd given her.

"He said her wrist is sprained, but not broken," Myra continued. She turned back to stir the pot over the stove. "She won't be able to use it much for a couple of weeks though."

The sound of a baby's whimper drew Leon's attention to the corner of the kitchen. He walked over to the crate he and Ruby had fixed with some blankets for the baby's temporary bed. Until they could find whoever she belonged to. Ruby had been taking the crate to her room with her at night to listen for and feed the baby. Leon supposed she wouldn't be able to do much for the baby with her sprained wrist now, though.

Little Catherine's face was scrunched, though her eyes hadn't yet opened. Reaching down, he gently lifted her and laid her against his chest where his heartbeat could soothe her.

"Has she been fed?" he asked, suddenly worried.

Myra turned back around. For a moment, he was struck by the expression on her face. It was curious, even surprised. He couldn't tell what about.

"Yes." She hesitated. "Ruby said the formula you all had been using hadn't been agreeing with her, so I took the liberty of mixing up a homemade formula my mother said she raised me on. I used some of the milk from the bottle in the cellar. I hope that was okay."

Leon cracked a grin. "It's fine, I guess," he said. "That's sheep's milk. I milk a couple of the ewes who have extra to feed the heifer."

"The heifer?" Myra looked completely lost.

"The calf that you were petting earlier," he explained.

His leg was killing him. The baby had settled into his chest, and instead of waking, her whimpering had subsided. She was back asleep. He risked hobbling to one of the chairs at the kitchen table and sitting down.

"Oh." Myra still looked puzzled. "You use milk from sheep to feed a cow? Shouldn't the cow be the one getting milked?"

"She's still a baby," Leon said. "Her mother died birthing her, and the rancher didn't want to take the trouble of bottle-feeding her, so I said I'd take her on." He tilted his head, studying the woman who stood across from him thoughtfully. "You didn't grow up around animals, did you?"

Myra tucked a curl behind her ear, lifting one shoulder in a shrug; a nervous gesture, he gathered.

"I could still be of help around a farm, if I needed to be," she said quickly. "I'm a quick learner. And I *like* animals. We just lived in town, and..."

"It wasn't a criticism," he interrupted her rush of words. "Just an observation."

"Oh," she said.

For a moment, they just looked at one another. Leon could tell her thoughts were racing, and his were doing the same. Her comment had made him wonder if perhaps she had changed her mind and *would* be willing to stay on and help out— at least while they had the baby.

He felt a moment of panic as he thought about trying to do everything himself.

Ruby had been right. He would have to tell her that...later.

"Can I fix you a bowl of soup?" Myra asked finally, glancing hesitantly at the cupboard.

"I'd appreciate it."

Having something to do seemed to renew her zest. She moved swiftly and gracefully to get down a large pottery bowl. Then she filled it nearly to the brim with a thick red bean soup that smelled so good Leon's stomach gurgled again. The baby stirred against his chest, making a small sound like a kitten. He patted her back gently.

Myra set the bowl in front of him, along with a large, fluffy biscuit. She obviously knew how to cook.

"Do you want me to take Kitten so you can use your hands?"

He looked up to where she hovered next to his chair.

"Kitten?"

"Oh..." She blushed slightly, prettily. "Catherine just seems like such a big name for such a little person. I started calling her Kitten just to myself. I'm sorry if I've offended..."

"No. I like it."

He more than liked it. His heart warmed at how perfect it was.

Reluctantly, Leon lifted the baby from his chest and handed her over. His and Myra's hands brushed lightly. He couldn't help but notice.

When was the last time he'd interacted with a woman who was not his sister? It was perhaps an odd thought to have in that moment, but he couldn't seem to help noticing. There was just something so feminine about Myra. It awoke a part of himself he hadn't known was sleeping. A part of him that noticed *everything.*

As she lifted the baby to her shoulder, she murmured, "Are you getting hungry again, little one? I'll fix you something nice, okay?" Her voice was sweet, and she looked perfectly natural holding the little one.

"Have you had much experience with babies?" Leon asked. He took a bite of the soup and nearly hummed aloud with pleasure. It was as good as it smelled.

"I often watched the children of my parents' friends and family members growing up," Myra said quietly. She held the baby against herself with one arm and moved to put a fresh pot of water on the stove as she spoke. "And I've always loved children," she added.

Leon grimaced slightly. He lowered his spoon.

"I'm sorry. For what I said earlier. About the baby being yours and you and Ruby scheming. It was… cruel and uncalled for."

Myra turned toward him, surprise evident on her face. After a moment, she nodded.

"Ruby told me how you just found Kitten on your porch," she said. "I... have a lot of empathy for that."

"You've had a baby left on your doorstep?" Leon asked, looking up in surprise from slathering the best biscuit he'd ever tasted in butter.

Myra shook her head, flushing. She flushed easily, the color rising through her porcelain cheeks like the blush of sunrise.

"I was a doorstep baby myself," she clarified softly. "My parents— my adoptive parents took me in and raised me as their own."

She lifted one shoulder again in that half-shrug.

"It's not an easy thing, I know. I always... kind of hoped I'd have the chance to do something similar someday. To pay back the generosity that was extended to me."

"It doesn't take that much generosity to take care of an orphaned baby creature," Leon said gruffly. Then, realizing he may have come across as rude, he added, "Not to make less of what your parents did or anything."

Myra nodded. Her eyes searched his face, and Leon found that he couldn't look away. The green irises were mesmerizing.

The moment was broken by the sound of Ruby's and Adam's laughter in the sitting room. Myra and Leon both turned quickly, the spell broken. Leon felt at once relieved and disappointed at the interruption.

The feelings stirring through him were strange and unsettling. And he wanted more of them.

"Sounds like Ruby's feeling better," he said.

Myra's eyes flickered to his again with a knowing look.

"Mm-hmm." A smile touched the corner of her lips. She was even prettier when she smiled.

"But if she's not going to be able to use that hand for a few weeks, we will definitely need help around here," he added.

Myra's gaze steadied on his face. She nodded slowly.

"I'd be obliged if you'd stay on to help with the house and the baby at least until then," he said abruptly. "Or until we can find Kitten's family."

For what seemed like an eternity, Myra was silent, studying his face. Finally, she nodded.

"All right," she said simply. "I will."

Chapter Seven

The man didn't know how to be still, Myra decided. Not like regular people. Pacing with the baby, petting the dogs, opening a window, mounting a horse— he did everything with a kind of vibrating energy that left her feeling like his power had been barely tapped.

His limp was pronounced. She was fairly sure his leg had been badly broken at some time and suspected he still lived with severe and nearly constant pain. But that hadn't kept him from striding all over the farm before coming into the house after he fetched the doctor. And it wasn't keeping him, now, from dragging furniture all over the house.

Myra wasn't sure exactly what his plan was, but she'd already seen him haul a large desk, a chair, and what looked like a chest of drawers down the hallway and out into the night.

Even when he was sitting perfectly still, as he had for a few moments in the kitchen earlier that evening, she could sense his thoughts turning, racing down one path and then another. His stillness was the stillness of a hunting wildcat, she thought.

But then she dismissed it because he didn't strike her as being dangerous. In fact, aside from his and Ruby's row when she'd arrived earlier that evening, she had seen him be nothing but gentle, with his sister, with the baby, with the animals...

She shook her head, surprised at herself for thinking so much about Leon at all.

If he was going to be her future husband, that was one thing, but it seemed clear that was not going to be the case. She couldn't deny that she was relieved she had been offered the place as the governess/housekeeper he now needed because of Ruby's injury.

In fact, she was struggling not to feel guilty about the injury. Ruby had been running after her, after all. And she was the only one who ostensibly benefited from it.

Well, the doctor, Adam, might have been benefiting from it a bit, too.

From where she stood in the kitchen, drying the last of the supper dishes, Myra glanced through the doorway into the sitting room. The doctor and Ruby sat on the couch, their heads close together. Glancing down at the baby sleeping in her makeshift cradle, she smiled and whispered, "I understand they have a working relationship, but..."

"Adam?" Leon's voice echoed from the top of the stairs. "Can you give me a hand?"

Myra couldn't help it. She slipped to the doorway of the kitchen and peeked around it. Leon already had a large, wooden headboard halfway down the stairs. He had his head down, wiping sweat from his eyes, and all Myra could see was the curly top of his head.

"What are you doing with that now?" Adam asked, stepping up beside her.

Leon looked up. His face was flushed under his tan with exertion. His eyes caught Myra's for a moment before flicking to Adam.

"I'm making the office into Myra's bedroom," he said. "It's just across from the kitchen, so it will be most convenient for her caring for the baby and all."

Myra blinked, momentarily overwhelmed. She had never dreamed that all his furniture moving was about doing what was convenient for her. No one, that she knew of, had ever done something to convenience her.

She seemed to be the only one surprised by this announcement though. Ruby nodded and smiled from the couch, and Adam clumped up the stairs to help with the headboard.

"I... please, you don't have to do all of this for me," Myra said as the two men struggled to work the large piece of wood down the narrow stairway. "I can just sleep on a mattress or something..."

"Too late now," Leon grunted.

"Whose bed are we pirating anyway?" Adam puffed.

"Don't worry, doc, it's not yours," Leon said cheerfully. "You're sleeping on the couch."

It's his.

Myra didn't know how she knew, but in that moment, she did. Leon was taking apart his own bed to set it up in a room that had once been his office. An office he had taken apart so it could be her room.

Of all of the feelings she'd had since arriving in Crested Butte only a few hours ago, this was the most complicated. Her heart actually hurt a little as she watched the men sweat and groan and haul the bed pieces into the little room across the hall. It was a hurt she'd never experienced before. It felt almost like a crack, hinting at something more just beyond.

"Myra?" Ruby's voice drew her from her thoughts.

She stepped into the sitting room.

"Are you all right? What do you need?" she asked.

Ruby looked up at her, biting her lip. Then, she patted the sofa beside her.

"Please, can we talk for just a minute more," she said softly, "before everyone heads to bed and this crazy day is over?"

"It has been a little crazy, hasn't it?" Myra agreed. She perched on the edge of the sofa and looked down at her hands, trying not to feel nervous. There was no need to be nervous just because someone wanted to talk to her. Especially when that someone was just another woman, the same age as her or even a little younger.

"I just wanted to say again how sorry I am about everything. I..." Ruby hesitated, studying the bruised wrist propped on a pillow in her lap. "I was selfish," she whispered, "when I posted that ad and when I sent that letter to you."

She looked up, her brown eyes swimming with tears. "Leon was right. I didn't think about how what I was doing would affect *your* life. And I know we just made things terrible for you when you got here. I hope... I hope you can forgive me someday."

Myra was still. She studied Ruby's face, her nerves melting away.

"I'll admit, I was angry at you about that earlier," she said finally. "But I already forgave you, Ruby. Please, don't worry about it anymore."

"Oh, I will," Ruby said. She smiled through her tears. "I think I need to be reminded a good many more times of just how selfish I can be so that I learn my lesson. But thank you, Myra. You really are amazing. Your letters didn't even do you justice."

Glancing around, she leaned closer, her smile growing conspiratorial.

"And I know you said you didn't really want to get married either, but... I just wanted to say, don't give up on Leon quite yet. He's a big softy under all that crust."

"What crust?" Myra said sincerely.

Ruby simply laughed, as if they had shared a jest.

The men came grunting through the sitting room again, this time with a long sidepiece of the bed. Once again, Leon caught Myra's eye for just a moment. And once again, she felt it. She didn't know what, but it was something important. She was sure.

"All right," she said quietly when the men had entered the bedroom, "I won't give up on Leon." Then, while Ruby grabbed her hand and squeezed it happily, she added internally, *and I won't give up on me.*

As badly as it had all started, she couldn't help but feel that this place, these people, would be worth the effort. That maybe reaching for something *she* wanted —for the first time in her life— was worth the effort.

She still wasn't exactly sure what it was that she wanted, but she'd caught glimpses of it even in the short time she'd been here.

There were the shining green fields of the ranch beneath the sunset earlier that evening— even more beautiful than she had imagined. There was the cozy kitchen and the anticipation of having it all to herself while she cooked meals for the family to enjoy. There was the baby, the poor little baby, abandoned just as she had been. And there were the dogs, all different combinations of white and black and brown.

Not least of all of this, there was the man who looked at her, *really* looked at her, as if she was something rare and beautiful and... worth it.

As if he had been summoned by her thought, Leon appeared in the doorway. He was limping more heavily than ever, but there was a spark in his eye and a quirk to his lips.

"Your room is all ready. Do you want me to haul your luggage in?"

Myra felt a bubble of laughter rise in her stomach.

"Please. If you would be so kind," she said as solemnly as she could.

Nodding, Leon picked up her single suitcase from where it sat by the door and carried it back to the room.

Turning to Ruby, Myra found her already watching her with a mischievous smile.

"What?" she asked. But she could already feel her face flushing.

"Oh, nothing," Ruby said, "just... I've got a really good feeling."

As she said it, something tickled Myra's face. She glanced up, startled to find dust trickling down from the ceiling beams. A low rumble sounded from somewhere seemingly far away. Then the world seemed to shiver around her.

It wasn't just her imagination, she realized. The earth was shaking. Quaking.

"Oh no," Ruby murmured. Her hand tensed around Myra's, squeezing until it almost hurt.

As the house gave another heart-stopping shudder, groaning in complaint, Adam and Leon reappeared in the doorway.

"We've got to get out of the house," Leon said, his voice sharp. "Everyone, quick."

Adam rushed forward, bending to help Ruby. Myra stood up and stumbled as the floor lurched beneath her. A hand reached and caught her elbow.

Leon. His brown eyes were inches from her own. He steadied her as she exclaimed, "What is it?"

"An earthquake," he answered. "I'm going to get the baby."

"I'll come with you."

"Hurry," he said.

His hand slid down her elbow, grabbing her hand and pulling her after him.

Chapter Eight

For the second time in as many months, Leon stood in the trembling darkness, facing the house. This time, though, the woman clinging to his arm was not his sister. In his other arm, Kitten stirred. She had somehow slept through him unceremoniously scooping her from her bed, and she continued to sleep despite the uncanny rumble vibrating through his bones.

He glanced over at Ruby, supported by Adam's arm, her face turned against his shoulder. Then he looked down at Myra.

As if she felt his gaze, she looked up. Her eyes were wide and luminous in the light of the rising moon. Her fingers were tight on his arm. She flinched as the earth vibrated once more beneath their feet, a fading aftershock.

"Does this happen often?" she asked in a thin voice. "Earthquakes, I mean?"

"Not too often." Leon tipped his head and amended his statement. "At least, not usually. This is the second one we've had this spring, but before that, we hadn't had one in years."

"What does that mean? Does it mean something that they're getting closer together?"

Leon shook his head. He felt responsible and helpless at the same time— a familiar but unpleasant feeling. "I don't know," he admitted.

"This one was a bit stronger than the last one," Adam commented. "It could mean that the first one was just a foreshock to this one." He paused before adding grimly, "Or they could both be leading up to something bigger."

Myra's eyes widened as she turned her attention to the doctor. "How big?"

Leon could see the same terror dawning on Ruby's face. He quickly realized this train of thought was not going to help any of them calm down.

"Never mind," he interjected. "That's unlikely. We've never had one bigger than this in Crested Butte."

Adam glanced over at him, his mouth opening as if to correct him. When he saw Leon's glare, he subsided.

Myra, however, still had questions.

"And why do we leave the house?" She turned back to Leon. "Is it likely to fall on us?"

"No. I mean, I don't think so." He frowned, glancing at the mostly sturdy little ranch house his father had built so many years ago. "I just wouldn't want to risk it."

There was no need to elaborate on his concerns about the state of the roof. Aside from the leak in his room, he had noticed two places where the cedar shingles had been blown loose. And he had no idea how the chimney was holding up beyond what he could see from ground level.

Realizing he was grinding his teeth, he forced his jaw to relax. *I've just got to hire someone to climb up and take care of that,* he thought reluctantly. *It's no blow to my pride that I can't do it myself.*

But it was. No matter how much he tried to ignore it. His leg didn't keep him from doing many things, but climbing a ladder and crawling around on a steep roof was definitely one of them.

"So... shall we go back in now that it's stopped shaking?" Adam's voice penetrated his reverie.

Leon blinked, returning to the present. For the first time, he noticed how chilly the night air was. Glancing down, he found that Myra had been watching his mind spin, her eyes thoughtful.

He cleared his throat. "Yeah, sure. We can go in."

Now that the ground had fully stopped shaking, it was quiet enough to hear the breeze rustling through the new oak leaves overhead. Weariness tugged at Leon as the four of them trudged back up the porch steps. He was reminded of what a long day it had been and how much of it he had spent on horseback.

No doubt Myra was tired too after her day of travel, he thought. And Ruby, after a day of trying to care for the crying baby. It was high time they all headed to bed.

Personally, Leon was very ready to put this strange day of upheaval behind him and start fresh in the morning. He glanced down at the sleeping babe in his arms. The stomach upset that had plagued her for several days gratefully seemed to have passed, at least for now. Perhaps it was the new formula Myra had fixed for her.

Once again, Myra must have been watching him.

"I don't know what you have been doing 'til now," her soft voice said at his elbow, "but I'm happy to have her sleep in my room tonight if you like."

Leon looked up, meeting her serious gaze.

"That is what I'm staying on for after all," she added with a slight shrug.

Leon nodded slowly. "She's been staying in Ruby's room, but after what happened today..."

"I'm sorry," Ruby began again.

Leon glanced at his sister. Raw regret was scribbled all over her face. She bit her lip, looking like a guilty child. He shook his head.

"It wasn't your fault you fell. And Kitten's technically not even your responsibility," he added, feeling a flash of his own guilt over all of the responsibility that had been piled on his unprepared sister. "You don't have anything to be sorry about."

"I think I do," Ruby said, still looking miserable. Her gaze flickered to Myra, tears springing to her eyes.

Leon didn't miss the way Adam's arm tightened around his sister... or the fact that Adam's arm was still around her at all. He didn't *need* to be supporting her now that the earth was no longer trembling.

Myra had released Leon's arm quickly the moment it had stopped. He didn't know why he had noticed that specifically, but he had.

"Ruby," she said softly now, stepping forward, "please, we've already discussed this."

Leon glanced down at her, surprised by the firm but gentle tone. Myra's face was both sympathetic and calm as she reached out and touched Ruby's arm lightly.

"You're exhausted," she said quietly. "Don't worry about it and just go get some rest. I'm happy to take care of the baby."

Ruby nodded. Her chin trembled as she pressed her lips together, the tears still glimmering in her eyes.

"Thank you," she said, her voice soft with relief. "I would love that."

Then, flushing, she glanced at Adam and Leon before returning her gaze to Myra.

"Before you take her, though, would you mind... that is..." Her flush deepened as she touched the wrap on her wrist. "I may need some help unbuttoning my dress and..."

"Of course," Myra said efficiently. "I'll help you first. If Leon doesn't mind keeping Kitten for a few minutes more?"

She glanced up at him as she said it. Leon nodded.

"I've got her," he agreed.

As the two women went up the stairs, he and Adam were left alone.

The doctor sighed, running a hand through his hair.

"What a night," he said. "I guess it's a fortunate thing Miss Barnes arrived when she did." His gaze was curious as he turned it on Leon. "Ruby tells me you've hired her on as a governess and to help keep the house."

What else had Ruby told him? Leon wondered. But he didn't ask. He simply nodded, glancing down at the baby in his arms.

"Figured I was going to need the help as long as the baby is here," he said gruffly. "Especially once Ruby moves into town."

"I'm sorry—"

Leon held up his hand. He'd had his fill of apologies for one night. And he couldn't blame Adam for wanting Ruby's help full-time, just like he couldn't blame Ruby for wanting to follow her dreams.

He had learned a long time ago that there was really no use in blaming anyone for anything: his parents for dying, God for taking them... once one started in on that, there was really no stopping.

"I'm not some kind of victim here, Adam, so you can all stop apologizing. Now go get some sleep. Your patients are going to want you clearheaded when you're stitching and medicating them tomorrow."

He looked up, catching Adam's awkward nod, the understanding that flashed across his face.

"You got it," he said, rubbing a hand across the back of his neck. "Thanks."

Turning, he headed for the sitting room and the couch that would be his bed for the night.

Leon went into the kitchen to get Kitten's crate. He might as well move it into Myra's room while she was busy, he figured.

An inexplicable something stirred in his stomach as he thought about her coming back down and the two of them being alone for a moment, transferring the baby before heading to bed.

I'm your mail-order bride, she had said.

He could still see her standing there in the drive, highlighted by the sunset, her chin up and her shoulders back, doing her best to hide the fear flickering in her eyes. She was beautiful, he admitted. And from what he had seen so far, she was capable and courageous.

So, why had she even answered a mail-order bride ad? What was she running from? What was worth crossing the entire country to marry a man she had never met? And why had she really decided to stay?

They were all questions that would need answering sooner or later, but in that moment, as he thought of her upstairs, tenderly helping his sister as if *she* was the nurse, all he could muster was gratitude that she was here.

He already wasn't quite sure what they would be doing without her.

Chapter Nine

The sound of Kitten's cries dragged Myra from her dreams. As they fell away, she let them go without regret, rolling to her feet almost before her eyes were open. The lingering anxiety that filled her told her all she needed to know. As usual, the dreams were not worth remembering.

She stumbled to the crate that was the baby's bed and bent, lifting the whimpering infant in her swaddle of soft blankets.

"Sh-sh, you're all right," she crooned groggily. "Everything is all right."

The baby quieted almost instantly, nestling against Myra in a way that sent a pang through her heart.

"Aw... were you having nightmares too?" Myra leaned her cheek against the downy curls, closing her eyes in the darkness. "You don't have to be afraid. I'm with you now."

Cradling Kitten snuggly against her shoulder, she shuffled toward the door of the little room. Two nights of being a nursemaid and already she had learned to navigate the simple space in complete darkness. With the number of times Kitten had woken her during those nights, she was more than a little afraid she might start making this trek in her sleep.

Blinking, she freed her fingers from the blankets just enough to pinch her own arm firmly, forcing herself to become more alert. The tiny bundle in her arms was depending on her.

Once she reached the hallway, she paused to light the lamp that sat ready on the little table against the wall. She carried it into the kitchen and set it on the table. The bottle of sheep's milk sat waiting in a bucket of water from the cellar spring.

As Kitten began to fuss and squirm again, Myra hurried to start a pot of water heating on the stove. The fire had burned low, and she had to pause to shove more wood through the small door in the stove's belly. It was difficult to do one-handed.

Kitten's cries grew in volume. Still feeling half-asleep and vaguely anxious, Myra jostled the baby gently against her shoulder, up and down, up and down.

"Sh-sh, little one," she shushed. "You're going to wake the whole house."

She glanced toward the stairs, her anxiety growing. So far, both Ruby and Leon had been easy to please. They seemed to look for things to appreciate about what she did rather than looking for reasons to complain, as her mother had always done. But Myra found she still couldn't relax.

It was just because they were so relieved to have help, she thought. Once the politeness wore off, their true colors would shine.

And it would not surprise her at all if it was Kitten's midnight wails ended up being the final straw. They were wearing the polish off of her own patience as she stumbled about the shadowed kitchen. Trying to fill the glass baby bottle one-handed, she nearly dropped the milk to the floor and found herself hissing through her teeth in frustration.

"I'm not mad at you, baby," she shushed distractedly, continuing to bounce the weeping infant against her chest. "I would never be angry with you— just with myself. If I could move any faster or more gracefully, I would certainly be doing so."

"What are you talking about?" a husky voice said from behind her. "That one-handed catch was one of the fastest and most graceful things I've seen in a while."

Myra's heart jolted with both surprise and recognition. She turned to find Leon standing in the doorway. He was in his trousers and shirtsleeves, his thick hair mussed and his brown eyes drowsy in the lamplight. As ever, he was accompanied by all three of the ranch dogs. One of them plopped down beside him and yawned pointedly.

"I'm so sorry she woke you," Myra whispered. Her heart felt as if it was being squeezed by her growing anxiety.

Just what I was afraid of.

Leon didn't look upset though. He limped across the kitchen and reached for the wailing baby on her shoulder.

"Here," he mumbled. "I'll hold the little beast while you get its food."

Caught off guard, Myra let out a strange little hiccup of laughter. Immediately, her face heated with embarrassment.

Leon didn't seem to notice. He took Kitten with practiced hands and put her on his own shoulder. Feeling more wide awake than before, Myra turned quickly back to the stove.

Behind her, Leon began to pace the kitchen, humming in a low voice. Kitten quieted infinitesimally, but Myra knew she wouldn't fully stop crying until her belly was full. With hands that had inexplicably begun to shake, she stirred the formula briskly, making sure it was well-mixed and evenly heated. Then she twisted the nipple into place at the end of the bottle and tested a drop against her wrist.

"All right," she said in a hushed voice, turning back to Leon. "It's ready."

She reached for the baby, but Leon shook his head. His eyes were less intense in the middle of the night, she thought as they met hers. It made it less intimidating to meet his searching gaze.

"Give me the bottle," he said, reaching for it with his free hand. "I'll feed her." He paused before adding quietly, "You look like you're about to fall asleep standing up."

Once again, heat flooded Myra's face.

"I'm fine," she said quickly. "I promise, I would never endanger the baby by doing something like that."

"Of course you wouldn't," Leon said easily. "I wasn't saying you would."

He plucked the bottle from her hand, bending his head to meet her eyes more directly.

"All I'm saying is that you look tired. I'm trying to give you a break here."

Was there an edge of sharpness to his tone, hinting that he was disappointed in her failure to bear up? Myra was too weary to be sure. All she was sure of, suddenly, was that he was right. She wanted desperately to sink into a chair, close her eyes, and drift straight into unconsciousness.

Even her lips and tongue felt tired, too tired to form any kind of objection. After a moment of muddled thought, she gave up on trying to even come up with one. Leon had already drifted into the living room and settled into the one rocking chair. The dogs followed him, sprawling in various positions of relaxation on the rug at his feet.

Unwilling to simply abandon him with the baby, in case he changed his mind and wanted to hand her over again, Myra followed him.

She sank into the soft, worn cushions of the sagging sofa and pulled her feet up under the hem of her dressing gown.

She was thankful she'd taken a moment to put it on over her nightgown. It struck her suddenly how improper her mother and Alice and everyone back home would consider her present situation. She was in her nightclothes, her hair hanging down her back in a braid, sitting alone with a man in the middle of the night.

She turned her head, letting it rest against the back of the sofa.

It doesn't feel improper though, she thought sleepily.

What *did* it feel like?

She blinked, watching as Leon rocked back and forth, his face bent to the eagerly suckling baby. They had left the lamp in the kitchen, and the living room was dim, lit only by the light's faint overflow. Myra could feel her body relaxing despite her determination to stay ready for whenever she was needed.

The word came to her slowly, like a bubble rising through her consciousness.

Safe.

She felt safe sitting here with the quiet sheep rancher she had come to Colorado to marry and still barely knew. Noting the dogs and the quieting babe, she thought, *There's something about him that makes all of us feel that way.*

"Why have you never married?"

The words slipped from her lips before she fully realized what she was about to ask. She sensed Leon's surprise in the way his head jerked upward. His expression was lost in the dimness though. As heat flooded her face for the third time in as many minutes, she was thankful that it also hid hers.

"I mean, I understand why you didn't want to marry *me,*" she added hastily. "But you—you're so good with Kitten, and you seem to enjoy her. I just wondered why you haven't started a family of your own."

Her sentence trailed off in jumbled breathlessness. It was followed by silence.

Myra no longer felt particularly safe or relaxed. She felt as if she'd just put her foot in her mouth and was about to pay for it.

It was too late to take the words back, no matter how much she longed to. She bit her lip and closed her eyes, waiting. For an angry retort to mind her own business or something like that— she wasn't sure.

When Leon's answer finally came, it was not what she expected.

"I'm only twenty-five," he muttered. "Don't I have time yet?"

Myra's eyes flew open.

"Of course," she stammered. "I didn't mean to suggest... I'm sorry..."

Leon sighed.

"You don't have to apologize, all right?" he said. "It's fine. You just surprised me is all."

Now she had managed to annoy him even further, she thought. She snapped her mouth closed, as she should have kept it in the first place. For a long moment, there were no sounds in the living room aside from the gentle creak of the rocking chair and Kitten's satisfied sucking.

Myra nearly jumped when Leon unexpectedly spoke again.

"The ranch keeps me busy," he said. "I guess I just haven't had time to even think about... courting a woman. Trying to win her love."

His words held a slight, ironic twist. Myra found herself puzzling over it, her embarrassment momentarily forgotten. Was he pessimistic about marriage in general, she wondered, or just about his own ability to procure it?

The latter option struck her as unlikely. Leon was a handsome, if somewhat disheveled, man and an apparently successful landowner. His character, so far as she had seen it, was brusque but not unkind. She remembered Alice's words about having half a mind to answer the ad Ruby had placed herself. It seemed to her that plenty of women would have the same inclination.

She caught herself preparing to say all of this out loud and quickly bit her tongue. A new surge of heated blood flared into her cheeks, and her heart skipped a beat at the near miss.

Come to think of it, sitting here alone with him in the darkness *was* starting to feel a bit uncomfortable.

"Why haven't *you* married yet?"

Now it was her turn to be stunned into momentary silence.

"I almost was," she said finally. She hadn't expected to admit this unless pressed to the extreme. But Leon's answer had felt honest if brief. She found herself wanting to be equally sincere in return. "It's why I was in such a hurry to leave home," she added softly.

"You didn't like the guy?"

She shook her head, bile rising in her throat at the memory. Then, realizing Leon might not be able to see the gesture, she said aloud. "No. Not at all. He was a lot older than me and...

not a good person. My parents —my adoptive parents— felt it was a good match, though. They intended to force me into it. So, I ran away."

Somehow, the story had tumbled out in its entirety. Myra was surprised by how much lighter she felt just getting it off her chest. She held her breath, waiting for Leon's response.

It didn't come immediately. Kitten finished the bottle, and he set it aside. Lifting the baby to his shoulder, he began to pat her back rhythmically.

"You mentioned you were a 'doorstep baby'," he said eventually.

"That's right."

"What I don't understand is how parents who loved you enough to adopt you as their own would turn around twenty-one years later and try to marry you off against your will," he said bluntly.

Just like that, tears sprang into Myra's eyes. She blinked rapidly, caught off guard. It took a second for her to be able to speak around the lump that rose in her throat.

"I don't understand it either," she murmured finally.

Maybe because they never loved me in the first place. The words were there, hovering at the front of her mind ready to be spoken. But she couldn't do it. There was a sick feeling of dread in her stomach, as if speaking them aloud to another person would make them true.

Besides, she wasn't sure Leon would understand it if she told him: Leon, with all his adoring dogs, whom Ruby told her he had adopted as a litter of puppies abandoned on the property. Leon, who bottle-fed a baby cow three times a day and helped newborn lambs learn to suckle. Leon, who had just now begun to sing in a quiet, husky voice to the little doorstep baby snuggled in his arms.

Myra very much doubted that the inscrutably kind Leon Sanders would be able to accept that a child could be unwanted or that there were people incapable of loving without expecting something in return.

So, she kept the thought to herself, feeling its potent burn like a firebrand in her chest, quietly sniffing back the tears that insisted on welling, and listening as he sang half under his breath:

Sleep, my child, and peace attend thee,

All through the night.

Guardian angels gather round thee,

All through the night...

Chapter Ten

The baby in his arms had been asleep for a good half hour, but Leon found himself reluctant to transfer her to her makeshift cradle. In the faint lamplight, her face was so tiny, and perfect, and peaceful. He felt he would never tire of looking at it.

His heart felt full and warm with the innocent trust placed in him by this unconscious infant. It was a familiar feeling, one he still marveled at when a puppy or lamb fell asleep in his lap. But with Kitten —an entire human being who would one day grow up to have thoughts and feelings and a life of her own—, it was at another level.

He glanced up at Myra. She was still curled on the couch, her cheek against the back cushion. It was the most relaxed he had ever seen her. She hadn't spoken or moved in quite a while. He was pretty sure she had fallen asleep.

No wonder, he thought. *After how hard she's worked the past two days, not to mention getting up with Kitten at night.*

The morning after her arrival, Myra set to work as if her life depended on it. She had cleaned almost the entire house, cooked three equally impressive meals each day, and cared for Kitten with devoted attention. In the midst of it all, she'd found time to help Ruby whenever she needed it and to keep her company as she convalesced.

Leon couldn't remember a time when the little ranch house had been filled with so much conversation. Most of the time, when he came in from working, Ruby seemed to be the one doing the talking, but Myra was an engaged listener. Her face was expressive, and she was quick to voice agreement or encouragement.

Ruby had come alive with her around.

If anything, seeing how Ruby enjoyed being around another person confirmed how right it was that she should move into town. She wasn't like Leon, who needed the quiet hours alone on the ranch. She thrived in constant contact with other humans, especially, he knew, when she could participate in caring for them rather than just being cared for.

"I feel so guilty letting you do all the work when you've only just arrived!" he'd overheard her exclaim as he was coming in for supper the night before.

Myra had laughed easily. "Please, don't worry about it anymore, Ruby," she had said in her gentle, cultured voice. "You *are* helping me by telling me where things are and how you prefer for them to be done."

"Oh, no, I'm not going to start bossing you about how to *do* things," Ruby had protested. "You do them the way you like, Myra. I'm just grateful that you've decided to stay and do them at all."

Myra's lips had crooked into an almost bemused smile at the comment, and she had looked up as if to say something else. But then, she had caught sight of Leon standing in the kitchen doorway, and a cloak of reserve had fallen over her.

She had been less reserved tonight, he thought with his own bemused smile now. Her question about why he had never married had caught him off guard. And perhaps that was what had given him the boldness to make the comment he had about her parents.

It may have been a bit harsh, he thought now. The way she had stilled after he said it spoke to her own shock and hesitation.

He just couldn't shake the sense he had that it wasn't just the unwanted marriage she had fled, it was her parents themselves; and it was something she was still internally struggling to reconcile.

Whatever it was, he realized he had been looking for a chance to push past the careful mask of politeness and people-pleasing that she maintained so religiously to who she really was underneath. And for a few moments, she had given him that chance.

Leon shifted in the rocker. His leg had begun to ache an hour ago, and it would only grow worse the longer he put off getting up and moving around.

Though it still appeared completely dark outside, a rooster crowed faintly from the henhouse. Piper, who had been sleeping on the rug at his feet, sat up. She glanced up at him, her tail thumping the floor. Then she got to her feet and sauntered over to the door. She looked back at him expectantly.

"All right, girl. You got it," he said.

His leg had grown so stiff, it took him a minute to stand up. He was also moving carefully so as not to wake the baby. Finally though, he managed to get his feet under him. The other two dogs stood up as he did and followed him to the door, stretching and yawning noisily on their way.

He opened the door and all three dashed out into the cool, predawn dark. Leon took a deep breath of the fresh, dewy air himself. It was rich with the scent of the grass and leaves that grew greener every day. It tugged at him, drawing him out.

After making sure Kitten was well-covered by her blanket, he gave in to the pull and stepped out onto the porch. He crossed its width and leaned against the railing, looking out over the ranch. Faint pink blossomed along the horizon, tinting the pearly clouds. Another rooster crowed, but they weren't the only birds awake. Robins and larks trilled in the trees and from the fenceposts, filling the air with song.

Reaching down with his free hand, Leon massaged his painful knee absently, soaking in the peace of the morning.

He wasn't sure how long he'd stood there when the scent of fresh coffee drifted out of the open door, mingling with the fresh air. A few moments later, Myra's soft tread sounded on the porch behind him. He turned to find her holding out a steaming mug. She held another in her other hand.

"Coffee?" she offered. Her expression was shy but open. More sincere, he thought, than any he had seen her wear before.

"It smells good. Thank you." He straightened from the rail and took the mug from her.

Myra cupped both hands around the mug she still held. Her gaze lingered for a moment over Kitten's peacefully slumbering face. Then she lifted it to the horizon, where the sunrise was growing more and more vivid. She drew in a breath, stepping forward to stand beside him at the rail.

"How beautiful," she murmured.

Leon nodded. "Sunrise is my favorite time of day," he confided.

"Mine too... when I've had enough sleep the night before," she returned with a gentle laugh. "Thank you for your help with Kitten last night."

"Of course."

He felt slightly embarrassed by the fact that she thought she needed to thank him for what he assumed was a common courtesy.

"There's no reason the responsibility of everything having to do with her should fall on you just because you're here now," he said.

He turned slightly to face her. She was still gazing toward the sunset, her face and hair glowing with a slight reflection of the colors.

"Same goes for the household chores," he added gruffly. "I hope you don't feel it's entirely up to you to do everything. I'm always willing to help if you need it. And not everything needs to be done all the time."

This caught Myra's attention. She turned her head, eyes widening.

"I'm sorry," she stammered after a moment. "Is there something you've noticed that I haven't kept on top of? If so, I'm only too happy to—"

"No." He cut her off abruptly and then winced at his own harsh tone. He took a breath, trying to rein in his frustration.

"I'm not criticizing you," he said as carefully as he could. "I'm encouraging you not to be too hard on yourself. You've hardly stopped working since you got here, and I just want you to know no one is going to mind if you take a break now and then. Or accept a little help."

She continued to stare at him with those wide green eyes as if waiting for him to take the words back and scold her. He attempted a smile to lighten the situation.

"The house is already far cleaner than it ever was when Ruby was taking care of it on her days off. And we've both eaten better in the past two days than... in the past two months."

Myra's face relaxed slightly. She still turned her mug in her hands nervously, though.

"Oh," she said. Then, hesitantly, she added a faint, "Thank you."

Feeling awkward, he turned back to the sunrise. She did the same. A moment later, she spoke again, slowly as if she was choosing her words with care.

"I've really... enjoyed taking care of the house and Kitten and cooking since I came here," she said. "But I will keep that in mind. I've actually been meaning to say something similar to you."

Leon glanced back at her, raising an eyebrow.

"Something about Ruby's subpar cooking and cleaning?"

Myra's face immediately flooded with red, erasing the faint freckles that had begun to show up in the morning light.

"No!" she exclaimed. "About helping each other. I've never lived on a farm before," she hurried on, "but I want you to know that I'd be happy to help with any farm chores it would be appropriate for me to do. Gathering eggs or... um, milking... whatever it would be. I like to be outside and around animals when I can be. You'd just have to teach me whatever you wanted me to do."

Her voice trailed off slightly as she finished, and she looked up at him, her gaze half bold, half pleading.

Leon studied her, marveling somewhat at what she had just offered. Finally, he lifted a shoulder.

"I suppose you could take over caring for the chickens," he said slowly. "If you really wanted to."

It was a job he particularly enjoyed as he found the chickens entertaining and easily pleased little creatures. It was especially pleasant in the spring, when a few of his hens invariably went broody and decided to raise a few chicks.

Myra's face lit up, and he found himself smiling at the picture that leapt into his mind of her discovering her first batch of chicks.

"Oh, yes. That would be perfect!"

"I don't want you to feel pressured, though," Leon said cautiously. "I know you have your hands full with the baby and the cooking. I'll show you how to do everything, but if you ever need for me to take the job back or even just fill in for you, you'll let me know, right?"

"I promise," Myra said happily. "What about gardening?" She had turned to fully face him now, her expression still bright and her posture leaned eagerly in. It did interesting things to his stomach, he thought, to have her standing so close, acting so confiding. "Do you have any gardens?"

"For vegetables? Not since Ruby went off to become a nurse," he admitted. "Since then, I've just been buying trucks off the neighbors."

"Would you consider having a garden again if I took care of it?" Myra pressed.

Leon couldn't shake his surprise that this slight young woman seemed so eager to take on even more work than they had already piled onto her. His admiration for her continued to rise.

"If you want one, I could till up a patch," he agreed slowly. "And pick up some seeds next time I'm in town."

"I don't want to cause you more trouble," Myra said quickly.

He shook his head, laughing slightly. "You're offering to grow fresh vegetables for us to enjoy all summer long, which will save me money and be great. If that's causing trouble, I can't imagine what you must think doing someone a favor to be."

Myra looked uncertain at first, but gradually, she let her face relax into a small smile. Their eyes locked, and Leon felt a strange zing of excitement. It was as if, he thought, they were partners of a sort, planning their adventures for the summer. It had been a long time since he had felt a similar feeling. Probably, he realized, since Mr. Harrington had passed on, leaving him to figure out the ranch himself.

Myra was the first to glance down, her face still slightly flushed.

"I should go start breakfast," she said. "Especially since Kitten's going to wake up any moment and want hers."

Leon followed her gaze to the sleeping baby in his arms.

"And I should go get breakfast for the animals," he agreed. As if in response to his words, a sheep suddenly baaed from the barn, and a horse whickered. He and Myra both laughed.

She reached for Kitten and he handed her over, hyper conscious of the way his and Myra's arms and hands brushed as they carefully made the transfer. Giving him one more quick smile, she was about to head into the house when the dogs started barking.

She and Leon turned to see a man riding down the drive.

Someone is out and about early, Leon thought in surprise. He stepped to the edge of the porch and watched as the man rode closer. His stomach tightened slightly as he finally recognized who it was.

Paul Graham. The new neighbor with the sour attitude. His face was difficult to make out at this distance, but Leon got the uncanny feeling that he was staring at Myra and the baby.

He turned toward her, nodding toward the house.

"Maybe you should go on in," he said tautly. Myra looked startled, but she didn't argue. Instead, she simply nodded and did as he said.

Leon made sure the door closed firmly behind her before he turned back to face the neighbor.

Paul Graham pulled his horse to a stop. He looked down at the dogs barking about its legs and declined to dismount.

"Sanders," he said, tipping his head slightly.

"Graham."

"I figured it was my turn to make a neighborly visit." Paul Graham's voice rang insincerely even as he plastered on a gracious smile. "My apologies if I caused any offense in our last conversation. I was a bit on edge, being so new to this area and all."

Leon hummed noncommittally. *Why are you really here?* The suspicion that clouded his emotions surprised him. He had never felt quite this way about anyone else before. Something about the man just didn't sit right with him.

"Your wife and child?" Graham asked, nodding toward the house. "You didn't mention you were married or a father when you were over my way."

"I didn't see any reason to," Leon said shortly.

He wasn't sure why he didn't correct his neighbor. If he stayed around long enough, he was bound to find out Leon and Myra weren't actually married. But it didn't matter right then. The desire to protect her and Kitten rose naturally within him. Claiming them as his own seemed the best way to do that at the moment.

"I suppose you all made it through the earthquake we had a few days ago all right," Graham said, his horse shifting under him.

"We did." Leon paused before forcing out dutifully, "You?"

"Unfortunately, my fences did take a hit. I've been working to fix 'em the past couple of days, but it's really a job that requires an extra pair of hands."

Leon bit his tongue before he could recall the man's own words to him about not needing any help on the 'dinky little place'. This, he realized, was the real reason for Graham's sudden neighborliness.

"If you could find the time to give me a hand, I'll happily pay you back with helping out over here, whenever and however you need it."

Leon found himself wanting to refuse, but he forced himself to stop and think before replying. Just because the man had bought the farm Leon had wanted to own himself, the farm he had partly grown up on, didn't make him an enemy. Neither did the fact that he had made a bad first impression give Leon a good reason to refuse him common neighborly courtesy.

Do for others what you'd want them to do for you, Mrs. Harrington had always said.

Swallowing the bitter lump in his throat, Leon nodded. He could not quite muster a smile.

"Sure," he said. "I'll give you a hand. Will tomorrow work?"

"Tomorrow will work just fine. I appreciate it."

Paul Graham tipped his head again. His gaze drifted over Leon's shoulder for just a moment before returning to his face. "You and your lovely wife have a wonderful day," he said.

He turned his horse and set off at a trot down the driveway. Leon watched him go, skin crawling.

Chapter Eleven

June 1897

"You're sure your wrist is up to this?" Leon stood next to the wagon, his head tilted to gaze up at Ruby with a doubtful expression.

She sighed. "I'm *completely* sure. And even if it does get tired, I'll just switch with Myra and hold the baby while *she* drives."

Myra stopped herself from casting an anxious glance at the reins in Ruby's hands. She had never driven a wagon before. She made an effort to give Leon an assuring smile instead, but it felt tight around the edges.

Still, it seemed to help. Nodding slowly, he stepped back and lifted his hand slightly in a wave. Ruby clucked to the horses and the wagon jolted forward. As Kitten whimpered against Myra's breast, she quickly turned her attention to comforting the baby.

She touched her soft face, her heart clenching at how hot it still felt. This was the second day Kitten had had a fever. Myra desperately hoped the doctor would be able to figure out what was causing it.

She lifted her head as they reached the road and glanced back at Leon. He was just turning from watching them go, surrounded by dogs and the calf. He ran a hand through his hair before replacing his hat.

"He worries about you," she said to Ruby.

"He worries about everything," Ruby responded, sounding exasperated. She tilted her head back, taking a dramatically

111

deep breath. "I haven't driven to town in nearly two weeks. This feels like freedom. Aren't you excited to be getting off the ranch for a change?"

She looked over at Myra, her smile expectant. Myra hesitated. "I would be more excited if it was for a reason other than Kitten being sick," she said gently.

Ruby's expression quickly altered, and she nodded. "Of course. I'm sure Adam will know what to do, though. He's a *really* good doctor, Myra. He could have been a doctor anywhere he wanted, but he chose Crested Butte because he grew up here. He wanted to come home and help the people he knew."

She bit her lip, glancing sideways. "If I tell you something, will you promise not to tell Leon? At least not until I have a chance to tell him?"

Myra nodded.

It wasn't like she and Leon did that much talking anyway, she thought. It had been nearly two weeks since the night they had chatted while taking care of Kitten. He had helped more than once since then, but their conversation had never returned to the deeper topics they'd begun to discuss then.

Which is proper for a governess and her employer, Myra reminded herself.

She quickly pulled her mind back to Ruby and the secret she was preparing to share.

"Adam sent a note the other day, when the grocer's boy made that delivery? He said how much he's missed my help in the clinic, and he said he's had the cottage cleaned out and repaired. It's ready for me to move in whenever I want."

"And... you think you'll want to soon?" Myra ventured.

Ruby cast another quick glance in her direction.

"I don't know," she said finally. "I'm so glad that you're here to help now, but I still feel bad about leaving you and Leon with everything. It's just... I love being a nurse. And it would be so much easier if I lived right there near to the clinic."

"And near to Adam?"

The moment she said them, Myra wished she could take the words back. She could hear her mother's sharp intake of breath in her head, followed by, *Myra, it is* not *your place ...*

But Ruby did not appear to think the comment was overfamiliar. She gazed steadily ahead, pink rising gently into her cheeks.

"I don't know," she said again. "I don't know how I feel about Adam— or even a relationship in general. Sometimes I think it would be the most natural thing in the world. Other times, I worry that it would ruin everything."

She turned to face Myra, biting her lip. "How *does* one know when marriage is right for them... or when they're in love?"

Myra shook her head. "I certainly don't know," she said. "I've no experience in that regard— except that I knew I didn't want to marry the man my parents had picked out for me."

"And yet, you would have married Leon? If the letter really had been from him?" Ruby asked. Her face was open and curious, but Myra felt her own face flushing now. She looked down, focusing on the baby in her lap.

"I don't know," she admitted. "Maybe. If there had been no other way."

"Well, I'm glad things worked out the way they did," Ruby said heartily. "I like having you around. You've already made our lives better. And I think you're a good influence on Leon."

"What do you mean?" Myra looked up, startled.

"About how you've made our lives better? Where do I even start? The house is far cleaner than it ever was when I was in charge, you're a much better cook, and with the garden in, we'll have homegrown vegetables all year. Kitten seems to be doing much better on the formula you made, and..."

"I meant about influencing Leon." Myra felt bad about interrupting, and she knew her face must be flushing with embarrassment, but she had to know.

"He's been coming in for meals," Ruby pointed out. "I think he's even put a little weight on, and he needed to. I feel like he's a little more relaxed too. He never liked me having to take care of the house on top of working in town. I don't know how to explain it exactly." Ruby shrugged helplessly. "It just seems he's breathing a little easier these days."

Myra nodded. She wasn't sure she understood what Ruby was getting at either, but it was some relief to know that her presence truly was appreciated.

"I'm glad you think so," she said softly. "I was so used to getting constant feedback from my mother growing up, I've been struggling to tell if my work is meeting standards. Neither you nor Leon ever criticizes..."

"Of course not!" Ruby exclaimed, turning wide eyes on her. "Why would we when you've taken so much on without us even asking?"

"I suppose my mother... saw things differently," Myra said.

They had reached the outskirts of town. Ruby waved to people she knew as she guided the horse to the front of the clinic. Myra climbed down carefully, cradling Kitten against her chest. The infant was quiet, blinking up at her with big, dark eyes. Her lethargy concerned Myra as much as the fever.

The doctor was less worried.

"It doesn't appear to be anything serious," he said after he'd given the baby a gentle examination. "Likely a little virus. You'll just want to make sure to keep her hydrated. Here..." He rummaged through a cabinet and pulled out a small packet. "You may try mixing a little of this powder into her formula. It's difficult for infants to get all of the nutrients they need from anything other than their mother's milk, and that can make them more vulnerable to illnesses. This should help."

"All right. Thank you, doctor," Myra said. Wrapping the baby back up, she glanced at Ruby, who had joined them in the examination room. Adam had been hard put not to glance her way frequently, and she could tell Ruby wanted a moment to talk to him alone.

"I'll just meet you out at the wagon," she said.

Tucking the drowsy baby against her shoulder, she let herself out of the room and crossed to the door of the clinic.

A man was just coming in, and he held the door for her. As she passed him, his eyes fell on the baby, and he did a double-take.

"Oh," he said, his eyes flicking from the baby to her hair and back to the child, "you're Leon Sander's wife, aren't you? I just caught a glimpse of you the other day when I came by to ask for his help with some fencing. That red hair is pretty unmistakable. I don't think I've met another person in town with hair quite like yours."

He smiled, a large but somehow insincere smile that showed a lot of teeth. Myra was flustered and uncomfortable, both with the way he was looking at her and the baby and by his assumption that she was Leon's wife. Or was it not an assumption? Had Leon *told* him she was his wife?

With an uncertain smile, she continued to inch away from the man, trying not to be impolite but anxious to move on. He didn't seem to catch on to her discomfort. Instead of heading into the doctor's office, as he had been prepared to do, he let the door swing shut and stepped toward her.

"I'm Paul Graham," he said. "Your nearest neighbor. Your husband helped me with my fences the other day. I told him anything he needs help with now, just let me know. But I haven't heard from him since."

Myra's stomach turned a somersault as the man referred to Leon as her "husband." She hoped her confusion wasn't completely obvious on her face.

"It's nice to meet you," she murmured. The man's eyes had returned to Kitten. He reached out as if to touch the edge of her blanket. Instinctively, Myra stepped back. Paul Graham's gaze flashed back up to hers, irritation quickly smoothed over with politeness.

"My apologies," he said stiffly. "Just… she doesn't really take after either you or Leon, does she? I'm assuming she is a she?"

"Yes, well, she's her own little person," Myra said. She was inching backwards again. To her relief, the man didn't follow her this time. He simply stood, looking after her until she turned and hurried to the wagon. As she climbed up and settled herself, she hoped Ruby would be out very soon so they could be on their way.

She felt unsettled, and she wanted to be back on the ranch. Where she felt safe.

Chapter Twelve

Leon had just finished positioning the cradle in Myra's room when he heard the sound of footsteps on the porch. The door opened, and Ruby's and Myra's voices spilled into the house.

"...good as new," Ruby was saying cheerfully. "Besides, it's just heating up the stew from last night, isn't it?"

"Well, I was going to make a few biscuits," Myra said, her voice soft and melodic.

"Then, *I'll* make a few biscuits," Ruby rejoined. "I'm insisting, Myra. I've done little enough to help since you got here, and pretty soon I won't have many chances. Go put your feet up and relax for a change. I'll call you when dinner's ready."

Feeling strangely nervous lest Myra catch him in her room, Leon quickly slipped into the hall and met the two women as they removed their bonnets at the door.

"Leon!" Ruby exclaimed in surprise. "I didn't expect you to be in at this time of day!"

Myra looked up, something flickering in her green eyes. When they met his, though, she said nothing. He stepped forward and took the baby from her so she could have both hands free to unlace her boots.

"What did the doc say?"

"He thinks it's a virus. Nothing serious," Myra said quietly. "We're just to make sure she gets enough fluids and try to cool the fever if it persists. He gave me a powder to add to her milk."

Once again, her eyes flicked to his. There was a question there, almost an assessment. He waited, holding her gaze, for her to ask it, but after a second, she let her eyes drop, her face flushing slightly.

He turned to Ruby. "I hear you're taking care of the supper fixings tonight."

"That's right," she said confidently. "And over dinner, I have something to discuss with you."

He nodded, already knowing what it would be.

"Well, if you're not going to be busy, then," he said, turning back to Myra, "there's something I'd like to show you."

She looked up, surprised.

"Me?"

"Yes. It's already in your room."

Still carrying Kitten, he led the way down the hall, conscious of Myra just behind him. At the door of her room, he stepped aside, motioning for her to go in ahead of him. She did, brushing lightly against him as she passed. She immediately saw the cradle.

"Oh!" she said. She stepped across the room to stand beside it. Her fingers brushed the smooth wood. Then she looked back at him, her eyes bright. "It's perfect. Did you make it?"

"Yeah. I figured Kitten had slept in a crate long enough. She needed a real bed. Something she could grow into."

Myra stilled at his statement, and he could see what she was thinking. Did he mean that he had given up on finding the baby's family? That he was going to keep her and raise her as his own? That he might require Myra's services for years to come?

Thankfully, she didn't ask any of the questions that crowded her brow. If she had, Leon still wouldn't have quite known what to answer. Instead, she said, "It's beautiful. I had no idea you did woodworking."

Leon leaned his shoulder against the doorframe beside him. "Mr. Harrington taught me a lot of things. He was a man of many trades, and a master at most of them. I'm not nearly as skilled as he was, but I can make do."

"Mr. Harrington— it was the Harringtons who raised you," Myra murmured, as if making sure she had things straight in her own mind. Ruby must have told her about the accident then. Good. It was a story Leon avoided retelling himself whenever possible.

"From the time I was ten and Ruby was five," he agreed gruffly. "Right up until they passed when I was seventeen."

"I'm sorry," she said softly. "It must have been... almost like losing your parents twice."

Leon felt the long-faded twist of pain that he knew would never quite disappear from his heart as she said the words. Myra's eyes were large and deep, the green having cooled like forest shadows. Rather than sympathy, her face showed a strange tension, as if she was as unsure of what to say in the moment as he was.

Finally, he just nodded. He looked down at Kitten to find that she had drifted asleep in his arms.

"Their ranch is the next one over," he said. "It felt as much like home as this one."

"I met the man who purchased it in town today," Myra said.

He looked back up at her quickly. "Paul Graham?" He couldn't seem to keep the frown from his face.

She nodded. Her gaze searched his.

"What did you make of him?" he asked finally.

"He... struck me as being a bit... too interested," Myra said. She was frowning herself now. Leon felt his gut tighten at her choice of words. Unexpectedly, anger rose within him.

"What do you mean?" he asked sharply. If the man had accosted her or made her uncomfortable in any way, he swore inwardly, he would head directly over there to have a word with him. And then maybe into town to have a word with the sheriff.

He felt sick at the thought that Myra or Kitten should ever be in any kind of danger.

"Oh, he just... asked about Kitten and commented on... on my hair—" Myra blushed "—and on how she looked nothing like either one of us." She paused, her color deepening as she glanced up at him. "He seems to be under the impression that we're married and Kitten is ours," she said finally, painfully.

Leon reached up, rubbing a hand through his hair.

"That's my fault," he admitted. "I don't like him much either, and... it felt like the best way to keep him away from you and her." It was his turn to feel the heat rise in his cheeks as he wondered how Myra would take this announcement. Maybe she would be annoyed by him trying to look out for her in this way, as Ruby often was. Maybe she would even be angered by the lie he had allowed to stand.

But she didn't react. Instead, after a moment, she simply walked over and took Kitten from him.

"Time she try out her new bed," she said softly. "I fed her a bottle at the clinic, so she should be good for a couple of hours yet."

Leon remained where he was, leaning in the doorway, as Myra carried the baby to the new cradle and bent to tuck her in. He could have gone. He realized that. He had shown her what he intended to show her. There was no reason for him to linger.

But he wanted to linger. Myra was still a mystery to him: her responses, the things she noticed, the things she said. And it was a mystery that drew him in like the novels he had read as a boy. If there was a way to solve her, he wanted to be the one to do it.

When Myra turned, she did not seem surprised to see him still standing there.

"What are you going to do now with all your free time since you don't have to fix supper?" he asked, grinning slightly.

Myra tipped her chin upward, an answering smile tugging at the corners of her lips as she thought for a moment. Slowly, shyness returned to her face. Once again, she looked as if she wanted to ask a question but was too afraid to do so.

"What?" he said.

"I think I'd just like to take a walk," she said. "I've always enjoyed walking. But... I don't really know my way around the farm beyond the garden and the driveway."

"I'll go with you." The words flew from his mouth as if of their own accord, but he was not sorry he'd said them. "Show you around," he added. "If you want me to."

As usual, Myra's expression was difficult to read. Her lips continued to sit in a pleasant tilt. Her green eyes searched his. Heat rose through his body as he waited for her answer.

"I would like that."

The spurt of energy that shot through him at her quiet words was completely unexpected. He did his best not to let it show. Turning, he gestured with his hand for her to go first. She slipped past him.

"Kitten shouldn't wake for a while, but I'll just ask Ruby to keep one ear out for her," she murmured, slipping into the kitchen.

Leon went to put on his boots, trying at the same time to slow the beating of his heart. What was this feeling that was flooding through him? He felt nervous and excited at the same time.

It's just a walk around the farm, he told himself.

With the woman who came out here to be your bride, a voice in his head reminded him.

It wouldn't have made any difference, he thought, if she hadn't been... well, Myra. Myra fascinated him in a way a woman never had before. He admired her and wondered about her.

Am I starting to have feelings for her?

He pushed the idea from his head the moment it appeared. It was too preposterous, especially after such a short time of knowing one another.

The dogs were already excitedly whining at the door, so he let them out. Immediately, Crocket's nose lifted into the air, and he went rigid. He barked, and the other two dogs joined him, perking their ears and glancing around.

Frowning, Leon stepped out after them and glanced around.

The yard was quiet, the long shadows of evening stretching from the house toward the fields.

"What is it?" he asked. But the dogs seemed as confused as he was. They ran in circles, Piper making it as far as the drive before she seemed to lose the scent of whatever it had been.

Finally, Leon called them back. They crowded around him, their postures tense, glancing about with alert eyes.

Uneasiness crept through him like a chill.

He determined to keep Myra close as they took their walk and keep a close eye out for anything that seemed out of place. Something was off... he just couldn't pinpoint what it was.

Chapter Thirteen

Warm air gushed through the open windows, stirring the stove-heated kitchen air without cooling it. Myra could feel that her cheeks were rosy red from the heat.

The day has been unseasonably hot for mid-June. She probably would have been wise to wait for some other day to make such a complicated dinner.

But she was feeling anything but wise these days. *Nervous. Giddy. Off kilter.* All of those would be better terms to describe her state of mind lately, and all of them had increased dramatically since Leon had driven Ruby away that morning in the wagon piled with her belongings.

He was planning to spend a good part of the day helping her move into the cottage and make a few repairs that still needed done there. But he would be back for dinner. And then it would be just him, Myra, and Kitten.

Myra's stomach stirred with renewed nerves as she thought of it. She paused in her dinner preparations to peek into Kitten's cradle. The baby was sleeping soundly. Myra touched her round, rosy cheek gently. It was warm and soft. She hadn't had a fever again since their trip to the doctor, for which Myra was grateful.

Hurrying back to the oven, she opened the door slightly to peek inside.

Her stomach dropped slightly. The mutton roast she'd spent all afternoon brining and basting somehow looked stranger each time she checked it. It was more gray than golden brown at this point.

She had not thought that cooking mutton would be that different from the pork and beef she'd fixed many times back home, but something was certainly not right.

Sighing, she decided to pull the roast out and hope for the best. If she continued to cook it, she was afraid it would go from gray to black. Besides, she needed to put her biscuits in.

At least the vegetables for the meal were going to be good. And the dessert. She had a huge pot of fresh peas from the garden ready to start simmering, and the rhubarb pie she'd baked early that day was cooling on the kitchen table. It would be perfect with whipped cream, she thought, but she had noticed that the sheep's milk did not have as much cream as cow's milk, and she didn't want to steal the extra fat from Kitten and Leon's calf.

Setting the pan of dubious mutton on the table next to the pie, Myra adjusted the peas over the heat and went to the door and peered out. Leon should be getting home any time now, she thought, her heart quickening. Would it be terribly awkward, just the two of them eating together? She hoped not. But it was hard to know.

She and Leon were both quiet by nature, and they had been happy so far to let Ruby fill in most of the gaps when all of them were together at dinner. But there were also times, she thought, when conversation between just the two of them came easily. Like when they took care of the baby together at night, or when he had taken her on the tour of the farm.

As she remembered walking side by side with him along the tidy fences and field rows, the flutter in her stomach grew stronger. She couldn't exactly pinpoint when Leon had started to make her feel this way. She had felt something since the beginning, she knew, when she first saw him standing there, holding the baby. But the strange thumps of her heart kept getting stronger— each time she saw him smiling as he bottle fed the calf, or bending to pet one of his three dogs, or taking Kitten from her cradle just because he loved to hold her while she slept.

Walking with him that day, hearing him talk so fondly about the lambs and the farm itself, there had hardly been a moment when her inner emotions had *not* been in an uproar.

At some point, she was going to have to figure out what that was all about. But so far, she had been too busy with the house and garden and Kitten —just trying to keep on top of things— for any introspection.

She hadn't even found time to draw or paint since coming to live here. Though her tension had eased slightly over the weeks of receiving no criticism from either Leon or Ruby about how she was doing with things, she still had a sinking sensation whenever she thought about them finding her playing at her hobby rather than doing something useful.

Her mother had only ever tolerated the art because she felt practice was necessary to make Myra a well-educated (and marriageable) young woman. Once she was married, she had always made it clear, Myra was unlikely to have time for such frivolity. And even though she *wasn't* married yet, her life was very similar to what it would have been if she was. Wasn't it?

The heat in her cheeks was unbearable. Opening the door, Myra stepped out onto the porch. Here the breeze was stronger. Even if it wasn't much cooler, it felt far more pleasant. She tilted her face to it, letting it blow away the flushed feelings and stop her hair from tickling her cheeks as it had been doing all afternoon.

The dogs were all lying about the yard, waiting for Leon's return. Piper lay closest to the drive, her chin on her paws. Crocket was further back in the shade of the oak tree, sprawled on his side, fast aslccp. Shell lay at the bottom of the porch steps, and when she saw Myra emerge, she leapt up and came to her, wagging her tail.

Myra bent to pet the dog, her heart warming. It pleased her to realize how easily she could tell the triplets apart now. And it pleased her even more to be recognized by them as a member of the family, a part of their home.

She looked up at the sound of the calf bawling. She was standing at the base of the stairs, chewing on a sprig of grass, looking up at her expectantly.

"I'm sure Leon will feed you when he gets home," Myra laughed. "We really need to name you," she added thoughtfully. Leon always just called her "the calf." He had admitted to her on their walk —laughing as the calf ran leaping and skipping ahead of them— that at first it had been because he didn't want to get too attached to her. She had been a weak, scrawny thing when he took her in.

No more, Myra thought, watching the sturdy red calf yank at another strand of grass curiously.

At an excited yip from Piper, Myra looked up to see the wagon coming down the drive. Leon was slouched in the driver's seat, his head slightly bowed. He looked up and spotted her on the porch. Myra's heart stood still for a moment. She felt nervous, almost embarrassed to have been caught waiting for him.

Then he lifted a hand in the peculiar, motionless wave he had. And her heart started beating again, a bit too fast. She lifted her hand to wave in return.

The smell of scorched peas drifted from the kitchen behind her. With a yelp, she turned and ran back into the house, almost tripping over Shell, who had been leaning against her skirt.

The peas had run out of water, and the bottom layer was stuck to the pot.

"Oh, no!"

Myra poured more water on them and worked her wooden spoon hard across the pan. Slowly the peas popped free, turning the water an oily brown as the burnt bits crumbled. Myra groaned. Closing her eyes for a moment, she waited until her pounding heart slowed slightly.

This was the first time she'd ruined a meal. Would Leon yell at her as her mother would have? She felt angry with herself for ruining a meal she had intended to be extra special. Now it was just going to be extra uncomfortable.

Fearing she had left them too long as well, she snatched the biscuits out of the oven without testing them and began to set the table.

She nearly had everything ready when she heard Leon in the entryway.

He came in a moment later, slowly, limping hard.

Immediately, she felt her worries over dinner fade a little.

"Are you all right?" she asked.

"What?" He looked momentarily confused. Then, as she glanced subtly at his leg, he followed her gaze and grimaced. "Oh, yeah. Just overdid it a little, I guess— hauling Ruby's furniture and climbing a ladder. It'll be all right come morning."

Myra nodded. She started to ask, then bit her lip. Leon crooked an eyebrow at her.

"What?" he said again. At the same time, he limped past her to the cradle in the corner. Myra hovered, watching his face

128

soften as he looked in at Kitten, feeling her heart tremble in response.

"I... I just wondered if you'd feel comfortable telling me what happened to your leg. Sometime." She could feel her face flushing, and it made her feel more awkward than ever. "You don't have to if you don't want to," she added hastily.

Leon glanced up. He didn't look surprised by her question, only somewhat resigned.

He sighed, then nodded.

"I'll tell you over supper," he said. "I was wondering how we were going to fill the silence without Ruby here to chatter." His voice was warm, affectionate as he said it. Myra giggled before she could stop herself, surprise breaking through her shyness.

"I was wondering the same thing," she said. "While I was cooking."

Leon nodded. "We're neither one of us big talkers," he agreed. "At least, I haven't heard you talk very much since you got here. Is that how you were before or was it just that Ruby never let you get a word in edgewise and I'm too intimidating?"

"You're not intimidating," Myra said immediately. Then, flushing again, she said, "I mean, not in a bad way. It's just..." She was only making things worse. "I was never around many people growing up, especially men, aside from my family and our priest and his sister."

"Priest?"

As Myra went into motion again, setting plates on the table and getting a knife for the mutton, he limped to the table and pulled out a chair, lowering himself into it with a stifled groan.

"Why, yes." Myra glanced at him, surprised. "Father Timothy. He took our parish when the old priest, Father

Malcom died when I was… oh, thirteen. He and his sister lived in the rectory, and I would often visit. Alice and I were very good friends. In fact…"

She hesitated, wondering at her own chattiness. Alice was the only one she'd ever chatted to so freely. She wondered what was making her so open and loquacious now: Leon's easy attention or her own nerves.

"In fact, it was Alice who showed me the ad for the mail-order bride that brought me here," she finished, somewhat reticently.

"Ah. Then, I suppose I have Alice to thank for that," Leon said. There were lines at the corners of his eyes, like he wanted to smile but was keeping it in for some reason. "Although, I'm somewhat shaken to learn that you're Catholic. I haven't seen you doing the rosary or lighting candles or anything like that since you came." His face sobered slightly as he studied her. "Do you make prayers for the dead?"

Myra dropped her gaze, focusing on popping the biscuits off the pan into a towel-lined basket. They felt ominously heavy. Surely she hadn't managed to spoil them as well!

"I make prayers for everyone I care about," she said quietly. "And I try to pray for people who have wronged me as well. After all, the Bible says to love our enemies."

Leon nodded slowly. "They preach that in the church here as well," he said. "Perhaps Protestant and Catholic beliefs aren't so far apart as I've been led to believe?"

"I… I don't know," Myra admitted. "But I'd be happy to go with you to your church, if you attend sometime."

"I do try to, off an' on," he said. "Ruby has always been more into it than I have. I suppose… being older than her when it happened, I found it more difficult not to blame God for our parents' deaths."

Myra looked up, surprised by this vulnerability. She answered carefully.

"Do you feel you've gotten past that now? Blaming God, I mean?"

"Yeah, I think so. Most of the time."

Leon's brown eyes looked especially dark as he looked back at her contemplatively. He was leaning back in his chair, apparently relaxed. She could feel his eyes still on her as she began serving their plates.

The mutton had not improved with sitting. She had to saw hard with the knife to get through it, and the gravy looked blobby. She had stirred the burned peas into the rest until they were difficult to see, but the entire batch still smelled a little off.

"That's when my leg was injured," Leon said unexpectedly. "In the same accident my parents were killed."

Slowly, Myra slid into her seat at the table. She pushed Leon's plate across to him, and he picked up his fork, but didn't immediately start eating.

"We were on our way home from a camping trip, up in the mountains," he said slowly, his voice low. "I'd been swimming and climbing and fishing all day, and I fell asleep in the back of the wagon. A storm came up, suddenly, and it made a flash flood."

His voice caught. Myra held her breath, her heart already aching for the ending she knew was coming.

"It pushed the wagon over the edge of the path and off the side of the mountain. I was thrown free, but the wagon landed on my leg and pretty much shattered my knee. My parents and Ruby were still in the wagon when it reached the bottom of the mountain. Only Ruby survived."

"How did you..." Myra caught herself and bit her tongue. Now was not the time to be pressing for details simply to satisfy her curiosity. But Leon looked up and lifted an eyebrow, waiting for her to continue.

"How did you get off the mountain?" she asked, flushing. "You and Ruby. Did someone come along and find you?"

Slowly, Leon shook his head.

"I dragged myself to the bottom of the ravine," he said. "Ruby had hit her head and was unconscious. At first..." He paused, suddenly fighting for control of his emotions. Myra felt sympathetic tears stinging her own eyes.

"At first, I hoped my parents were as well, but... they were both already gone by the time I got to them. One of the horses, miraculously, had broken free before the wagon went all the way down, and I... somehow got me and Ruby onto him. We rode him to town for help."

"And how old were you?" Myra breathed.

"Ten," Leon said simply. "Ruby was five. She had amnesia for a week, didn't even know who I was and never really remembered what happened. But she's irrationally terrified of storms. The Harringtons, our neighbors, took us in, and Mr. Harrington helped me take care of this property as well as his own until they passed away when I was seventeen and Ruby was twelve."

He paused, swallowing.

"The Harringtons were like a second set of parents to us. Their death was sudden too. Otherwise, I think they would have left the farm to us. It sat vacant for eight years until Paul Graham bought it."

Myra suppressed a shudder at the reminder of their neighbor. She lifted her fork, with a few peas and a tiny piece of mutton on it, to her mouth and took a bite. Across the table, Leon began to eat as well.

The mutton was like leather. No matter how long Myra chewed, it wouldn't turn into something swallowable. And the peas tasted acrid and bitter— scorched. Grimacing, she glanced across the table to see if Leon was spitting his bite back onto his plate. But he was taking another bite, chewing and swallowing as if nothing was wrong.

She forced herself to swallow the bite and reached for her water, washing it down with a generous swallow. It seemed shallow to bring up the disaster so immediately after Leon had bared his heart to her. So, instead, she offered him a biscuit. He took it with a swift smile in her direction.

Myra felt warmth spill through her once again. She still forgot, even after nearly two months, how different Leon was to her adoptive parents. He was kind. And it seemed to her all of a sudden that it was the nicest characteristic a man could possibly have.

Chapter Fourteen

July 1897

"Leon!" Ruby threw herself across the threshold and into his arms, startling him so much he stumbled slightly. "I've missed you," she said against his shoulder.

Regaining his balance, he let his arms fold around her.

"Missed you too, sis," he chuckled. "I've forgotten how to be ready for a sneak attack like that."

"How have you all been getting along without me?" Ruby asked eagerly as they released each other. He grabbed her hand to help her up into the wagon, and she settled herself, reaching up to touch her smooth, brown bun as if the hug might have knocked it askew. "Has Kitten grown? I'm so looking forward to spending two whole days with you all! I expected to see you all at least sometime in the past two weeks." Her tone turned reproachful.

"We've been keeping busy," Leon said. "And yes, Kitten grows every day. She started rolling over last week, and she loves playing with her toys."

He circled around the wagon, fully conscious of how strange the moment felt. First, Ruby looked different. He couldn't put his finger on exactly what it was, but he had never not seen his sister for two entire weeks before. There was a sparkle to her that he didn't remember, and a sort of distance. He supposed it was from the experience both of them had had the past two weeks that had not been shared.

He supposed it was the opposite of the feeling that had been growing between him and Myra. They *had* been sharing experiences over the past weeks. Dinners together had grown more and more comfortable, conversation flowing more and more casually. Sitting here next to Ruby, he couldn't help but think of all the details that he and Myra had shared that it would take far too long to fill his sister in on.

There was no reason she needed to know about how the lambs were growing or the garden producing though. Likely, she wouldn't find it interesting anyway. The fascination was all his own, he guessed, and it had a lot to do with the copper-haired housekeeper who had grown to feel more like family than anything.

He was conscious of Ruby's eyes on him as he settled beside her and took up the reins, clicking to the horses.

"Is the sheriff still looking for her parents?" she asked at last.

Leon shrugged, a chill spearing through him.

"I suppose he is," he admitted grudgingly.

When had finding Kitten's parents stopped being his fondest wish and become his greatest dread? He couldn't pinpoint an exact moment. He suspected it had happened gradually over the course of evenings and nights with her and Myra, passing her back and forth when she was fussy and just watching her in delight when she was happy and sleeping and learning to play.

He thought of the way Myra's face lit with beautiful affection as she smiled at the baby and his heart stung freshly. If he lost Kitten, he would lose Myra. It was more than likely. Surely she wouldn't stay on just to take care of him and the little, leaking ranch house.

"And how have you and Myra been getting along?" Ruby asked next, as if she could read his thoughts. He felt heat crawling up his neck and hoped she wouldn't notice.

"Fine."

"Just fine? Honestly, I thought you might be getting fat by this time on her fabulous cooking," Ruby chuckled.

Leon smothered a grin as his mind flew back to their first dinner together after Ruby had moved to town. He didn't exactly know why or how, but somehow, Myra had managed to ruin everything she tried to cook that evening. He had tried not to react to the gray leather mutton, the scorched peas, and the undercooked biscuits, but Myra was eating the same thing, and she let it pass without comment.

"You might as well take the leftovers to the dogs," she'd said as he was pushing his chair out to leave. He had looked up, startled, to find her meeting his gaze with an expression that was half defiant and half nervous.

"Oh, and I named the calf while you were gone," she added irrelevantly. "Her name is Brigid."

"Brigid?"

"Brigid was a dragon-slaying Catholic saint. I hope you don't mind."

The humor of the moment had been too much for him to hold back his chuckle. The moment it burst out, he looked to Myra, afraid of hurting her feelings, but after a moment of confusion, she'd simply looked relieved. Then, she started laughing too.

"What are you smirking about?"

Leon jerked his mind back to the present at Ruby's demand.

"Oh... nothing," he said quickly. Shrugging self-consciously, he hurried on. "How about you? Have you been keeping busy?"

As Ruby launched into a recitation of her past two weeks, he relaxed. His mind, however, continued to race.

Was he truly in danger of letting his feelings for Myra show when he didn't even intend to? And if so, did Myra have an inkling of them? He found himself searching back over the past two weeks of their cohabitation, seeing everything through new, self-conscious eyes.

Had he been too familiar at times? Too open and sincere? Myra had never made him feel so. In fact, the warmth of her personality was much to blame, he thought, for drawing him out of himself as much as she had. But maybe that was just who she was. Maybe it really had nothing to do with him. Maybe she didn't dread the day, like he did, that Kitten would be taken away and she was free to move on with her life.

She'd come out here to get married and have her own family, he remembered. Likely, she still wanted that, and he was keeping it from her.

He was so mired in self-doubt and worry, he had trouble keeping up the proper responses to Ruby's conversation as they continued to the ranch.

As he guided the horse down the drive, the dogs leapt from their spots in the yard where they lay keeping watch, barking. He saw a flurry of movement on the porch— Myra. She seemed to have been working on something, her lap full of material of some kind.

As the wagon rolled into the yard, Ruby called out and waved. Myra turned, smiling, then hurried into the house.

A moment later, she reemerged, her hands free. Ruby skipped up the stairs and hugged her. From Myra's momentarily stiff reception, Leon gathered that the exuberant greeting surprised her even more than it had surprised him a bit earlier. As her green eyes met his over Ruby's shoulder, he raised his eyebrows, smirking slightly.

He watched as her expression responded, softened with humor. Then, his heart beating a bit fast, he set about unhitching the horse and putting away the harness. The women had gone inside by the time he walked up onto the porch thirty minutes later.

He glanced at the rocker where Myra had been sitting when they arrived, wondering again at her hurry to get her work out of sight. A square of white paper on the wooden floorboards caught his eye.

Stepping across to it, he bent with some difficulty to pick it up. It appeared blank until he flipped it over.

A strange whooshing sound filled his head as he digested the paper's contents.

It was a sketch, beautifully and intricately done. It showed a man seated in the rocker Myra herself had just vacated. His left leg was stretched out somewhat stiffly in front of him, and his head was bent over the baby in his arms. Even with his face turned slightly away, the gentle expression was clear, as was the identity of the man.

It was him. And it was Piper sitting next to the rocker, her uneven ears cocked as she peered up at him and Kitten.

Myra must have drawn it. It must have been what she was doing when they arrived. It was astonishing, though, for him to consider that this piece of art had been created by her slender fingers holding a pencil to paper. Of course, she was talented— in everything she did. But she had never given any indication that she was an artist.

The thing that set his pulse throbbing most though was the emotion the picture seemed to convey. As if she'd somehow captured the scene through the eyes of the viewer— which would have to be her. The depiction suggested not only his affection for the baby, but the affection of the one watching...

But no. He blinked, forcing himself to come back to the real world. He couldn't be making assumptions like that, he thought, his face heating. It was dangerous. Everything he'd been feeling and thinking recently was dangerous. This seemingly peaceful life they had shaped for themselves balanced on the knife's edge of finding out who Kitten really was.

It was precarious— far too precarious for him to be feeling this deep, soul-tugging desire to hold everything just the way it was, close to his heart, and never let go.

Chapter Fifteen

Myra found herself distracted the next morning, despite Ruby's stream of cheerful conversation. She didn't have any excuse, she told herself. Kitten had been sleeping through most of the nights recently, only waking for a feeding before going right back to sleep. She had felt flustered ever since Ruby and Leon had almost caught her wiling away the time drawing while she waited for them to arrive from town the evening before.

She hadn't started out to get lost in her sketching. Once she had prepared everything for supper —she was playing it smart and keeping things simple this time— and tucked Kitten in for her nap, she had felt antsy. She needed something to do while she waited for their return, and her thoughts had drifted again to her long-neglected pencils and paper.

Images drifted through her mind that she hadn't even realized she had been capturing and storing away for later. Many of them —an almost embarrassing amount— featured Leon. Nearly as many were of Kitten. As she pictured their features rendered in smoothly-shaded black and white, her fingers had itched for her pencil... and she'd finally given in.

She had spent a good two hours just sitting on the porch sketching, and the time had gone by so swiftly, she hadn't even noticed it was gone until the dogs barked and she looked up to see the wagon pulling into the yard.

Her drawings and supplies were still in a heap in the top drawer of her bureau where she'd stuffed them before rushing back out to greet the siblings.

"I told him we would all be there, naturally," Ruby said cheerfully.

Myra turned around, realizing she had completely lost track of the conversation. Her eyes caught Leon's. He was leaning back in his chair, Kitten on his lap, gnawing toothlessly at an apple slice. He was watching her lazily across the table, his dark eyes inscrutable. She felt herself growing flushed and more flustered than ever, although she didn't know why.

"I'm sorry," she stammered, "You told who we would all be where?"

"Reverend Valoy," Ruby said. "I told him we'd be in church Sunday and stay for the potluck after. Practically the entire town is going to be there."

"Oh..." Myra stood still, the spatula she'd been using to flip pancakes hovering just above the skillet. Conflicting emotions rushed through her at the thought of participating in a community-wide event. Excitement, nerves...

"Myra's Catholic," Leon said. "She might not want to go."

His eyes watched Myra steadily, his lips quirking slightly. She couldn't tell if he was recalling fondly the close conversations they'd had over the past weeks or making fun of her. She felt her shoulders stiffen slightly.

"Of course I'd like to go," she said. "I'd love to meet the people of the community."

"That's what I told him," Ruby said, happily stabbing up another bite of pancakes. "I told him *all* about you."

Why in heaven's name? Myra thought, her heart beginning to race again.

"Myra?" At the sound of Leon's soft pronunciation of her name, she yanked her attention back to the present. He was watching her with a slight frown. "Are you sure?" he asked. "We don't have to go if you don't want to."

141

"She said she wanted to!" Ruby protested, looking back and forth between them with an injured expression.

"But she looks like she's about to panic," Leon pointed out.

Myra felt a warm gush of feeling, both grateful and somewhat frightened by the fact that he saw her so clearly.

"It just feels like it's been so long since I was around anyone other than you three," she said, attempting a weak laugh. "Aside from popping into the grocer's and the feedstore a couple of times. I won't know many people at all... but truly, I'm looking forward to meeting them, Ruby."

She gave the other woman a warm smile before turning back to the pancakes.

Would they look forward to meeting her, though? Leon and Ruby had been so kind in their acceptance of her, but suddenly, she was barraged with memories of her mother's criticisms: that she was too quiet until she spoke out of turn. That she didn't know how to dress or carry herself or be properly charming in a conversation.

Above all, she found she didn't want to embarrass Leon and Ruby, after the way they had put their trust in her. Especially Leon. Her face flushed as she admitted to herself —and she was glad her back was turned so he couldn't see— that it had felt almost like being a family the past two weeks without Ruby. She had found herself imagining more than once what it would be like if they really were a family. If Leon had married her when she came like the ad said he would. Or if he might decide to marry her...

She refused to let her thoughts go down that path. He had given no indication that he felt that way about her. She was counting eggs before they hatched, jumping to conclusions... all things her mother had spent years trying to teach her not to do.

Maybe she had been right in calling Myra a slow learner.

Flipping the remaining pancakes onto a plate, Myra did her best to compose her face before she turned to set them on the table. She could feel Leon's eyes still on her, but she refused to look up and meet his gaze.

***

Eyes were on her again as they entered the church the following day. She could feel them, hear the murmur of interest that scuttled among those settling into their pews as she and Leon and Ruby slipped into the church moments before the service began.

She felt her face flushing and hoped that her hat would hide most of it. She had spent extra time this morning, choosing an outfit from her meager store, pinning up her hair, tying the hat on with a ribbon.

"Oh, you look so lovely," Ruby had exclaimed as they walked out to the wagon together, the younger woman carrying Kitten, whom she'd been doting on since arriving. "See? It's a good thing to get dressed up and off the farm sometimes, isn't it?"

Agreeing with a nervous laugh, Myra had looked up as Leon offered his hand to help her into the wagon. His eyes met hers, but he said nothing.

He said nothing now as he stepped aside for the two women to slip into the pew. He followed them in, angling himself slightly so that he didn't have to bend his knee hard in behind the pew but could let his leg stretch out slightly toward the aisle. Watching the grimace that flickered across his face before he quickly hid it, Myra felt her heart pinch.

From what he had said and the way she watched him favor the leg subconsciously, she knew he must be in pain nearly all of the time. She wondered if the constant pain kept the grief and trauma of the accident that had caused it and taken his parents' lives as painful and fresh.

Pushing the dark thoughts from her mind, she turned forward, doing her best to focus on the first Protestant service she had ever attended.

She found that she fully enjoyed it —the hearty singing of hymns, and then the surprisingly personable address given by the tall, young Reverend Valoy.

"You do know that Protestant reverends don't have to remain celibate like Catholic priests, don't you?" Ruby whispered, leaning close halfway through the service.

Myra nodded, glancing at her, puzzled as to why she would bring it up. When she saw the sparkle in Ruby's eye, she understood. Was the girl now trying to set her up with the reverend? After writing an ad to get her out here to marry Leon— and then telling her not to give up on him?

She was surprised by the sharp little stab of anger that speared through her. Quickly, she tried to squash it, but her heart still felt pained. Did Ruby agree, then, that Leon would never change his mind about marriage?

But she hasn't seen how things have changed the past two weeks, Myra found herself arguing.

She was unfortunately very distracted by her thoughts the rest of the service. As it ended, the reverend announced the potluck, and the congregants eagerly flooded out of the church to the picnic tables in the yard, where the food was set out among much good-natured laughter and chatter.

As they allowed themselves to be swept out with the other churchgoers, Myra took Kitten back from Ruby, needing the security of the baby in her arms. She was conscious of Leon at her back as well, and of how safe and belonging it made her feel.

And she was conscious of missing his presence when they were eventually separated by the groups of men coming to greet Leon and women coming to meet her. As Myra smiled, her heart pounding, Ruby began to make introductions with relish.

"Myra, this is June Daily. Her husband, Hal Daily, runs the lumber mill in town."

As the older woman pressed Myra's hand and cooed over the baby, Myra felt her chest tighten further. There was something about the woman's measuring glance, even beneath her genial smile, that reminded her of her adoptive mother.

"I declare," the woman exclaimed jovially, "the way you and Leon came in to church and out of church together with that darling baby between you, I would have sworn you were a happy little family! I was prepared to ask you exactly *how* you managed to snag that young man's heart when every other lady in this town who's pined after him —including my own daughter— have tried and failed. But Ruby here tells me you're only here as a governess for poor little Catherine."

"Oh, yes, that's correct." Myra smiled, her arms tightening around the baby despite herself.

"Well, I'll tell Sophia she still has a chance then," Mrs. Daily beamed. "I'm sure she'll be relieved."

Don't you dare! Myra wanted to cry. She held herself back at the last moment, lightheaded with mortification that the thought had even crossed her mind. She tried and failed to hold on to the other names and faces as Ruby introduced her to more women.

Eventually, they made it through the line, filling their plates. Glancing around, she spotted Leon at a table with several other men. She headed toward it, unheeding of whether Ruby followed or not. Leon glanced up at their approach and then stood.

"Sheriff," he said to the man beside him, "this is Myra Barnes. And the baby, of course."

"Happy to meet you, Miss Barnes," the sheriff said, tipping his large white hat, "as I'm sure all of the other single bachelors around here are." He chuckled. "I'm warning you, Leon, you've only got a short time to snatch this lovely girl up before someone else will happily step into your place."

Myra froze in the act of setting her plate on the table, feeling her face flame. Leon looked equally flabbergasted, but his answer when it came was not what Myra had expected.

"I think you've got the wrong idea, Sheriff," he said stiffly, "Myra is simply here as a governess for Kitten. I mean, Catherine. I meant it when I said there's nothing more between us."

It felt almost as if he had slapped her. Inwardly, Myra could feel herself reeling backwards. Of course, she'd told herself she might be imagining any kind of affection from him—she'd told herself he was just being kind—but... to say it right out like that with everyone listening (she was sure Mrs. Daily was right behind her listening) felt devastating.

Heat flooded her face, and hot tears prickled at the backs of her eyes. She recalled the moment she had realized that Ruby had sent the ad and that she was unwanted on the Sanders farm. It felt the same way now. Just as then, she wished she could sink through the ground and disappear.

Instead, she managed to murmur something like, "I think Kitten needs her bottle now."

Then, she spun, blindly, hurriedly, ignoring Ruby's call, and rushed toward the church, where at least she would be alone, away from the eyes that now felt judging, mocking, as they followed her ignominious flight.

Chapter Sixteen

Leon's ability to keep up in a social situation had never been great, and he could feel it draining away by the moment. As Hal nattered on about the recent demand for pine at the mill, he found himself zoning out, his eyes searching the crowds for Ruby and Myra.

He soon spotted his sister, sitting noticeably close to Adam's side at a nearby table, in animated conversation with the young reverend and Sophia, the Dailys's adult daughter across the table. But Myra was nowhere.

Frowning, Leon realized he hadn't seen her since she had hurried abruptly off to the church, saying something about feeding the baby.

His mind flashed to the strange incident she had reported having with Paul Graham and the way the dogs had behaved later, as if someone had been lurking around. Ruby would call him paranoid, as she often did, for his sudden unease, but he was standing from the table before he'd even realized it.

Hal cut off in surprise, and he glanced down.

"Sorry, Hal. I'll be back," he said quickly.

He hurried to the church, taking the steps as quickly as his leg would allow him to. The big wooden doors creaked as he pushed them open and stepped inside. The church was stuffy and quiet, making his footsteps that much more noticeable as they clumped up the aisle.

Myra was seated in the pew where they had sat for church. She looked up, startled at the sound of his approach. Then, her countenance fell into an expression of quiet disappointment.

"Hoping for someone else?" he asked, attempting to make light of the situation. It struck him as strange that Myra had chosen to hide out here in the church building with all the socializing going on outside— though personally, it seemed like a pretty good idea to him.

Myra didn't answer. She simply shook her head, looking back down at Kitten. The baby was asleep. Maybe that was why she hadn't come back out.

Grunting quietly, Leon slid into the pew beside her, stretching his leg out with a sigh of relief.

"It's all a little overwhelming, isn't it?" he said.

Was he trying to make small talk? As Myra nodded again, he was overcome by the strangeness of it all. He could sense that something was off with her. He had never been so attuned to another person's moods, but also, Myra was easy to read. Her face was like a glassy lake, reflecting and rippling with every emotion.

It made him even more uneasy that she seemed to be trying to hide it from him.

"Hey. Is something wrong?"

Without even realizing what he was doing, he reached out and took her hand.

Finally, he had her attention. Myra's head snapped up, her big green eyes meeting his. They were glistening with tears. His heart somersaulted.

"What's the matter?" he asked. "Are you hurt? Sick? Did someone say or do something...?"

"We should go back out. Otherwise people *are* going to think there's something going on between us," Myra said thickly. There was anger in her voice, he realized. Thinly concealed and

149

somewhat shocking. He had hardly ever seen Myra angry. Not, he thought, since that first day, when she had turned on her heel to walk away and leave him.

His heart sped up at the thought. He tightened his grip on her hand.

"What do you mean?" he asked. "What are you upset about?"

"You know what I mean!" she exploded quietly. "You're the one who just said it!"

"I was... I..." At a loss, Leon spun back over in his mind what he had been saying before Myra had turned and left the table. "When I was talking to the sheriff?" he asked, lighting finally on the moment. "Everyone just seemed to be assuming we were together," he explained, his own cheeks heating as he recalled some of the comments he'd gotten upon joining the men after church. "I wanted to be sure no one thought there was anything... untoward going on."

"Well, it sounded like you were just throwing me out there for anyone who wanted to take a crack at me," Myra said. A tear shook itself loose from her eye and tracked down her cheek. With one hand tucked under Kitten's head and the other still imprisoned in Leon's grasp, she swiped at it with her shoulder, an angry and impossibly young-looking gesture.

"I'm sorry," Leon said. His voice emerged husky and desperate. His stomach felt like a rock as he realized how it must have sounded to her. "I didn't mean to do that."

"You could have at least... made it sound like you didn't despise the idea of us being... together." The anger had drained out of Myra's voice when she spoke again, and only the hurt remained. At her plaintive tone, Leon felt a mixture of self-loathing and strange, unwelcome hope.

"I didn't... I don't..." He paused, closing his eyes briefly as he composed his thoughts. "Myra, I don't want you to feel like you're bound by any kind of expectations," he said finally, "based on what brought you out here in the first place."

He wasn't going to say the words *mail-order bride.* Not ever, if he could help it.

"I don't," she said sharply.

He blinked, fastening his gaze to hers again. She was looking at him, her eyes like fields in the sun.

"I don't feel bound by any expectations," she added more softly. "And I hope you don't either. I don't care how things started." Her tone was suddenly intense with feeling. "All I care about is where things have come since then. I'm not thinking about the past. I'm thinking about where things could go in the future."

What was she saying? He felt that he was being exceptionally dense, but he was so afraid of reading into her words and once again messing things up. He bit his lip, struggling with how to respond.

"Okay," he said finally. "Well, that's what I want too. I want you to feel completely free to pursue whatever the future holds for you."

He watched as some of the light faded from Myra's eyes.

Abruptly, she nodded. Her gaze fell away from his and she tugged on her hand. He released it immediately, startled to find he was still holding it.

She busied herself with arranging the blankets around Kitten's face. Leon leaned back in the pew beside her, feeling drained and at a loss.

"Okay," he said again after a moment. "Do you want to go back out and visit some more? Or do you want to go home?"

"I want to go home," Myra said quietly. "Please."

His heart gave another painful lunge as he considered that she might be speaking of her real home— the home she'd come from to come here and be thoroughly disappointed in him. But he quickly shook the unreasonable thought away.

She was talking about the ranch. That was her home. For now.

"All right," he said. "Let's go. Here, I'll take the baby."

As they made the familiar exchange, their hands and arms brushing, the scent of her hair in his nose, Leon had a sense of deep pain and loss. As if something beautiful had just been in his grasp and he had failed to hold on and let it slip away.

Chapter Seventeen

Monday morning dawned gray and drizzly, but Leon still headed outside as soon as breakfast was over. Myra watched him go, feeling the hollow place inside of her that had been there since the day before, when he'd denied being associated with her before the entire church.

Even this morning, she thought, he was avoiding her. The easy feeling that had been growing between them had been missing even as he thanked her for the breakfast before leaving.

"Mmm, it's been so nice to spend these days here." Across the table from her, Ruby wrapped her hands around her coffee mug. "I almost don't want to head back into town at all. Especially with this weather."

Myra shifted her attention to Leon's sister, smiling as she pulled her thoughts away from herself and her own disappointment.

"*Almost*," she echoed. "You really are happy to be living there now, aren't you?"

Ruby nodded, her own smile wistful.

"I miss the ranch," she said. "And the dogs and Leon, even in his grumpiest moods." She narrowed her eyes at the door before rolling them toward Myra. Somehow, having Ruby comment on his mood helped Myra not to feel it so heavily. The two laughed quietly together.

"But I don't miss the long drives to and from the clinic," Ruby continued. "And I like being closer to so many of my friends and the events in town..."

"And Adam?" Myra pressed gently.

Ruby's eyes flashed toward her, widening.

"I don't know why you're trying to look so surprised," Myra admonished gently. "Anyone can see he's infatuated with you, Ruby. And I noticed you two were together for the entire potluck yesterday. What's the matter?" she added as Ruby dropped her eyes, her smile wavering.

"I... I don't know. You're right," the younger woman murmured. "I do like him. I feel about him... like I've never felt about anyone else. But I'm not sure I'm ready for all of that yet— marriage, babies, housekeeping." She glanced around before turning back to Myra, her gaze pleading. "It all seems to come so naturally to you, but I've never been good at any of this stuff. I'm good at nursing, and I want to keep doing it. I don't know if I can do that and also let myself fall in love and get into a relationship."

Myra nodded slowly, sobering.

"Just for the record, it doesn't come naturally to me," she said. "I was just taught a lot of this from a very young age. But also... I think I understand what you're saying." She hesitated. If Alice was here, she thought, she would have some wise, soothing advice for the girl. All Myra could say though, was what was on her heart. "I don't think you should have to give up something you love for something else you love. But Adam's a doctor. Surely there's a way you can have both him and nursing."

Ruby attempted a smile. Then she took a deep breath, reaching up to tuck a strand of hair behind her ear. "Well, he hasn't asked me anything yet," she said quietly. "So, I guess I don't have to decide just now." She cocked her head, looking at Myra thoughtfully. "What about you?" she asked. "Have you ever liked a man like this? I know you came out here in answer to my mail-order bride ad, but... have you always wanted to get married?"

Myra could already feel her face flushing. How could she admit to Leon's sister that *he* was the only man she had ever felt attracted to in that way— especially since he had basically shown that he was revolted by the idea? She busied herself with brushing a few crumbs from the table.

"I suppose I always wanted to get married," she said. "But it was always sort of a vague idea in my head. I never had anyone in particular in mind. One thing I was sure of was that the man my parents picked for me was *not* someone I could ever be happy with."

"Would you have married Leon if he'd gone along with it?"

She had asked the question before, but still it startled Myra. As did the realization that her answer had changed since the last time they'd discussed this.

"I... I suppose so," she whispered finally.

"Well, I wish he would have, then," Ruby said stoutly. "I still say he doesn't even know what's good for him or what he wants— and I had the right idea in bringing you out here. You're one of the nicest people I've ever met, Myra. I honestly can't believe you stayed on after all we put you through that first day."

At Ruby's sincere announcement, warmth flooded through Myra, dissipating some of her tension.

"Thank you," she said, smiling up at Ruby. "I'm very happy to have met you too. And Kitten." She smiled down at the baby, who sat contentedly in her lap, chewing on her favorite thing right now, an apple slice. With no teeth she couldn't get anything off of it, so there was no danger of her choking, but she seemed to enjoy the texture against her tongue.

Myra had the passing thought that the baby might actually be about to get teeth. It was early yet, but not unheard of.

"Even though you all didn't get married," Ruby was saying, "it still might have been a good thing you came out here. There are a lot of really great young men—"

"No," Myra interrupted quickly. She felt herself flushing deeply as she met Ruby's eyes. "Don't try and play matchmaker with me, Ruby," she added more gently. "I've had that experience, remember? And it didn't end well. When the right man comes along, I'll know it."

Ruby nodded slowly, a smile twitching at the corner of her mouth. "All right, Myra, I'll let you pick your own man. But I have to approve before he can marry you, all right?"

"As long as I get to approve whoever *you* marry," Myra shot back. As Ruby cackled, she had the lifting realization that the two of them were really becoming friends. She had never had a friend that she could swap jokes with and who really cared about what happened to her, other than Alice.

It was a good feeling.

"It's a deal." Ruby stuck her hand across the table, and Myra laughingly shook it. "We'll look out for each other. And keep each other's secrets," she added meaningfully, blushing slightly.

"It's a deal," Myra echoed. "Are you driving back into town by yourself today?" she added as she stood and began to clear the table.

"No," Ruby laughed, her face flushing further. "Adam is coming to pick me up. We're just going to start clinic hours a little later today."

As she said it, the dogs began barking outside. She ran to the door and opened it. Adam's buggy was just pulling in front of the house. She waved and then turned to grab the bag she had packed and set by the stairs.

"He's here!" she said. "Are you going to come out and see me off, Myra?"

Tucking the baby against her hip, Myra followed her outside. Her heart quickened slightly as she saw Leon appear in the barn door. For a moment, he seemed to meet her gaze across the lawn. Then he crossed to the wagon to greet Adam.

"Your new neighbor's been in town," she heard the doctor say. "Making his rounds to all the businesses, introducing himself like he's planning to become a fixture."

Myra didn't miss the slight grimace that crossed Leon's face. But all he asked was, "Is he keeping it friendly?"

"Oh, yes," Adam said wryly. "Very friendly. So friendly, some folks are already feeling rather suspicious of him. You know the saying, No one needs to be that nice unless they've got something to hide."

"Now that strikes me as quite unfair," Ruby said, halting just before she reached the buggy and crossing her arms across her chest. "Everyone is so suspicious and judgmental about newcomers here, it makes me sick."

Adam, who had climbed down from the buggy, his face lighting at the sight of her, and reached for her bag, looked somewhat surprised by her outburst.

Myra felt another warm burst of affection. Although Ruby had said little about their early departure from the potluck the day before, she realized she hadn't missed Myra's discomfort. She was speaking up as much on Myra's behalf as on the new neighbor's.

Myra immediately felt bad about how she had written the man off simply because she hadn't liked the way he looked at her or the questions he'd asked. She determined to give him another chance and be as kind to him as possible the next time they met.

Chapter Eighteen

Myra straightened from bending over the bushy rows of beans and shaded her eyes. Kitten still slept soundly on the quilt she had spread in the shade of the oak tree nearest the garden. The dogs were ranged out about her, flopped in various poses of relaxation but carefully spaced to keep the baby in the midst of their group. Brigid grazed nearby, her tail flicking lazily at flies.

The peaceful little group made Myra smile, a feeling of deep comfort and amazement filling her being. Sometimes she still found herself wondering how she had come to be in such a beautiful, safe-feeling, *home-feeling* place.

Resting her hand against the small of her back, Myra didn't immediately get back to work. Instead, she briefly closed her eyes and took a moment to simply be grateful. It was a habit Alice had encouraged her to pick up shortly after the two of them had started to grow close. Though Myra had never disclosed in detail her struggles with trying to please and be happy with her adoptive parents, Alice must have picked up on it.

Myra imagined she had been in an especially despondent state of mind on the day Alice had decided to share this bit of wisdom.

"Do you know what I've learned to do whenever I'm feeling discouraged or discontent about something?" her friend had commented gently. "I've learned to stop for a minute and take stock of all the things I can think of to be thankful for."

Myra could almost see the sparkle in Alice's blue eyes as she recalled the conversation.

"I'll admit, sometimes it's harder than others, and I start to think my list is pretty short. I start to think I've got a *reason* to be unhappy," the priest's sister had shared. "But if I just keep going, all of the many blessings God has given me start to become clearer. I start to see the rainbows through the rain."

It used to be hard for me too, Myra remembered now. More often than not, it had taken her long moments of contemplation to think of even a few things to add to her prayer of thanks. Not anymore.

I'm thankful for the warm sun against my shoulders, she thought, her eyes still closed. *And the sweet smell of hay being cut.*

She opened her eyes, letting her gaze travel past the oak tree to the horizon beyond. Leon's team, pulling the big hay cutting machine, was just visible against the blue sky. Leon himself was a vague silhouette, perched atop the machine.

I'm thankful to be living on a farm in the wide-open world, Myra continued, her heart swelling with genuine joy. *To have my own garden and to be living with a man who...*

There her thoughts stumbled. A man who what? Who was kind? Who seemed to appreciate everything she did? Who made her feel as if this was her home as much as his?

The feeling of joy in her heart had tightened until it was almost painful. She knew how the thought ended. *A man who makes me feel and think things I've never felt before. Good things. Happy things.*

A man she cared about.

Myra blinked and lowered her eyes. The bucket of beans at her feet was full nearly to overflowing. She dropped the handful of velvety green vegetables she'd already picked on top of the heap. Then she picked up the bucket and headed toward the shade tree to join Kitten while she snapped them in preparation for canning.

She was nearly to the tree when Piper suddenly sat up, looking past her toward the drive. The dog whined. Immediately, Shell and Crocket leapt from their repose, barks ready in their throats.

Myra turned as the dogs dashed past her toward the house. A buggy was coming up the drive. It slowed as it reached the yard, but the woman seated inside did not get out. The dogs circled, tails wagging, keeping up a racket.

The woman waved.

"Halloo!" she called. "Myra, dear. It's me, Mrs. Hal Daily? We met at church!"

Myra lifted her hand to wave back. Her stomach twisted slightly at the memory of the potluck where she had met Mrs. Daily. But she didn't allow herself to dwell on it. Hurrying on to where Kitten was lying, she gently gathered the baby into her arms. Careful not to wake her, she carried the babe with her as she approached the buggy.

"I told Hal to talk to Leon when they were helping poor elderly Mr. Jake with his haying last week." Mrs. Daily leaned out of the buggy, blossoms bobbing on her elaborate bonnet, "but you never can trust a man to do as he says he will. So when I realized I'd be passing by Leon's farm, I just had to stop in."

"Please, come in," Myra said. "The dogs are friendly. I can fix us some cold tea—"

"No, no, I'm afraid I haven't the time," Mrs. Daily interrupted cheerfully. "I just wanted to make sure Leon will be coming to the Thanksgiving festival at the church on Friday. I hope you'll be there as well," she added belatedly, with a firm smile.

"Thanksgiving?" Myra wondered aloud. "Doesn't one usually celebrate that in November? It's not yet August!"

"Oh, certainly," Mrs. Daily agreed, "but I'm talking about our little local festival. It's always held on the first Friday in August, when the gardens are at their peak. Hasn't Leon told you about it?"

The woman's voice was so amazed as she asked this question that Myra felt herself bristling protectively.

"Why, yes, I believe he did mention it." The lie slipped from her lips effortlessly, even as guilt twisted in her chest. "I'm sure if it's an annual event, he's planning on it." What she wanted to say was that she and Leon would be there together, but with one lie already sticking in her throat, she found she couldn't utter another so boldly.

"Just tell him to make sure and stop by Sophia's booth," Mrs. Daily said emphatically. "She's bringing pies this year— every kind of pie that can be made out of summer fruits and vegetables. And no one makes a pie like my Sophia. He won't want to miss it."

"*I* certainly don't plan to miss it," Myra said with forced cheerfulness. "Thank you so much for stopping by, Mrs. Daily. Please give Mr. Daily and Sophia my regards."

After sputtering for a moment at what could only be taken as a polite dismissal, Mrs. Daily promised to do so and turned her horse.

"By the way, I was just over at your neighbor's place," the woman said in parting. "I know you'll be mortified to know that he was under the impression that you were Leon's wife and the baby was your own child! I set him straight on that account, as I'm sure you'll be relieved to hear."

The dogs gave a few final barks before turning to saunter back to their shade tree.

Myra stood still, staring after the buggy with agitation— almost righteous indignation. It was almost as if the woman was intentionally rubbing in the fact that she had no claim on Leon. And what right had she to go around telling people things they didn't need to know?

Too upset to go back to work and with at least an hour before she needed to start dinner, Myra knew what she needed to help her work through the thoughts and emotions raging through her. Whenever Alice's peaceful tricks of gratitude and such hadn't worked, Myra had always had another balm to turn to: paint and canvas.

She had no canvas here, but when she'd been laundering the curtains in the house earlier that week, she'd fingered the coarse white linen of the one in Ruby's bedroom and had the thought that it would no doubt hold paint well. She could replace it before Ruby's next visit.

Myra hurried about the house, gathering her supplies: the curtain, the paints and brush, a bottle for Kitten. She carried everything back out to the shady spot under the tree. As she was preparing to set up, though, her attention was drawn to the creek, a little further from the house. She had yet to go down and check it out, though its burbling often drew her.

She was no longer resisting the beautiful things that drew her. She felt she needed their balm to heal her harried spirit. Tucking the linen more firmly under her arm, she started for the creek. The dogs and Brigid immediately joined her, trotting eagerly ahead.

The creek was set deep between its two ragged banks. However, there was a narrow deer path down the side, and next to the water the bank was flat and stony. Carefully balancing with her loaded arms, Myra made her way down the trail. She settled in, Kitten happy on her quilt beside her, the linen spread flat across one of the largest, flattest rocks she could find.

The dogs waded into the water, lapping it up. Brigid nosed at the tall grass that grew up among the stones. A dove cooed from one of the trees that towered above them. For a moment, Myra just watched, absorbing the peace of the moment. She watched the sun turn the creek's ripples to clear gold and the shadows of the leaves dance across the calf's back.

Her eyes settled on Kitten's face. The little girl was awake now, smiling and waving her arms as if to reach for the tops of the trees she saw flickering above her. A smile touched Myra's own lips. Picking up her brush, she began to paint.

In the rippling golden shadows of the creekbank, Myra lost all track of time. A warm feeling of focused pleasure and fulfillment enveloped her, making it feel as if she and the dogs and the cow and the baby and the trilling treetop birds were enclosed in a world of their own. Her brush moved over the canvas, adding layer after layer until the shadows and light fairly danced with life.

She was yanked from her reverie by Piper giving a happy yip and leaping up the creekbank to run off in the direction of the field. The other dogs, and finally Brigid, were quick to follow. Turning to look, Myra felt a start of surprise when she saw Leon, surrounded by wagging tails, bending to pat the various heads pushed against him.

Slowly, she felt herself returning to where and why she was. Her stomach twisted as she noticed that the sun was low in the sky behind him. It was dinner time. And she had made nothing.

Myra nearly dropped her paintbrush. Her hands shaking, she rushed to gather up her supplies and the sleeping baby, tucking her against her shoulder. Taking a deep breath, she hurried up the creekbank path to meet Leon on his way to the house.

Chapter Nineteen

Leon's skin was sticky with sweat and hay dust as he trudged in from the field. His leg, back, and shoulders ached, and his head was starting to join in from the heat and sun. Leading the horses into the barn, he moved through the familiar routine of unhitching and brushing them without really thinking about it.

Both his father and Mr. Harrison had drilled into him that a farmer was nothing without his horses. Their care always came first. Still, as he worked, he felt the intense anticipation of sticking his head under the pump in the barn yard and letting the cold, clear water gush over him and wash away the heat and ache and grime.

He wondered what Myra had made for dinner tonight. His stomach rumbled as he thought of the mouthwatering scents that probably filled the house at this moment. Under his purely physical hunger for rest and good, he discovered he was also eager to see Myra and Kitten. He had grown accustomed to their welcoming faces, the way Myra turned with a smile to greet him, and Kitten reached up with her little arms.

His heart warmed just thinking of them and his movements became quicker and lighter.

They, he realized, were starting to feel like home.

He fed both horses a scoop of grain, then turned them out into the pasture. As they sauntered off, their tails swishing flies away, he turned back toward the house.

He paused as his eyes caught on the door of the lambing barn. It was ajar. He frowned, turning toward it automatically. He couldn't have left it open because he hadn't been in the barn for several days now. The lambs were old enough now that they and their mothers had rejoined the main flock, so there were no chores needing done since he'd cleaned all the enclosures.

Was it possible Myra would have gone in for some reason? But what could she possibly need in there?

Leon found that his heart rate was speeding up slightly. He trusted the dogs to keep strangers from making free on the property. That's why he had trained them to stay about the farm buildings instead of following him to the fields as they would have otherwise done. But they couldn't be everywhere at once. And *someone* must have opened that door.

Where were the dogs anyway?

He pushed through the door slowly, ears straining for any sound, eyes quick in the dusty dimness. But the small building was empty. It still smelled faintly of the sheep and hay that had filled it only a few weeks before. Studying the dusty walkway, Leon wondered if he could see the faint tread of boot marks along its length. It was difficult to tell in the faint afternoon light spilling through the door behind him.

He was still extra alert as he exited the barn, closing and latching the door carefully behind him. Suddenly everything seemed strange or out of place. That bucket tipped over by the fence— hadn't he left it upright this morning? Of course, that could certainly be the fault of one of the dogs. Or more likely, Brigid, searching for snacks.

Where *were* they anyway?

He began to feel worried about Myra and Kitten. If the dogs weren't about, anyone could have walked into the house. He spotted an open window on the side of the house which he knew for sure *he* hadn't left open. His pace had quickened now to where he nearly stumbled as he hurried across the barnyard.

Movement from the trees surrounding the creek caused him to jerk his head around, spinning on his heel. Relief flooded him at the sight of Piper and Crocket leaping into sight over the bank, running toward him with panting tongues and wagging tails. As he bent to pat them, Shell and Brigid appeared over the bank, gamboling along at their own pace.

"What were all of you doing down there at once?" Leon asked. "Leaving the whole property and Myra and the baby unguarded?"

Only Piper seemed to catch the light scolding in his tone. She pricked her ears, cocking her head at him in puzzlement. Then, turning back toward the creek, she waited, her plumed tail swishing. A moment later, Leon saw the top of Myra's head appear among the trees. Then she was hurrying up the path toward him. She held Kitten against her shoulder, and her other arm was full of what looked like curtains and other various objects. Her face was stricken and Leon felt another pang of panic. But then she spoke, and the reason for her anxiety made itself known.

"I'm so sorry," she gasped, "I lost track of the time. Dinner isn't ready yet."

She bit her lip, slowing as she approached him. Kitten squealed and reached her arms out. Leon took her, settling her in the crook of his arm as Myra shifted the rest of her load to bear it with both arms. He caught sight of a worn paintbrush and flashes of color on the curtain. Myra's sleeves were pushed up nearly to her elbows, and there were streaks of a rusty brown and green on her slender hands and forearms.

She noticed him looking and blushed, hastily pushing her cuffs back down to their proper place about her wrists.

"I'll make something quick," she said. "Biscuits and... there's some smoked ham. It will only take me a minute to stir-fry some squash..."

He wasn't sure how much she was talking to him and how much she was talking to herself, but it seemed she would continue until she got some kind of reply or permission to get on with it.

"How long have you been down there?" he asked, glancing past her at the shady creek. "Did you leave the window open in the house?"

Myra stammered to silence, blinking.

"I— I'm not sure," she said. Her eyes drifted past him to the farmhouse, her brow crinkling. "I came down just after Kitten's nap," she said. "I don't remember opening a window, but... well, I must have."

There was still a tight knot in Leon's stomach left from his few moments of panic. He didn't intend to be harsh, but the words spilled out, intense with his worry.

"You can't just be wandering off and leaving the house for hours like that," he said, frowning down at her. "Especially not without checking that the windows are closed and letting someone know where you are going. You're not in some quaint little town anymore," he added. "Out here, anything can happen. We have to be careful. *You* have to be careful."

He was not watching her face as he said it. His attention had been caught by the dogs, who had tired of the conversation and started off on side trails of their own. Crocket had his nose to the ground, following an invisible trail across the ground. Piper was wandering toward the lambing barn. Did they sense the same thing he did? That something was amiss?

"I'm sorry," Myra murmured. "I... I didn't realize."

"I'm going to go into the house and make sure everything is okay," Leon said. He watched as Crocket's tracking led him closer and closer to the open window. Leon's heart was beating hard again. There was no reason for anyone to sneak into his house. He knew almost everyone in the community and they all knew he had little worth stealing, even if they were so inclined. But anything could have entered through that open window: a rabid coon, a snake, an owl.

He turned back to Myra. "Here, you take Kitten and wait out here," he said. Then he hesitated as he saw her face. Her eyes were glistening with tears, and her shoulders were hunched with tension.

"What?" he asked, startled. "What's the matter?"

Myra blinked at the way the question burst sharply from his mouth. But she didn't reply. Instead, she simply shook her head and muttered again, "I'm sorry."

Leon felt a surge of frustration rising from within the agitation that had already stirred him. He was confused, knocked off balance by all that was happening. His headache had grown worse, pounding behind his eyes. He was still hot and sticky, and he probably smelled, he thought belatedly.

He took a step back from Myra. Then, registering how full her arms would be when he handed the baby back, he said, "Give me your stuff. I'll carry it so you can take Kitten."

"No, that's all right." Myra shook her head again, her hands tightening about the paint-daubed linen. Leon was in too much of a hurry to make sure things were all right in the house to have time for her hesitancy.

"Give them to me," he said. He reached out and took the things from her only slightly resistant grip, then handed Kitten back to her. "I'll be right back."

He whistled, calling the dogs back to stay with Myra as he went into the house.

His footsteps sounded loud on the board floorboards of the entry, but he didn't want to pause to remove his boots. He also didn't want to be caught without them if he did meet up with someone or something.

Trying to breathe evenly and quietly, he limped through the sitting room and the kitchen. In Myra's bedroom, he lowered her painting supplies to the chair by the bed. It took him only a moment to check the room for anything that shouldn't be there, but he felt like an intruder himself the entire time he was in there. It no longer resembled the office it had once been at all. Even the smell of it was different, softly feminine and herbal— lemongrass or lavender. Maybe a mixture of both.

He finished checking the upstairs and found nothing. Slowly, the tightness in his chest had begun to ease. His stomach was still vaguely unsettled though. He was no longer anticipating the unmade dinner. He wasn't sure he'd be able to eat it if Myra made it. And she had seemed so flustered. He would tell her it didn't matter, that they could simply eat later. Or that she could get something for herself but not to worry about him.

He stepped outside with the words on his lips. They died as he caught sight of Myra. She had seated herself on the bottom step of the front porch, and she was trying in vain to hush Kitten, who had begun to cry lustily. At the sound of his step, she turned, swiping hastily at her cheeks.

She was also crying. Full-out crying. And the look on her face was still that look of stricken dread.

"She's ready for her bottle," she said, lifting her voice to be heard above Kitten's impatient wails. There was a slight tremble to her tone that matched the streaks on her cheeks.

"You can go on in," Leon said. His tongue felt thick and dumb. Was she upset because he'd told her to be more careful? Or had something happened that she hadn't told him? He felt his heart pinch as he watched her stand up, cradling Kitten and wiping once more at the tears on her cheeks, sniffing quietly. As she passed him to go in, he couldn't help it. He reached for her arm, to stop her and ask her what the matter was.

She flinched away from him. As she turned wide, startled eyes up toward him, his stomach dropped. The words he had planned to say fled, leaving his mind blank and unsettled.

Kitten's wails increased.

Ducking her head, Myra slipped past him and into the house.

With no idea of how to fix whatever was going on between them, Leon let her go.

Chapter Twenty

Dinner that night, when she finally got it fixed, was quiet. The most awkward it had been since their first together. Myra felt close to tears the entire time. Leon didn't complain about the hastily mixed biscuits or leftover stew. He said nothing else about her neglect that afternoon.

He wasn't going to. Deep down she knew this. It had been a constant since the first day she had been here. Leon and Ruby had tempers —she had seen them in plain evidence that first day— but they cooled quickly. They did not continue to exact punishment on whoever had messed up like her adoptive mother had. In fact, aside from the few stern words he had turned her way, there had been no repercussions to her complete irresponsibility that afternoon.

But she found that she couldn't quite shake the fear that it was yet to come. She had been trying so hard not to mess up since she had come that she really hadn't. Not in any serious way. But she had grown comfortable, and in growing comfortable, she had grown lax. It was what her mother had always told her would happen.

She spent the evening so deeply wrapped up in her thoughts, she hardly noticed how Leon was taking everything. He seemed preoccupied with himself. He came in when dinner was nearly ready, his hair wet and his shirt damp from where he had rinsed off under the pump. She noticed how red-brown his arms and face had grown in the sun. Everything about him, now, she thought, was the warm brown of late summer.

But his manner was cool, closed in on himself. He ate the stew and biscuits without comment, and when Kitten woke again and started to fuss, he pushed back his chair and went to pick her up. When Myra rose to fix the baby's bottle, he stopped her.

"I'll get it," he said simply. His voice was neutral. There was nothing unkind in it, but Myra found her eyes prickling with tears yet again. Maybe *this* is how he would punish her, she thought. By simply being quiet, not allowing her to help out or atone for the disappointment she had given him.

She spent extra time cleaning the kitchen until it was sparkling that night, then went to her room early, as soon as he had gone back out to do the evening chores.

Kitten fell asleep easily, tucked into the blankets of her handmade crib. For a moment, Myra stood watching her, her gaze sliding over the smooth wood of the cradle every few moments. Such care had gone into it, it was impossible not to see. And for a doorstep baby, one to whom Leon owed nothing in reality.

Turning away, she spied her painting supplies on the chair next to her bed. She felt her face flushing as she thought about what Leon must have thought when he saw how she had been wasting her time all afternoon. Walking slowly over, she picked it up and unfolded the hastily bundled curtain.

A few smudges marred the painting, but still, the glimmering moment she had captured by the creek remained. She felt her soul settling slightly at the sight of Kitten's sleeping face, dappled with golden light.

She would make it up to Leon, she thought. She had done it with her parents time and time again. She could do it with him. She would win back the easy camaraderie that had grown between them. And she would learn from her mistake. No more wandering off on side trails just because they drew her. No more getting so comfortable she forgot her place as a governess who hadn't even been welcomed at first.

No more thinking that her employer perhaps thought of her as something more— even as a friend. This, she thought, had been the wake-up call she needed. She had been getting too settled in, feeling like this was more of a home than she had ever had. She needed to be reminded that she could lose it just as easily as she had lost the others in the past.

Myra tried in vain to swallow the lump in her throat. When it wouldn't budge, she finally gave in. Throwing herself on the bed, she buried her face in the pillow and had a good cry.

***

Morning came blanketed in a fine, silver mist. The sunrise was brilliantly red, painting the sky behind the barns and green pastures more beautifully than Myra ever could have done. She stole glances at it constantly as she fed the chickens and gathered the eggs. Leon was out in the pasture, filling water troughs and feeding the sheep their morning grain.

She stole glances at him as well, wondering how the day would unfold.

She wanted to stand outside for a long moment and just soak in the beauty, but she was anxious to fix a good breakfast and get a start on her chores. There would be no loitering today, even if she had to do something extra like washing all of the windows to fill her time.

Eggs were scrambled and bacon was filling the kitchen with smoky savor when she heard the door open and Leon's uneven step in the entry. She quickly checked the leftover biscuits she'd set on the edge of the egg pan to reheat. Then she poured a cup of fresh coffee, setting it at Leon's place at the table.

She had turned back to the stove by the time his step sounded in the doorway. She heard him pause. Then his chair scraped the floor as he took his place at the table. Slowly, she served up a plate of eggs and bacon with two biscuits on the side, putting off the moment she had to turn to him and see the displeasure on his face.

He spoke before she had finished.

"Red skies in the morning."

"What?" She turned to him, confusion momentarily banishing her dread.

"It means there's bad weather coming." His eyes were steady and brown. "Not good for the Thanksgiving festival."

"Oh, yes... Mrs. Daily mentioned that to me," she said. She became aware of the plate of eggs tilting in her hand. Stepping across the space between them, she set it on the table. Leon tilted his head back to keep his gaze on her face. There was something in his expression. Not condemnation. Not anger. More like...regret.

It gave her a strange feeling inside— like sinking and lifting at the same time. She found she could not look away.

"Do you want to go?"

"Go?" Her brain felt slow, foggy.

"To the festival. I thought you might like to go." He lifted a shoulder in a half-shrug. "Most of the community will be there."

She blinked, finally dragging herself from the daze she seemed to have been drawn into. She took a step back, toward the stove.

"You just said bad weather was coming."

"It may hold off 'til evening. Likely will."

She was so confused. This was not what she had expected. It seemed he was purposefully trying to give her something nice after what had happened yesterday rather than punishing her in any way. And she had to admit, from the few weeks of getting to know the sheep rancher, that this fit his character.

She felt her shoulders beginning to loosen, the dread falling away. Maybe it had been true all this time. She had been waiting for the façade to fall away and for him to show his true colors. But maybe that had been unfair, a scar from her past experiences. Maybe his colors had been true all along. Still, she gave him one more chance.

She shook her head. "I should stay home and make up for the work I didn't get done yesterday." She could feel her cheeks warming. "When I wasted all that time down by the creek. Besides, you said... you said we shouldn't just leave the house..."

"I spoke too sharply yesterday," he interrupted softly. "I'm sorry."

Her heart gave a great thump, and then settled back to beating regularly, though at a slightly accelerated rate.

"The dogs will look after the house. And there's no reason why you shouldn't spend time doing the things you like when you can. You've done so much since you came— I think you deserve an outing."

Warmth and relief were swelling within her like the sunrise that morning.

"All right," she said finally. Her voice sounded breathless. "When do we leave?"

Leon's face relaxed. She hadn't even realized until then how tense it had been.

"As soon as we're done here," he said, gesturing toward the full plate before him and the kitchen in general. "I'll help you clean up."

Myra felt like singing as she filled her own plate and joined him at the table. Suddenly, the ease between them was back. They discussed how to keep Kitten happy in town for the entire day (milk in the doctor's icebox and a nap at Ruby's cottage), and Leon told Myra the booths they must be sure to visit. She noted with some guilty satisfaction that he did not mention Sophia's pie booth as one of them.

When they finished, Leon did indeed help her clear the table, and dried the dishes as she washed. Then, as she readied Kitten and everything they would need for her, he hitched the horses to the wagon.

Despite Leon's warning of bad weather on the way, the day looked beautiful as they set out for town. The sky over the mountains was cobalt blue, shot through with the wispiest wisps of happy-looking clouds. The air was warm and thick, but a breeze stirred it, making it bearable.

Myra's excitement grew as they neared the edge of town. Color and excitement fluttered down every street. As they entered the main street, she saw groups of men and women and children and families everywhere, wandering among the booths and participating in games and activities. The air buzzed with joy and companionship.

Leon helped her down. She stood by the wagon, a bubble of nerves rising in her stomach as she waited for him to unhitch and care for the team. Some of the faces she caught glimpses of in the crowd were familiar from the one church potluck she had briefly attended and a couple of trips to town for groceries. But most of them were strangers.

"Are you all right?" Leon said at her elbow.

She turned to him, laughing breathlessly at herself. "I'm just not used to being around so many people."

"Since moving out to the sheep farm, you mean?" he asked with a wry, understanding smile. The smile and the proximity of his brown eyes so close to hers made her heart do a backflip. Shifting Kitten in her arm, she forced herself to answer naturally.

"Since all my life," she clarified. "I… didn't go out much at home. I've never been to a social or a festival. I've never even seen one that came close to this."

Leon nodded, a ghost of his smile remaining, though his eyes had gone a shade more serious.

"Small towns can be like big families," he said. "We all help each other and sometimes hate each other. Stuff like this helps remind us we're all each other has—and we've got to stick together."

The way he said the words, still staring into her eyes, made Myra's heart jump yet again. She barely suppressed the quick intake of breath that came with it.

Before Leon could say anything else or she could reply, a shrill voice called out, "Leon! Myra! You're here!"

Myra turned just in time to catch sight of Ruby before the other woman threw her arms around her. The hug was tight but brief as she immediately drew back to pinch Kitten's rosy cheek affectionately and then hug Leon with equal ferocity.

"I didn't think you would come!" she exclaimed, her eyes finding Leon's. "You never said a word about it, and I've always had to talk you into it in years past." She whirled suddenly back to Myra. "Did *you* talk him into it? Was it hard?"

Myra couldn't help but smile back as Ruby's eyes sparkled above her impish grin.

"I didn't even know it was today," she confessed honestly. "Until Leon suggested we go."

"Oh! Oh, is that how it is then?"

Ruby's eyebrows arched as she turned back to her brother, planting her hands on her hips.

Realizing what she was insinuating, Myra wished she had bitten her tongue. She felt herself shrinking slightly as she waited for Leon's quick reply that there was "absolutely nothing" between them. But a second passed and it didn't come.

Instead, Leon said, "Since we weren't able to stay long at the potluck, I thought it was high time Myra had a chance to get to know the community a bit more—and they her."

Was he blushing? Myra snuck a second glance at his muscular, suntanned neck. It definitely looked a shade redder than it had a moment before.

"Well done, Leo," Ruby said. She reached out and gave him an admiring whack on the arm. Then, she turned to Myra. "I'll take you around and introduce you again to everyone I know. No one is going to expect you to remember them from when you just met them a few weeks ago."

Leon cleared his throat. "I was thinking we'd stick together, actually," he said. As Ruby turned back to him with dramatic slowness, he rushed on. "There's Kitten, you know. We were planning to pass her back and forth as needed and..." He trailed off as Ruby continued to simply gaze at him with a smug, knowing smile.

He was definitely blushing now. Myra felt her own face heating, and she wasn't even positive what was going on. All she knew was that a gush of joy filled her when Leon declined to leave her to the tender mercies of the town women and declared he wanted them to stay together.

"Very well, then," Ruby said finally, sweeping the hem of her skirt away from them. "I'll leave you to it then. If you need anything, Adam and I have a little medical booth set up outside the clinic. We're trying to pass out helpful information in fun ways as well as being available in case anything happens—like little Bobby Collins nearly knocking out his front teeth bobbing for apples." She glanced conspiratorially at each of them in turn. "That's already happened in case you were wondering. Anyway, one of us will be there at all times."

As she flounced away, looking fully satisfied with herself, Myra couldn't help but think *both* of them were likely to be wherever they were that day. Ruby's voice had warmed as she said Adam's name even more than it usually did. She must be letting him in a little, letting herself at least consider the possibility of love.

As the word crossed her mind, she glanced back over at Leon. His eyes were on her, and for some reason, it sent immediate heat rushing to her cheeks.

"Are you ready to explore all our little town has to offer?" he asked. He reached for Kitten, and Myra let him have her. He nestled the little girl against his shoulder in that easy way he had, making her heart squeeze with affection. Then his brown eyes turned back to her, and he offered the crook of his free arm to her. She took it, hesitantly, excitement filling her like soda fizz. *What* was happening?

"What do you want to see first?" he asked.

"Oh...I don't know." She laughed nervously. "I have no idea what there is to see."

"Well, then, we'll just start at the beginning and work our way clear to the end," he offered with a wink.

And that's what they did. Booth after booth, they stopped and chatted with the person attending it. They test-tasted sweet, chewy kettle corn and pork rinds, honey, and homemade candy. Myra pored over the booths that displayed the community's arts and crafts—extravagantly colorful and almost mathematically geometric quilts, knit items, hand-thrown pottery, metal-working...

One booth displayed dishes on which the woman attending it had painted tiny pastoral scenes. Myra was both astonished and delighted by the intricate details. She thought of the curtains she had already painted on. Were there other things in the house that she could decorate and still use—like these dishes? She thought of a large, plain blue teapot and a blank wall that she always found herself staring at when she felt dismal.

She stopped herself before her excitement could get ahead of her. Nothing in the house belonged to her. She would have to get Leon's permission to do anything with it.

Without really intending to, she cast a questioning sidelong glance at him. He was watching her, a slight smile on his face that completely mystified her.

"You're thinking of trying it, aren't you?" he said.

Myra was slightly stunned. She knew she had a transparent face, but no one had ever read a desire of hers so clearly before.

"I...well, yes. But of course, I wouldn't presume..."

"You can paint whatever you want," Leon said. "If your painting is anything like your sketching, you'll be doing every item in the house a favor."

Myra caught her breath. He had seen her sketch then, the day he and Ruby had nearly caught her drawing on the porch.

She must have dropped the paper in her haste. And he thought it was *good*.

"I'm not sure Miss Schmitt here would appreciate the competition" —he nodded to the woman with enough charm to make her chuckle good-naturedly— "but maybe if you pick something else to specialize in, you could have a booth of your own next year."

Myra was still trying to catch up when he added with a twinkle in his eye, "Tapestries maybe. Or curtains."

Even as she flushed with embarrassment, Myra's heart began to sing. *Next year,* he had said. The thought that he was anticipating her staying that long filled her with happiness. She carefully averted her eyes before he could see the hope shining there. He didn't even seem to realize he had said anything important. She didn't dare draw attention to it and risk him feeling uncomfortable or backtracking.

"I hope you don't mind about the curtains," she said bashfully as they moved on, walking slowly toward the next booth.

"I *will* mind if you keep hiding all of your art from me," Leon said. He paused, noting her deepening blush. "I mean, if you don't want me to see it, that's okay. I just..."

"I would like for you to see it," Myra interrupted. "I just...I didn't know you would be interested."

The hesitating, extremely thrilling back and forth was interrupted as they strolled past a group of men gathered outside the sheriff's station. The sheriff himself leaned against the wall in their midst, listening more than talking. He tipped his head to Leon as they went by.

"I'm telling you it's the same thief," one of the men was saying emphatically. "The way he's hitting our ranches and homes one by one. And all the thefts are the same! He only takes as much as one man can carry."

"Seems like he's just taking a sample, sometimes," another rancher cut in. "Like a couple pieces of silverware, just to prove he was there."

"Are you saying there's a larger gang somewhere, and this is just one of them testing the waters?" the sheriff said in a slow, even drawl.

The man shrugged, agitated. "I don't know, *sheriff*. Is that what the evidence tells you?"

"Meaning our places could be hit again?" the first speaker asked, his voice rising with anxiety. "What are you going to do about this?"

Myra realized that Leon was moving faster, gently tugging her along. She fell back into step with him, her mind spinning.

"What were they talking about?" she asked after a moment.

Leon shrugged his shoulder slightly, looking uncomfortable.

"There have been some robberies locally," he said briefly.

"Is that...why you were so worried about me leaving the house open?" she asked, understanding dawning.

"That and a lot of other reasons," Leon said. "But let's not talk about that right now. This is supposed to be a holiday. And you're supposed to be forgetting about that episode."

"I am?" Myra asked, marveling. She stared up at Leon, noting that his jaw had tightened slightly. Was he upset with her again? Or just upset about the robberies? She blinked as he suddenly looked down at her. His brown eyes were strangely tumultuous, gazing from beneath furrowed brows.

He didn't say anything though, and a moment later, they walked past a booth that made them both stop in their tracks. Myra drew in a deep breath of the sweet, warm scent that floated from the pan over the fire. Her mouth began to water.

Leon's face relaxed as he noted her reaction. He grinned crookedly. Then, he navigated them over to the stall.

A bent, white-haired woman was bent over a pan of spitting oil, testing some sort of crispy nest of dough with her fork before she lifted it out onto a nearby cheesecloth. Her much younger assistant, a girl of about twelve with chestnut hair and a cheerful smile, gave the hot, fragrant mass an expert sprinkle of sugar.

"Myra," Leon said, "this is Mrs. Petersheim and her granddaughter, Alma. They're famous about these parts for their...what is it called again?"

"Drechderkuche," the old woman said, looking up with a knowing smile. She and Alma chuckled together, and Myra immediately saw the resemblance between them.

"We're calling them funnelcakes now," Alma piped up. "See?"

She held a funnel above the oil for her grandmother, moving it in a circle as the old woman poured white batter through it into the oil. It sputtered and the circular wreath immediately began to brown.

"Will you have one, Mr. Sanders?" Alma asked brightly.

"You know I will," Leon responded with a laugh. Turning, he handed the sleeping baby back to Myra. Then, as she watched, intrigued, he paid a few coins for the hot treat, which Alma handed over wrapped in brown paper.

"Let's find a place to sit," Leon said. "Where we can enjoy this to the fullest."

They eventually found a bench just inside the alley between the General store and the post office. Leon sat down and Myra sank down beside him. She watched as he tore the funnel cake in half. He handed it to her, smiling. The caution was gone from his dark eyes as they shared the moment together. She found herself grinning back, her heart lifting as if on wings.

Never had she experienced anything like this, she realized. The festival, the camaraderie, the sharing of a snack. The realization added a tinge of pain to the big, warm emotion that crowded her inside. She almost thought she could cry—or laugh aloud—or...throw her arms around Leon and hug him.

She nearly gasped as the idea crossed her mind. Quickly, she covered her confusion by taking a huge bite of her half of the funnel cake. Sweetness and oily richness exploded in her mouth. It was soft and crunchy at the same time, gently sticky with the layer of sugar.

Leon laughed aloud as she widened her eyes with delight. Then, still laughing, he pointed to Kitten. Looking down, Myra saw the baby was reaching for her cake, mouth in an "o" of excitement.

"Oh no, you don't," she chuckled around the mouthful of heaven. But before she could stop him, Leon had pinched a tiny, tiny piece from his own cake and tucked it into the infant's mouth.

"Leon!" Myra exclaimed. "Cake should *not* be a baby's first solid food! Especially *fried* cake!"

"You're right," Leon chuckled. "It will spoil them for anything else. Look at her."

Myra looked down again. Kitten was sucking at the fragment in her mouth, and her face was a picture of delighted absorption. As soon as Leon moved to take a bite of his own cake, she reached out, shouting for more. Myra couldn't help it. She laughed along with him.

His eyes met hers, and something leapt between them, like a spark. Myra felt her breath catch.

"You...have sugar on your chin," Leon said with a chuckle. Myra thought she heard a slight catch in his voice as well, though. Her heart thumped as he reached out and swiped his thumb gently against her face, just below her lower lip.

"Th-thank you," she murmured.

"Mmm," Leon hummed. His face had gone serious, his brown eyes deep. It was, Myra realized, only inches from her own. And before she could blink, he closed the space. His lips brushed hers, as light as a butterfly and warm like the sun.

Shock blasted through her, along with another emotion she didn't have a name for. The next moment, she was kissing him back.

And then it was over, and he was leaning back, and everything had changed.

Chapter Twenty-One

The storm promised by the red skies that morning hit just as Leon was finishing evening chores. Fat drops of rain rattled down like hail, pounding the house, and wind whined around the windows.

He took off his boots and hung his dripping jacket on its peg. His thoughts went to Ruby, as they always did when it stormed. Even though she couldn't remember the circumstances of the accident that had taken their parents, storms had always terrified her, as if something inside of her still held the memory.

But Ruby was safe in town. Probably still with Adam, actually, he admitted to himself. The two had been nearly inseparable all day. Ruby had about her a more joyful and carefree attitude than he had ever known her to have, so he couldn't bring himself to be anything but happy about the development.

As he moved toward the kitchen, the sound of Myra's voice slowed him. She was humming quietly, occasionally letting the words of the lullaby slip through.

Hush, little baby, don't say a word,

Daddy's gonna bring you a mockingbird...

Leon's heart swelled with feeling as he paused outside of her room and peered in. Myra stood by the cradle, her back to him, gently rocking it as she sang.

Leon had never felt about anyone the way he was beginning to realize he felt about Myra. She had gone from being a stranger to being someone who made his house feel like home. From being a necessary evil to a fixture he wasn't sure he could live without. He thought about the kiss they had shared in town. It had been brief, impulsive—but she had not seemed dismayed. In fact, her eyes had shone like two stars when he pulled away.

Ruby hailing them from the end of the alley had prevented them from saying anything about it then, and though he had waited, Myra had not mentioned it on the way home. Now, Leon wasn't sure how—or if— he should bring it up.

What he was sure of was that his entire being ached to do it again.

Myra's voice had grown softer and her rocking slower as Kitten finally drifted off to sleep. Now, she turned toward him. She did not seem surprised to find him standing there watching her.

"Storm's hit," he said. He wasn't sure why. Anyone could hear the weather stomping about the house. But Myra smiled and nodded.

"Are you hungry?" she asked, crossing to join him at the door. "I know we ate before we left the festival, but..."

"Yes," he said, "I'm starved."

Myra's laugh came easily. Her eyes lingered for just a second on his face as he stepped aside to let him by. They were warm and green and full of invitation. He followed her to the kitchen, leaning against the doorframe as she put on the kettle and began slicing bread.

"I have some gravy left from this morning," she said. "I'll just heat that up, and we can have it on toast with tea."

"Tea?" he lifted an eyebrow. The conversation was meaningless, he knew it. But he wanted it to continue forever, just like their gentle banter at the festival.

"You don't drink tea?" Myra asked, turning to glance at him over her shoulder.

"More of a coffee person, I guess," Leon said.

"Coffee would keep us awake," Myra commented. "A little tea with milk will do the opposite. My friend, Alice, prescribed it for everything. After today...I could use a little something to help me calm down."

Leon's heart quickened slightly. This was it, he thought. The opening he'd been watching for to discuss the kiss.

"I hope you had a good time today," he started hesitantly.

Myra's hands stilled over what she was doing. Then she turned toward him, leaning back against the counter. The lamplight spilled over her, highlighting her slender figure and the smattering of freckles across her nose. Her hair had that sunset color that had first caught his attention.

"I had a magical time today," she said softly. "I've never had a day quite like this one."

Was she talking about the kiss? Or just the festival?

"It is a pretty special event for a little town like this one," he said carefully. "It's been going on for as long as I can remember. I...remember going with my parents when I was very young. And then with the Harrisons in the years after that."

He watched the emotions flit across her face like dark shadows.

"I wish I had a memory like that," she said softly. "Even just one. But my real parents abandoned me only days after I was born."

"Do you have any good memories with your adoptive parents?" he asked quietly.

"My adoptive parents hardly let me leave the house most of the time." Her voice was flat but resigned. "And they never spent time with me when they could help it. I..."

Her gaze, which had drifted to the floor, flickered back to him, hesitant.

"Two sets of parents, and neither of them loved me. I used to wonder if something was wrong with me," she finished softly, "that just made me impossible to love."

Leon's heart squeezed at the pain in her face and voice. He felt momentarily almost guilty for the fact that he, on the other hand, had two sets of parents that had loved him extravagantly.

"That's not on you," he said, his voice coming out hoarse with emotion. He cleared his throat as Myra looked at him, startled. "I don't know why your birth parents couldn't keep you or why your adoptive parents didn't give you the love you deserve, but neither of them is your fault. Everyone who meets you loves you," he added, his heart rate quickening. "Ruby and Kitten... and the dogs and Brigid."

She gave a shaky laugh, which encouraged him.

"If my parents were still around— or the Harrisons," he added, "they would have loved you."

Myra blinked. Her eyes, so green and luminous, suddenly filled with tears.

Leon could hold himself back no longer. Crossing the kitchen in one long, uneven step, he gathered Myra in his arms. His lips found hers, easily and eagerly, as if the brief kiss they'd shared earlier that day had been a map, leading him here.

Myra's slight gasp was the only sign of her surprise. She melted into his arms willingly. He felt her hand against his neck, the flutter of her pulse like a bird's wings, as she responded and the kiss deepened.

Thunder rumbled outside, and a cold drop of water splashed against Leon's face. He and Myra pulled back at the same time, breathless and blinking with surprise. He looked up at the ceiling where a dark well of water was preparing to lose another drop. Then, he looked back at Myra.

Her face was flushed, her lips slightly parted. She was smiling.

"I'm sorry," he said. "That's the second time I've done that without asking permission." He kept his arms around her, and she didn't pull away.

"Don't be," Myra said softly. "I didn't think the day could get any better until you did that."

Leon's heart leapt. At the same time, another cold drop of rainwater released from the ceiling and hit him square on the nose. Myra giggled, but her expression had begun to turn worried.

"Is the roof leaking?" she asked.

"Has been for a few weeks now," Leon admitted grimly. "A few of the shingles need replaced. It's just...not an easy task when you've got a steep roof and a bad leg. I'm sure one of the neighbors would be willing to help, but...I've been putting off asking for it."

"The new neighbor offered to help with something like that, didn't he?" Myra questioned innocently. Leon felt his arms stiffen slightly around her.

"I... Yeah, he did." Leon didn't add that he neither liked nor trusted the man. What reason did he have really for either? That Graham had been rude the first time they met? That he'd outbid him in purchasing the Harrisons' farm? It wasn't much to go on.

He didn't want to think about the surly new neighbor or the leaking roof at that moment. All he wanted to do was stare into Myra's glowing green eyes, and maybe lean in and kiss her again.

There was a quiet clatter from outside. Both of them jumped as all three dogs suddenly leapt up from where they had been dozing by the door and started barking, loudly and frantically.

Leon let go of Myra and rushed to the window. As the dogs barked and pawed at the door, he pushed aside the curtain and peered out. The storm had nearly worn itself out. The rain was just a gentle patter now, and the flickers of lightning were distant and infrequent.

Lamplight spilled from the window as Leon lifted the curtain, glimmering on the wet ground. Leon jerked his head to look as a dark object hurtled across the farthest corner of where he could see and vanished into the night.

"That was a man," he said. Immediately, he wished he could snatch the words back. Myra gasped, and when he looked at her, he saw her face had gone pale. He knew that she was thinking of the robberies that had been talked of in town that day.

The dogs were still barking, the sound wearing away what was left of his calm. He made a quick decision.

"I'm going to go out and look," he said, heading for the door. "Lock the door behind me, and don't let anyone in until you hear my voice."

He went to the cabinet in the living room where he kept his handgun and withdrew it. Myra's face became even bleaker as she watched him load it. She followed him to the door. As soon as he opened it, the dogs dashed out into the darkness, baying. He was about to follow when he felt Myra's hand on his arm.

He turned to her.

"Be careful," she whispered. The light in her green eyes made him certain that he would be. He needed to come back to her—and finish what they'd started.

Chapter Twenty-Two

As soon as Leon had disappeared into the darkness off the edge of the porch, Myra closed and locked the door. Then she went around the inside of the house, checking that all of the windows were also closed and latched. She ended up in her own room, gazing down at the baby. Kitten was sleeping peacefully, oblivious to all that had happened in the last few minutes.

Leon kissed me. Again, Myra thought. The thought was like a lifeline that she held onto. He had said that his parents would have loved her. And she...

She cared about him—so much. It had come to her softly over the weeks they had spent together. First, she had felt safe with him, then happy, and now... Now she never wanted to lose what they had. She wanted it to stay, to grow, to become something more.

Myra paced back to the front room. Her eyes snagged on the water still dripping slowly from the kitchen ceiling to the floor. Moving mechanically, she got a towel and mopped up the small puddle that had formed. Then she pulled a bowl from the cabinet and set it in the spot to catch the water.

Back in the sitting room, she swept aside the curtain a small amount and stared out into the darkness until her eyes ached. Finally, she saw a light, a lantern exiting the horse barn and coming quickly toward the house. As the dark figure barely lit by the lamp got closer, she recognized Leon's slightly rolling stride.

She opened the door less than a second after he called out. The dogs were with him. They crowded in around his knees, shaking off water.

Leon's face was grim. Myra's heart, which had leapt upon his return, sank a little.

"He took something, didn't he?" she asked.

"The harnesses for the team," Leon blurted out. He reached up, running a hand through rain-dampened hair. "It's almost as if..." He trailed off, his eyes dark with anger and contemplation.

"What?" Myra asked.

"Well, what use does a burglar have with a used harness?" Leon shook his head. "And yet, taking it makes all kinds of trouble for us. I can't cut hay without that harness. I can't take the wagon to town." His breathing grew rough as his frustration mounted. "It's almost like he did it...just to be difficult. That sounds stupid," he added immediately.

Myra shook her head, frowning. Her heart twisted to see Leon so upset. "It's not stupid," she said. "And maybe if you tell the sheriff it will give him a clue as to who it is. At least he didn't steal any sheep," she added, reaching for his hand.

Leon refused to be comforted. "I'm not taking any chances," he said, his jaw hardening. "I just came in to leave the dogs and get my slicker. He can't have gone far. I'm going after him."

"No!" The word burst from Myra's mouth before she could even think about it. She grabbed Leon's hand, wrapping her fingers around his calloused ones. He looked down at her in surprise. "It's too dangerous," she insisted, her heart pounding. "What if he has a gun and is just out there waiting for you? And it's too dark to track him without the dogs."

"I don't want them to get hurt," Leon said.

"I don't want *you* to get hurt," Myra rejoined. "Please, Leon. Wait until morning. We'll go to the sheriff and get help."

He wasn't pulling away from her. But he didn't seem to be relenting yet either, she thought, tightening her grip on his strong hand. He just stood there, looking down at her with a bemused expression.

"This isn't the civilized town you grew up in," he reminded her, "where the sheriff and all his deputies take care of crime so no one else has to deal with it. Crested Butte is a tiny town out in the middle of nowhere. We don't even have any deputies. Out here, everyone has to pitch in to see that justice is done."

"Fine," Myra said. "Then everyone can pitch in with you tomorrow. When it's daylight."

"He'll be long gone by then," Leon grumbled. But now, his eyes had dropped to her hand on his arm, and he was less taut.

"He won't be," Myra said. "You just said yourself that you didn't want to take a chance he doesn't come back this very night." She seized on an inspiration. "If he does and you're out looking for him, the entire ranch and me and Kitten will be left unprotected. And if...if anything happened to you, it would be even worse."

She felt almost selfish appealing to his fear of what would happen to her and Kitten and the ranch. But it worked. Leon's shoulders slumped.

"Okay," he said after a moment. "But I'm going to sit out on the porch and keep watch 'til morning."

"I'll sit with you," Myra said quickly.

Leon's brown eyes bore into hers, growing softer and warmer than she had seen them since the kiss before all of this had happened.

"You shouldn't," he said finally, gently. "One of us should be well-rested. Kitten will need that."

There was wisdom in what he said.

"Well, then, keep the dogs with you at least," Myra said, a lump rising in her throat.

All she wanted in that moment was to go back to what had been happening before the shadow of the man ruined everything. She wanted Leon to gather her in his arms again and kiss her. She wanted to hear him say what she was beginning to hope he might feel toward her.

Leon's gaze traced her face, and for a moment, she thought he might actually do it. But then, he simply nodded.

A moment later, he slipped back outside.

"Lock the door," he said over his shoulder.

With trembling fingers, Myra did. Then, she went to the window and pushed the curtain aside just long enough to see Leon settling into the rocker on the front porch, gun by his side.

She let the curtain swing closed. For a long moment, she simply stood there, breathing, noticing the way her heart beat, Leon's face swimming before her gaze. Then, she turned and went back to her bedroom. But she didn't immediately prepare for bed. Instead, she stood for a moment looking down at Kitten, who was sleeping peacefully. Then she gathered her painting supplies and canvas and went to the kitchen.

She spread the canvas on the table and prepared her paints and brushes. When she began to paint, it came easily. Her fingers did not hesitate over a single detail. Rather, they rushed, trying to keep up with the flickering image in her head.

Myra had never really been one to name her paintings. Usually, she just thought of them as the name of the most prominent person featured, since all of her paintings featured people to some extent or another.

This painting, especially. It held only the head and shoulders of a man with tousled brown hair and serious eyes. There was pain in his eyes, and determination, and kindness. His shoulders were broad and firm.

The Protector, Myra thought, her mind with Leon on the dark, damp porch. *That's what I'll call it.*

She painted until midnight, when Kitten woke wanting a bottle. Peeking outside, Myra saw Leon still seated in the rocker, his head up, his foot keeping it going with a steady rhythm. The dogs were dark shapes on the porch floor around him.

Never had Myra felt so safe and cared for. It flooded her chest with warmth. If only she could let him know how much she appreciated it.

The only way she could think of that night was to leave the painting spread on the kitchen table rather than hiding it away, as she had the rest of her paintings. It made her stomach flutter nervously to think of what his reaction might be.

As she finally slipped into her nightdress and snuggled under the covers, after offering up a prayer for the protection of her protector, she allowed her thoughts to once more slip away to the kisses. Both of them.

They had been so tender, so endearing. So impulsive. Lying there in the dark, staring wide-eyed at the ceiling, she found she could hardly believe they had happened again. But she wouldn't have imagined such a thing. Not from Leon. She could only believe it because it was true. Wonderfully, life-changingly true.

Chapter Twenty-Three

As soon as dawn began to lighten the sky, Leon took the dogs and did a complete circuit of the property. He checked every barn and shed and walked every fence line. At the far end of the north pasture, he found a single strap of leather about a foot long. It had broken off the harness, meaning the burglar had left the property heading in this direction.

With the rain that had continued to fall in a steady drizzle all night, though, his trail had been entirely wiped out.

Which was probably his plan, Leon thought.

As he walked back to the house, he contemplated what lay north of the ranch. Nothing really. His ranch was the last before a wide stretch of empty land where the cattlemen sometimes grazed their herds. That could mean the burglar was holed up out among the buttes and canyons. Or he knew enough of the lay of the land that he was just trying to throw off any trackers. He could have circled back around, headed into town or back to one of the ranches.

Myra had breakfast ready when he stepped into the house. She had fried potatoes and ham and had doused her already thick, smooth porridge with cream. He took a deep appreciative breath as he settled at the table. Myra turned to offer a shy smile and a cup of hot, black coffee.

"I figure you're tired to the bone," she said.

"And I still have to ride into town and see the sheriff," Leon agreed. "You and Kitten should be fine while I'm gone," he added, frowning slightly. "Assuming this is the same burglar they've been talking about in town, he's never hit anywhere in the daylight. Still, if he hadn't stolen my harness, I'd take the wagon and we could all go."

"We'll be fine," Myra said. She began to pile food onto a plate. As if, Leon thought, she could make up for his lack of sleep with sustenance. Well, maybe she wasn't so off. The smell of everything was already reviving him.

As Myra set the plate in front of him, he looked up to thank her and stumbled over his words. The look in her green eyes took him back to yesterday, and the intimacy they had shared. He wasn't even sure how she did it, but he immediately found that he wanted to do it again.

He yanked his thoughts from that train of thought, dropping his gaze to his food. He was confused by the emotions that whirled through him in Myra's proximity. Not that they were contradictory in any way. They were all positive. All of them made him feel taller, stronger, gladder than he had ever felt before.

He just wasn't sure he understood what they meant. And he wasn't sure he was ready for where they might lead him. He thought of the shock he had felt when Myra had introduced herself as his bride. Now, when he imagined her saying the same thing, the feeling that surged through him was both stronger and deeper.

It was a nervous feeling, but also a thrilling one.

"The dogs will keep us safe," she added, turning back to the stove.

Oh, yes. The burglar. His trip to town. Heat rose in Leon's neck as he focused intently on shoveling the delicious breakfast into his mouth. He was acting like a fool, and at the worst possible time. Whatever Myra was meant to be to him, and he to her, it could wait until after this present situation was dealt with.

It was almost a relief to push it to the back of his mind.

Kitten woke as he was finishing, and Leon paused just long enough to give her a hug and a tickle, enjoying the way her giggle bubbled out of her. She was such a happy baby, he thought as she beamed into his face. He never would have thought it by the serious dark eyes that had stared up at him from the blanket that first night.

Coldness settled in his bones as he remembered. Kitten wasn't his, any more than Myra was. That suddenly felt unbearable.

"You're wondering about her parents, aren't you?" Myra said. He looked up to find that she'd paused in cleaning up the kitchen to watch them together. "I do it all the time," she added softly. "They're really missing out, aren't they?"

"I still don't understand how someone could do that. Just give up such a bright, wonderful person," Leon said. He continued to look at Myra as he said it, and he saw that she understood he was saying it about more than Kitten. His heartbeat quickened as she flushed and smiled, returning to her task.

The image of her face stayed with him as he rode into town. He reached the sheriff's office and was reaching for the door when it banged open and Tim George stomped out. The brawny rancher glanced at Leon and raised his eyebrows. His face remained set and angry as he scoffed, "Don't tell me the thief's hitting the sheep farmers now too! How many of your woolly little beasts did he take?"

Leon took a second to catch up to the abrupt question.

"None," he said. "He hit my equipment. Took some harnesses."

"Huh. Maybe he's intending to hook my cows to a cart and drive away with the rest of this town. Right under our blessed sheriff's nose, I might add." Tim raised his voice as he said the last sentence pointedly over his shoulder. Then, he let the door slam behind him and stomped on down to where his horse was tied to the hitching rail.

After watching him for a second, Leon went into the office.

Sheriff Stabler looked up with a slight sigh. His naturally grim face was even more drawn than usual.

"You come to yell at me too?" he asked wearily. "I'll tell you what I told everyone else. I'm doing my darndest to find this fellow, and I'll keep on doing it, okay? Here, fill out a report of what was stolen."

He shoved a sheet of paper across the battered desk in Leon's direction. Reluctantly, Leon took it up.

"You're getting lots of folks coming in here with things stolen?" he asked cautiously.

The lawman nodded. "Cattle, feed, field equipment, even small things like silverware and pies. Just the other day, luggage was snatched right from the back of Surely's wagon. It's like the lowdown thief just grabs the first thing he can when no one is looking."

"What does that make you think?" Leon asked curiously.

"That it's someone who lives around here," the sheriff said promptly. "Someone we probably see every day and hardly give a second thought."

"But the burglaries just started recently."

"Yeah, about the time that Paul Graham fellow moved in."

Leon and the sheriff both turned as the third voice spoke up. Neither of them had heard the door open. Okie Smithers, the only other sheep farmer in Crested Butte that Leon was aware of, stood inside. The short, wizened man pushed up the brim of his hat.

"Don't tell me I'm the only one who's noticed it. And it's awful odd, isn't it? A fellow just buying up a big farm like the Harrison place and living on it all alone, hardly doing a thing to keep up the property or start any kind of stock on it. Must drive you near crazy," Okie added with a nod to Leon.

"I try not to think about it," Leon mumbled honestly.

"He's not alone out there, though," the sheriff contradicted. "I took him and his wife out there the day they came. She looked like she was about to give birth any day too, so I expect he has a kid out there now too."

Okie shook his head, giving Leon a knowing sideways glance.

"No, sir, sheriff. Ask anyone who's been out there. Graham lives alone."

"Yeah, he told me point blank it was just him," Leon joined in. "You sure it wasn't just a sister or something coming out to look over the place with him?"

Sheriff Stabler was looking slowly from Leon to Okie, his gray eyes thoughtful.

"Well, now, this here *is* rather interesting," he said. "Because he introduced her to me as his wife. Said they were going to be living there, raising a family and being right happy."

"Suppose she had other ideas," Okie said. "Anyway, I vote you check in on him because he's the first person I thought of when I found what was missing from my place this morning. I understand he's not too keen on sheep farmers."

"And what exactly was taken from you?" the sheriff asked.

"My gates," Okie said sourly.

Leon had only been half listening, his mind prodding at something he wasn't sure he wanted to uncover ever since the sheriff had mentioned Graham's missing pregnant wife. This, however, pulled his attention back.

"Your..."

"Yup. Sheep scattered from here to yonder. It's going to take me days to get them all rounded back up, even working with the dogs. You ask me, that's just plain spite. Ain't nothing no burglar can do with no gates."

All the no's were a bit much to untangle, but Leon had to agree. He recalled now that Paul Graham had been snide about Leon's sheep farming as well. If this burglar did have something against sheep ranchers, he supposed his own place might have been hit worse had the dogs not started barking.

That was something to be thankful for at least. Of course, the man could come back.

"Exactly how are you fixing to take care of this situation, Sheriff?" he asked.

"How about you let me worry about that, Sanders," the sheriff said testily. He was looking over Leon's shoulder, and Leon turned to see that three more men were hammering up the steps to the station, all wearing the same expression of frustration and anger that he and Tim and Okie had come in with.

It was apparent the sheriff was going to have his hands full.

"You know we can always form a posse," he suggested. "Go after the fellow when he makes his next hit."

"And who's to say he's not connected to a larger gang?" the sheriff asked sharply. "I've been getting word from neighboring towns that they're being hit with robberies as well. We could ride into something we're in no way prepared for." He shook his head. "Listen, you boys go home and let me handle this my way. Got it?"

Leon was anxious to get back to Myra and Kitten and the ranch anyway. Tossing his finished report on the desk, he took his leave. His mind churned as he brushed past the men hurrying in. There was no telling how helpful Sheriff Stabler would be. There had to be some way to keep his ranch safe himself. And he was going to figure it out.

Chapter Twenty-Four

The rain of the night before had washed the air clear, and the sun glistened on every leaf and quivering drop. But Myra was too nervous to venture any further than the chicken coop. She snatched up the eggs, chucked feed at the hens, and scurried back to the house. She spent an hour cleaning and tidying, then carried a bushel basket of beans she'd picked the day before the festival out to the porch.

Here she would be able to see anyone approaching and run inside if necessary.

She spread a quilt on the worn boards and put Kitten on her stomach with the few little toys Leon had picked up for her within easy reach. The baby smiled and grabbed for them, sticking them in her mouth the moment her fingers closed around one.

Myra watched her for a moment, smiling before getting to work snapping the beans. The dogs had settled in various positions around the yard, somehow managing to look completely relaxed and alert at the same time. Brigid wandered among them, her tail flicking, grazing on the sparse grass of the yard.

Myra smiled again as she recalled watching Leon rubbing each of the dogs' ears before coming in for dinner one evening recently. Brigid had waited her turn and seemed to enjoy it just as much as Piper, Crocket, and Shell.

"I'm pretty sure you think you *are* a dog," Myra said aloud as the calf nosed at Piper's side, trying to get her to pay her some attention. The calf looked up and bawled an answer. Myra chuckled. "Mm-hm," she said, "and I don't know if Leon's ever going to be able to bring himself to treat you like a cow and stop letting you wander all over the yard loose like that."

She turned her eyes back to the driveway, wondering when Leon would be home. Somehow, even just saying his name aloud made him feel nearer. But she was eager for him to actually be here, petting his animals and making Kitten giggle and looking at Myra in that way he had that made her feel like she was about to sprout wings like an angel and lift into the air.

Her heart pattered at the memory, and her thoughts skittered to the painting she had finished last night and left on the table for him. He hadn't said anything about it, but it had been gone when she came in to get breakfast.

Had he liked it? She hoped so, but she wasn't sure she'd ever come up with the courage to ask if he didn't bring it up himself.

From what he'd said at the festival, he did like that she painted, and he didn't just think of it as a frivolous accomplishment as her adoptive parents had. He seemed to think it had some meaning or use. He had said it wasn't a waste of time.

The ways in which Leon was the opposite of everything her parents had been were still almost more than Myra could comprehend sometimes. Whenever she had thought of...

She hesitated, blushing even though only she knew the thought that was about to cross her mind. Lifting her chin, she let it continue.

Whenever she had thought of becoming a wife, as she always knew her parents intended her to, she had felt a sense of weariness. She knew now that it was because inside, she was imagining a lifetime of trying to please someone and live up to their standards, as she had spent her childhood trying with her parents.

But living with Leon had changed all of that. For the first time, she found that just by being herself, she was being enough. She had found someone who appreciated her—*her*, not what she could do for him. And it was life-changing. It made each day and even the future expand with infinite possibilities and joy.

"I feel free," she murmured.

Shell lifted her head from where she lay at the top of the porch steps. A whine sounded in her throat. The next moment, Piper and Crocket leapt to their feet, barking toward the drive.

Myra squinted at the horse and rider coming down the long path. Her hand was on her skirt, ready to stand, grab Kitten and hurry inside if need be. Was it Leon? Or...

The man lifted his hat in a gentlemanly gesture, and Myra knew who it was. She felt a momentary chill down her spine. Paul Graham. The last time they had met, she had felt distinctly uncomfortable. But...

She remembered Ruby scolding all of them about being neighborly and unprejudiced. Myra had committed to being kind the next time she ran across their neighbor. Gathering herself, she stood up and stepped to the top of the stairs.

Paul Graham reined his horse to a stop a few feet from the steps. The dogs trotted around him, their barks few now, but their bodies still stiff and alert.

"Hullo, ma'am," Graham said, snatching his hat off entirely now. Underneath, his hair was combed almost impossibly neat and shiny. Myra could almost smell the pomade from where she stood. "Is Mr. Sanders about?"

Myra hesitated. Neighborly or not, she didn't want this man to know she was home alone.

"I can't say exactly when he'll be in," she compromised. "You know how busy ranching is this time of year."

"I do indeed." Graham wiped a dramatic hand across his forehead. "I've been doing a good bit of hard work myself this morning. I should have stopped at the well on my way out. I'm parched."

He was giving her a clear opening. Myra hesitated a second more. Then, she said, "I'll bring you a glass of water."

She stepped over and picked Kitten up, then turned to tell the man she would be right back.

He had dismounted and was standing at the base of the stairs. The dogs walked stiff-legged around him, glancing frequently at Myra, as if for instruction. Her voice froze in her throat. What was she supposed to tell them? To keep him away from her?

He wasn't even looking at her, though. His eyes had landed on Kitten, and he was staring at her with a kind of mesmerized fascination.

"She's grown since last I saw her," he said quietly. Another chill ran up Myra's spine.

"Yes, babies tend to do that," she laughed uneasily. "I'll be right back, Mr. Graham."

"You don't want to juggle the baby and the water," Paul Graham said quickly. "Here, I'll hold her for you."

Chapter Twenty-Five

Leon was more frustrated after leaving Sheriff Stabler's office than when he first rode into town. The lawman had absolutely no answers to the problem—a fact that was making a lot of the ranchers in the area very angry.

I don't want to take a life, but I'll do what I have to in order to protect Kitten and Myra. I'll be hanged if I let anything happen to them.

He stepped into the general store and waved at old Seth, who owned the place. Gritting his teeth, Leon walked toward the harnesses. He inspected them, wanting one that was good quality but wasn't too expensive.

Growling in the back of his throat, he carried the harness to the counter.

Seth looked at him and raised his eyebrows. "Didja break yours beyond repair?"

Shaking his head, Leon swallowed his anger. "No. Someone stole mine last night. That's all they took, too. Of all the things to steal... It just doesn't make sense."

"There's been a lot of that going around lately. I hear many ranchers complaining about the thefts. Sometimes the person steals odd items, like your very well-used harness. I heard one of them fellas saying that his gates were stolen. Other times, it's cattle. I reckon that at least a couple hundred head of cattle have been stolen recently."

"I know. I just came from the sheriff's office." Leon could hear the frustration and anger in his own voice.

Seth nodded sagely. "You aren't the only one who's angry, and not just at the thief. People are starting to get frustrated that the sheriff isn't catching this guy." He sighed as he carefully wrote the price of the harness down on Leon's credit sheet. "If the sheriff isn't careful, he's going to have a lynching on his hands. Most folks think that it's that new guy who bought that ranch next to yours who's been doing all the stealing."

"That's what I've heard." Leon nodded toward the paper. "I'll pay that at the end of the month."

"I know you're good for it." Seth put it back in the box where he kept everyone's accounts. "Have you met the fella?"

"Yeah. He came by the house, wanting to know if I could help him fix his fence. I agreed, of course." Leon rubbed his face. "It's funny that he wanted to fix the fence surrounding an overgrown pasture to keep in the cattle or sheep he didn't have."

"He's been in here a few times. I don't cotton to him. There's just something about him that doesn't sit right." Leon sighed. "But my mother said that I shouldn't judge a person until I get to know 'em, God rest her soul."

"My ma and Mrs. Harrington would have said the same thing. But then Pa and Mr. Harrington would have warned me to trust my gut because that's what keeps a man alive."

Seth nodded. "I agree with that advice. You take care and drive safely home."

"I will. Thanks."

He was just about to mount his horse when Ruby ran up to him.

She petted the horse. "I thought I recognized the baby." She slipped him a piece of carrot. "Why are you in town? Are Kitten and Myra with you?"

Leon shook his head. "No. They're back at the house." He explained what had happened.

Ruby's eyes opened wide. "Really? Just the harness?"

If Leon weren't so angry about the intrusion, he'd have laughed. Everyone had the same reaction—including himself.

"I've heard that some people are frustrated and getting angry. All the ranchers seem to have been struck." She looked around. "I think a few of the places in town have too. They say it's that Paul fella who bought the Harrington place."

"That's what I hear. Have you encountered him? The sheriff said when he arrived, he was with a very pregnant woman, who he introduced as his wife."

Ruby shook her head. "No. The only baby we've given birth to lately is Mrs. Jergenson's. There were a few others, but I think they were handled by Midwife Tucker. Maybe she helped Paul's wife, too?"

"I don't know. When I first found Kitten, I asked him whether he had a baby. He said he didn't."

"It's all very interesting." Ruby kissed her brother on his cheek. "I best be getting back to help Adam. Young Fred Jones was bucked off the horse, and it stepped on his head."

Leon started to head back to his own place, but curiosity got the better of him. When he'd been at Paul's ranch to help him with the fencing, there hadn't been any sign of a wife or a baby. Plus, when Catherine had first arrived on his doorstep and he was actively trying to figure out where she might have come from, he'd stopped by Paul's place, and he said he was the only one who lived on the ranch.

Of course, I hadn't gone near the house, and his wife might have been there, especially if she had recently given birth when I was helping him. She might not have arrived until later.

However, the idea of Paul having a wife and child didn't sit well in Leon's gut.

Who was the woman Paul was with when the sheriff met him? Was that really his wife? The man didn't mention a woman or child the entire time we worked on the fence. If a man just had a baby, I would think that he'd at least mention it, being a proud pa and all.

He exhaled sharply.

Of course, I didn't mention anything about Kitten or Myra. But then, Kitten isn't my biological daughter, and Myra isn't my wife.

A sick thought formed in his stomach.

What if Kitten…?

He shook his head to dispel the thought.

No. There's no way…

I'll just tell Paul that I was stopping by to let him know that there's a thief in the area who's been stealing from all the ranchers nearby. That would be the neighborly thing to do, wouldn't it?

Plus, speaking to Paul would let him get a reaction from him. If the man was guilty of something besides making everyone uneasy, then he might show a sign of it.

Leon wiped the sweat off the back of his neck. The sun was warm and almost blindingly bright. The peaceful prairie was a sharp contrast to the turmoil in his stomach. The grass waved gracefully in the breeze, and the wildflowers painted a beautiful picture. White fluffy clouds floated lazily in the sky while a herd of antelopes grazed in the distance. The mountains that surrounded the area always called to his soul. It was a scene that never failed to take Leon's breath away, even after all these years.

At that moment, though, he was so lost in his thoughts that he didn't even notice the scenery.

He wanted to get back to Kitten and Myra. Something told him that he needed to, but he was almost to Paul's place.

It still burned his soul that Paul had managed to buy the ranch before he could. Paul had been arrogant about it as well.

Finally, he reached the familiar house. His stomach churned when he saw the outside of the house. He slid off the horse and dropped the reins, petting his neck. "I'll be right here."

He carefully walked up the wooden porch steps. One of the steps had been broken since the last time he'd been there.

Leon knocked, but no one answered. Knowing he shouldn't but unable to stop himself, he slowly turned the doorknob and stuck his head inside.

"Hello?" he called out loudly.

There was no answer.

"Hello? Is anyone home?"

Still no answer.

He took a couple of steps inside. It looked as though a dust devil had swept through the house, covering everything in several layers of grime.

The furniture, which Paul must have brought in, looked as though it would disintegrate if someone were to sit on it. The only thing that looked half decent was the kitchen table and chairs.

A foul odor of mold, possibly accompanied by the scent of a dead rat, made him want to gag. The thick buzzing of flies made him cringe.

A few pieces of bread that had turned blue sat on the counter. Shards of broken dishes were scattered across the floor, and the walls had several fist-sized holes. Yellowed curtains swung in the slight breeze that slipped through a cracked window pane.

No woman has lived here recently. I don't know any woman alive who'd let a house get this bad unless she was so sick she couldn't get out of bed.

The thought unsettled him, so he quickly went upstairs to check the bedrooms. They were empty except for a lot of spiderwebs. One of the bedroom floors was stained with blood. The blankets were soaked with the dried, dark red substance.

"What in the Hades happened here?" he muttered to himself. "He certainly doesn't have the happy family life here that he presented to the sheriff."

As he stared at the bed, he wondered if the woman had given birth there.

If so, where is she, and where is the baby? Did Paul do the unthinkable? Did he hurt his wife and child? Or did she take off, leaving the baby behind...on my doorstep?

Leon shook his head. He'd been in the house way too long. He didn't want to be caught nosing around if Paul returned, although he got the feeling that he wasn't even living here.

Who could stand to live in this filth? Mrs. Harrington would turn over in her grave if she could see the house that she always took such good care of.

He walked back outside and circled the house. There were only boot prints belonging to a man. There were no women's.

"I don't know who was with him when Sheriff Stabler saw him, but she certainly isn't here now," Leon said as he mounted the horse.

He couldn't shake the feeling that something sinister had happened to the woman and her baby.

I hope that I'm wrong and that they're living happily somewhere else.

But deep down inside of him, he knew that he wasn't wrong.

"Something's not right here. Paul's hiding something. It might be that he's running with the gangs. Right now, I don't have time to figure it out."

He limped over to his horse and petted him on the neck. "You're such a good boy."

Leon hoisted himself into the saddle and turned the horse toward his own homestead.

Like Seth had said, Leon had tried to give the man the benefit of the doubt. As the sheriff mentioned, there was no evidence that Paul was involved in anything illegal. It was just a coincidence that the burglaries had started after the man moved into the area. Paul would be a likely scapegoat, especially since the people weren't exactly accepting of strangers.

Myra had been the exception. There was something about her that drew people toward her. It was her awkward, shy, but sweet nature.

Leon was antsy to get back to the house. No matter how he tried to reason out the situation, he was certain that it had been Paul who was snooping around the place last night and had stolen the bridle.

What if he waited until I left the ranch to pay Myra and Kitten a visit? Myra could protect herself—unless she was taken off guard.

He knew he couldn't force his horse to go any faster. The heat and the fact that Sampson had been working nonstop since early that morning would tire the beast if he pushed him beyond his usual walk. Finally, the homestead came into view. His heart stopped when he saw a familiar horse standing near the house. Paul was holding the baby, and Myra was staring at him with wide eyes.

Chapter Twenty-Six

The last thing Myra wanted to do was to let this man hold Kitten. Although he'd not done anything that would make her think there was something off about him, she still didn't trust him. She couldn't put her finger on the reason, but he set her teeth on edge and sent an icy chill down her spine.

"That's quite alright," Myra said, glad that her voice held steady. She didn't want Paul to know that she was uncomfortable.

She started to scoop up Kitten to take her into the house with her, but Paul got to her first. Myra wanted to scream, "Give me back my baby," but she bit her tongue. She didn't want to do anything to upset the man. Something deep down in her gut told her that he was dangerous if crossed.

He looked at her with narrowed eyes. "I just want to hold the baby. I should have one about this age."

His voice was calm, and Myra got the idea that he was trying to be charming. But there was an edge in his voice that took her breath away. He looked at her as if challenging her. Myra was afraid that if she tried to take the baby from him, he might hurt her or Kitten.

Stay calm. He can't sit here all night holding the baby.

Myra quickly went into the house and returned with a glass of water, hoping that he'd give her back the baby. He didn't.

"It's a beautiful day for sitting outside. I notice you have a nice vegetable garden going, and you've planted a few flowers. It looks nice."

Myra was in no mood to make small talk with him, but she was going to do whatever would keep him happy until she got her baby back—she'd already come to think of Kitten as her baby.

"Thank you," she said stiffly.

The baby squirmed in his arms.

"I think Kitten wants to get down. She likes to move around a lot."

The dogs whined but seemed to understand that they, too, needed to be calm. They lay on the porch near them. The calf was close by, as usual, and was eyeing the scene.

"Kitten?"

"That's her nickname." Something told Myra not to explain the real reason behind it to him. "Sometimes when she's happy, she makes kitten noises. It's adorable."

"I see."

Paul was focused on the baby and tickled her under the chin. Kitten wasn't having any of it. She turned her head and reached for Myra.

Myra held her arms outstretched for the baby, but Paul ignored her and the fuss the baby was starting to make.

"I think you should give her back. She's starting to get fussy."

Paul pretended like he didn't hear her.

Myra tried to figure out what to do. She couldn't go into the house and get the rifle. Paul could take off with the baby. Even if he didn't, she couldn't guarantee that she wouldn't end up hurting the child.

Myra's heart hammered against her ribs, and the hot August sun that had been so welcoming earlier beat down on her, making it hard to breathe. She felt the trickle of sweat dripping from her neck and trickling down her back, like a line of spiders walking along her spine.

Kitten began fussing louder, and her face turned bright red. Myra's heart nearly stopped when Paul's hands tightened around the infant.

"I said, I think you should give her back now," Myra repeated, her voice stronger this time.

"Babies can wait. My wife always said I was good with children."

"She really needs to stay on her schedule." Myra tried to sound firm, hoping she didn't come across as helpless as she felt.

Paul's eyes darkened. "You know, I came all this way to visit. Seems mighty inhospitable of you to rush me."

Myra swallowed hard and tried to control her racing heart. She forced a smile on her face. "I don't mean to be rude, but babies need to be kept on a schedule."

The calf moved closer, as though she sensed that Myra was upset. Piper growled in the back of her throat.

"Your animals are very protective. That's a good thing since I've heard that there's a gang in the area and a thief that's been hitting all the ranches."

Kitten was starting to whimper, and Myra was desperate to get her back but felt helpless.

"I've heard about that," Myra said, desperately trying to keep her voice steady. "We actually had an intruder last night who stole a harness. That's such a strange thing to steal."

"It does seem strange." Paul seemed amused by the situation.

The sound of hoofbeats made them both turn their heads. Myra nearly cried with relief when she saw Leon's familiar form on Sampson.

Leon dismounted, dropped the reins to the ground, and leapt toward them. He looked from Myra to Paul holding the whimpering baby, then back to Myra again.

The look on his face made Myra a little nervous. His brows were furrowed, and his lips were pressed into a thin, white line. She didn't want him to do anything rash.

Myra forced a smile on her face. "Leon, Mr. Graham just stopped by for a visit. Since you weren't home, he asked for a glass of water and wanted to hold the baby."

To Myra's relief, Leon seemed to understand what she was trying to tell him. "Good to see you again, Mr. Graham. How's the fence holding up?"

"It's good for now. I haven't managed to get any cattle yet, though. I was thinking about waiting for the spring."

Paul was bouncing Kitten in his arms a little too roughly. It took every ounce of Myra's willpower not to jump up, punch the man in the throat, and take her baby back.

Leon stepped forward, trying to seem relaxed, although Myra recognized the guarded look in his eyes. He extended his hand to Paul with a small, tight smile that let Myra know Leon was on edge.

Paul shifted Kitten to one arm so he could shake Leon's hand. Both men squeezed hard, as though trying to outdo each other.

"Thank you for keeping an eye on Kitten while Myra rested," Leon said, reaching for the baby. "I can take her now."

Paul tucked Kitten in closer to his chest and shook his head. "Oh, I don't mind holding her at all. The little one and I were just starting to bond."

He tickled Kitten's chin again. The baby turned her face away and whimpered.

Myra held her breath as Leon eased himself onto the porch, his movements slow and deliberate, like he was trying not to scare a new foal.

The tension in the air was so thick that it could be cut with a knife. It was oppressive and weighed against Myra's chest like a ton of bricks.

Leon draped his arms over his knees and tried to seem relaxed, although Myra could see that his muscles were tense, like a cat about to pounce on an unsuspecting mouse.

Kitten whimpered again, and Myra's fingers itched to jump up and snatch the baby away from Paul. Only the fear that she would set Paul off and he would hurt the baby kept her frozen in place.

"How long were you in the area before you bought the old Harrington Ranch?" Leon asked, obviously trying to keep his voice conversational and polite.

"Not long. My wife and I were just passing through and saw the place. It seemed like a great opportunity."

Paul started bouncing Kitten in his arms faster, the motion jarring enough to make Myra feel as though she was going to explode.

"Where is Mrs. Graham staying? I'm sure she and Myra would love to meet since we're neighbors."

Myra bit her bottom lip when Paul's face darkened with anger, and the vein in his neck throbbed.

However, Paul made every effort to keep his anger out of his voice. "She wanted to travel back east to see her kinfolk. She'll be back in a few months after I get everything settled."

Myra cleared her throat. "Where were you before this?" she asked, hoping her voice sounded pleasant.

Paul's gaze flickered toward her, as though he was assessing her question, and then back to the squirming baby. "We moved around quite a bit, although we were mostly in Oklahoma Territory."

Leon stretched out his hurt leg. "Oklahoma Territory is very nice. It's good cattle country. I've gone through there on a few drives when I was a teenager."

Paul nodded. "That it is." He shifted the baby to his other arm.

She let out another whimper and turned her head to look at Myra, who was still sitting on the edge of the chair as if she was about to jump up and tackle the man holding her baby.

Paul stared at the baby, studying her features. "This baby doesn't look like either one of you."

Myra's heart skipped a beat, and she didn't want to tell the man the truth. Her gut instincts told her that would be very dangerous. "She's my late sister's daughter. Sheila died in childbirth, and I agreed to raise her as my own after Sheila's husband decided he couldn't take care of a child by himself."

Paul raised his eyebrows and looked at her. "Interesting story."

Swallowing a groan, Myra tried to remember to breathe. It was clear that Paul didn't believe her.

224

"I'm very sorry for your loss."

His words sounded very insincere.

Paul stood up, and both Leon and Myra jumped to their feet as well.

The dogs leapt up too, staring intensely at the intruder. Shell bared his teeth as a low growl rumbled from his throat. Even the calf took a step forward as if she was about to headbutt Paul or do anything she could to protect her people.

Paul seemed oblivious to the hostility that surrounded him. After handing the baby to Myra, Paul grinned, but his eyes were hard.

"She doesn't look anything like you. You know, if the baby isn't yours, you can't keep her, and she'll end up in an orphanage if the sheriff is notified. They are terrible places, I've heard."

"I assure you, she's my niece," Myra said coldly.

"Yeah, okay. Y'all take care now." He tipped his hat, mounted his horse, and rode away.

Leon and Myra stood rooted in that spot, watching him leave.

Myra exhaled a loud, deep breath and hung her head. She felt as though all of her strength and energy had drained out of her body.

Leon put his arm around her shoulders. "Let's go inside."

Myra sat on the couch, holding the baby she'd come to see as her own in her arms.

"Who's such a pretty girl? Who's a good girl?"

Kitten reached up, pinched Myra's nose, and yanked a lock of hair that had escaped her bun.

Leon sat next to them. "How long had he been here?"

"It seemed like forever, but I guess it was just half an hour or so. He asked for a drink of water, and when I reached for Kitten, he snatched her up. He wouldn't give her back to me. I didn't dare try to fight him because I was afraid he'd hurt her."

Leon's ears turned red, and Myra knew he was furious. He, too, loved the baby as though she were his own.

"I was willing to give the man the benefit of the doubt even though he set my teeth on edge." Myra brushed a lock of hair out of her face. "I've heard, though, that children and animals are the best judges of character. Even Brigid didn't like him."

"I noticed that," Leon said. "I'm sure she would have gotten her licks in if the dogs had attacked."

Kitten started fussing, and Myra leapt to her feet. "It really is time for her bottle."

She quickly warmed up the milk, and then, as Kitten greedily sucked, Myra looked at Leon.

"What are we going to do? I don't think we've heard the last of him." She trembled, and a hint of tears appeared in her eyes. "I don't want to lose this baby. I love her too much."

Chapter Twenty-Seven

Leon stood up and walked around to where she was feeding the baby. He hugged her awkwardly.

"No one is going to take the baby from us. First, the sheriff already knows about her. I went to him as soon as I found her, trying to figure out who she might belong to and why she was left on my doorstep." Leon leaned against the counter. "Second, the orphanages are already full. They aren't going to take children away from people who want them, especially if the child is being treated right."

Myra nodded, seemingly reassured by his words. "I'm going to hate not being able to go outside without constantly being on guard." She adjusted the baby in her arms. "I guess next time, the second that there's a hint someone is approaching the property, I'll grab the baby and the dogs, run into the house, and lock the door."

"You'd leave the calf outside?" Leon asked teasingly. "How could you? Brigid wants to be a part of the family, too."

"She can come, too. The more the merrier. She'll be a good protector when she gets bigger." Myra smiled. "You know, you're never going to be able to eat her."

Leon chortled. "I know. I figure that she can either be a milking cow or a breeder. It's much harder to eat animals you consider to be friends."

Myra looked down at the baby, and her smile faded. "You know I love this little girl as though she were my own child. I can't bear to lose her."

"We won't."

She looked up at him and tilted her head to one side. "Paul seemed very interested in Kitten. He kept glancing at her, and then he made those comments about how she didn't look like either of us."

"I'm afraid I might know why. You heard him say that he had a wife. Sheriff Stabler said that when Paul first came to town, his wife was very pregnant, as if she was about to give birth."

Myra nodded.

"Before I came here, I stopped by his place to see if she was there. The house was filthy. There were at least six inches of dust on the furniture, and it smelled like something had died in there. I went upstairs on the off chance that his wife was bedridden." Leon took a breath and rubbed his eyes as though he was trying to erase the image of what he saw. "One of the rooms had a lot of blood in it. There was blood on the floor and on the bed."

Myra furrowed her brows. "You mean like if someone gave birth?"

He nodded.

Myra's eyes widened as she realized what he was saying. "You think that Paul's wife had the child and that Kitten is Paul's daughter."

"That's what I'm afraid of. If she was trying to get away from him, she might not have been able to take the baby with her. I'm the closest neighbor, so she might have thought that I was better than the devil she knew." He sighed. "My guess is that she left the baby on my doorstep to protect her."

"You have to give her credit for not leaving the child behind. It can't be easy to go on the run with a new infant."

Leon crossed his arms over his chest. "I think she was a very brave woman if that's the case."

Myra's face had turned ghostly pale. "If Paul is her father, we can't let him have her. That man doesn't know the first thing about raising a baby."

"We'll make sure and keep her safe. I have a feeling that Paul isn't going to last long in this community anyway, especially if he's the one who's been rustling cattle and stealing equipment." Leon ran his hands over his face. "Seth, who runs the general store, thinks that if the sheriff doesn't get him soon, the ranchers in the area will form a lynch mob. They'll get a tall tree and short rope, and that'll be the end of that problem."

Myra shuddered. "I don't want to see him lynched unless he's done something to really deserve it."

"My guess is that he has. And he would know and understand the consequences of his actions. The usual punishment for cattle rustling is the same as horse theft—hanging."

"What are we going to do about Paul meanwhile, though? I'm afraid he's going to keep coming back. He might catch me off guard, like if I'm tending to the vegetable garden, hanging laundry, or doing some other chore where Kitten isn't right next to me."

"I think we need to talk to the sheriff again. I know Sheriff Stabler is tired of people coming to him about the rash of burglaries and other problems that have been going on, but this was a direct threat to the baby."

She looked up at him questioningly. "Is that wise?"

Leon patted her shoulder. "Yes. Like I said, he already knows about the baby and has made no effort to take her from me.

Plus, he has his hands full right now with everything else that's going on."

Myra nodded but didn't say anything. Kitten finished the bottle, so Myra picked her up and started patting her back.

"When are you going to go?" she asked quietly.

The fear in her voice twisted Leon's stomach.

"We'll go in the morning. It's getting dark, and I don't want to chance meeting up with him when I can see three feet in front of me." He took the now-sleeping baby from her. "I won't leave you here alone again. I bought a new harness, so we can take the wagon."

Relief washed over her face, and her shoulders relaxed. "I'll make dinner then if you want to put her to bed."

Leon took Kitten into Myra's room and laid her in the cradle. She sighed, and it looked as though she was smiling in her sleep. He couldn't resist giving her a little kiss on the forehead.

He and the dogs went outside to move the sheep into the large enclosures designed to keep them safe at night. This was their last night at the pasture closest to the house, which meant the dogs wouldn't be nearby either, since it was their job to guard the sheep overnight.

I need to get another puppy or two just to guard the house, Kitten, and Myra.

During dinner, they avoided discussing Paul Graham, as he'd already taken up too much time and energy. Instead, Myra told Leon about the squash, tomatoes, and bell peppers she was harvesting from the garden and what she intended to do with them.

Leon discussed how it was time for him and the three dogs to move the sheep from the northern pasture to the western pasture. He had five pastures that he rotated the sheep through to prevent overgrazing.

They talked about how fast Kitten was growing and how she'd be crawling before too much longer.

However, Leon didn't fail to notice how Myra walked around the house, checking all the windows, before going to bed that night. She also made sure she had a two-by-four next to her bed in case someone got to her room before she could get to the rifle.

They were up with the sun the next morning. He let the sheep out of their enclosure, milked the cows, and dealt with the chickens while Myra took care of Kitten and made breakfast.

After they ate, she packed a bag for Kitten, including milk in a bucket of ice, and they headed to town.

Leon noticed that Myra's head was on a swivel, as if she expected the boogeyman to jump out from behind a rock or tree at any moment.

"I feel silly being so nervous," she admitted. "He did hold the baby for too long and didn't seem inclined to give her back, but he didn't do anything threatening."

He smiled at her. "I know what you mean. If you're being overly anxious, then we both are."

They reached town and headed straight for the doctor's office. Ruby looked up in surprise when they walked in.

"Is everything okay? Is Kitten sick?" she asked anxiously.

"No, but there's been some..." Leon looked at Myra, "...developments. Is Adam available?"

"Yeah. He just got finished pulling about a hundred quills from Old George's face and chest and treating him with salve."

Leon shook his head. "When will that darned dog learn? Miss Margaret really needs to keep him in her house or only let him out if he's on a rope. He gets a face full of those things every time he runs loose."

Ruby smiled and shook her head. "I know. I think the score is porcupines thirty and Old George zero."

Adam stepped into the reception area and smiled. "I didn't expect to see you in town today."

Myra explained Paul's visit the day before and how he was holding the baby. She looked at Leon and then said, "We think that he's Kitten's father."

Ruby's eyes opened wide, and she gasped. "You can't be serious."

Adam rubbed his chin. "It makes sense. His wife and child disappeared soon after they got here. A woman's badly beaten body was found yesterday morning by some hunters about three miles east of here." He shook his head and closed his eyes. "She had a small bag with her. Judging by my investigation, she'd recently given birth. I think she was so weak after being beaten that she just collapsed."

"Oh, my heavens." Myra put her hand up to her mouth, and tears sprang into her eyes. "That poor woman."

"She had a letter addressed to her in the bag. The only name found was Elizabeth. She was buried in the cemetery with just that name." Adam grimaced. "It was only me, Ruby, the sheriff, and the pastor there to send her off."

Leon's lips tightened. "That answers some questions about why he's mentioned a wife, but she's nowhere around, and there's no sign of the woman the sheriff saw or a baby since she was pregnant."

"That monster," Myra breathed. "There's no way he's getting his hands on the baby, whether he's the father or not."

Leon put his hands on Myra's shoulder. "We won't let that happen."

"You two stay here with the door locked. I'll go with Leon to talk to the sheriff," Adam said.

The two of them walked to the sheriff's office, and Leon described what had happened the afternoon before and his theory about the baby's parentage.

"I agree. And don't worry, I won't let him take the baby from you. He has no proof that the child is his." Sheriff Stabler stroked his gray-streaked beard. "Sal, who owns the saloon, came in this morning. Last night, he heard Paul boasting that tomorrow night, he was going to get back what belonged to him. I think he means to go after Catherine tonight at your ranch."

"We should organize a little surprise party. I'll go back to the ranch and take care of my nightly chores while Adam and you wait for Paul to show up." Leon said. "Would that give you enough evidence to arrest him?"

"It would, indeed. I'll even mention that Elizabeth came to us, and she was badly hurt. We'll see what his response is."

"We'll have lunch, then head out to the ranch. I put a couple of saddles in the wagon this morning, in case Myra and I needed them," Leon said, feeling relieved that they had a plan to deal with Paul once and for all.

Then, he could have time to really think about his feelings and relationship with Myra.

Ruby and Myra weren't thrilled about being left behind, but neither Adam nor Leon wanted the women anywhere near the ranch if there was going to be trouble.

After they ate, the two men got ready to leave.

Seeing the fear in Myra's eyes made Leon's breath hitch. He placed both hands on her shoulders and looked into her eyes.

"Everything will be fine, I promise." He brushed a kiss across her lips and looked into her eyes. "We'll be back soon."

Leon just hoped that he'd be able to keep his promise.

Chapter Twenty-Eight

Myra flinched when Ruby turned the key, and the deadbolt clicked into place. Then, Ruby secured the doorknob lock as well.

"Adam keeps a lot of drugs here, like morphine. He doesn't want someone getting in and stealing the drugs." Ruby smiled. "Adam is certainly very cautious."

She stood in the foyer next to the door, watching Adam and Leon ride away. A sense of dread oozed through her veins, making her feel sick to her stomach.

Kitten must have felt her tension because she squirmed and let out a loud cry.

"Let's put the baby down on the floor with her blanket and toys," Ruby said. "You'll not do her any good if you squash her."

Myra smiled weakly. "I don't like this."

"Neither do I. Let's go into the sitting room. You know this is Adam's house as much as his office."

Ruby quickly spread a blanket for the baby and laid Kitten on her back. The baby babbled something and rolled over onto her stomach, grabbing some of the blocks.

"I think she just told you something," Myra said.

Laughing, Ruby nodded. "She's going to be sassy, just like her father." When she saw the look of horror on Myra's face, Ruby added, "Leon is her father now. Just as you are her mother."

Myra stood still, in shock for a moment. She knew she loved the baby as though she were her own daughter, but hadn't thought of herself in the true capacity of being her mother.

I'll do a better job than the mother who raised me. Kitten will always know that she is loved, no matter what.

Love for the baby flooded her heart. Myra sat down, never having felt such a powerful emotion before. Kitten, unaware of Myra's deep feelings, hammered blocks together and drooled on the blanket.

After several minutes, fear for Leon's, Adam's, and Sheriff Stabler's safety crept through her veins. A million thoughts ran through her mind.

What if Paul brings his entire gang and they outnumber the men? What if they do more than just break into the house? What if they burn everything down and kill the sheep, dogs, and other animals?

Myra jumped to her feet and paced around the room, wringing her hands.

Ruby's voice interrupted her thoughts. "You need to sit down. You're going to wear a path in Adam's sitting room and rip your hands off your arms."

Sighing heavily, Myra turned around to look at Ruby, who was sitting on one of the chairs, patiently sewing a gown for Kitten.

"I'm just so worried. I'm terrified that it won't be just Paul who shows up. What if the entire gang comes down on the ranch?"

Ruby nodded. "I understand. I do. I'm scared, too. That's my brother and my...and Adam. But wearing out your boots isn't going to save them." She looked out the window. "If you want, we could make dinner. We'll just have some chili and cornbread, so there'll be plenty when the men get back."

"Alright," Myra sighed. "It's getting close to Kitten's bottle time, too."

While they cooked, Ruby told stories about her and Leon's childhood that kept Myra laughing.

"One time, Leon convinced himself he could herd hogs like sheep. He went into the sty and tried to drive them back into the enclosure for the night. The boar, named Boris after a grumpy neighbor, wasn't having any of it. Boris was the kind of pig who just wanted to be left alone to do his own thing. He took after Leon like the devil was inside of him." Ruby laughed. "The devil was inside the pig, that is. Leon hit the fence and slid through like melted butter just as that pig hit the fence hard enough to break the board."

Myra chuckled, picturing poor Leon, with his limp, trying to outrun the angry boar.

"Then, there was the time when the Harringtons had some friends over. Their daughter went to school with us, and Leon had a crush. Leon decided to show off. He got on an unbroken three-year-old colt and took it into the pond to break it. The colt managed to buck him off. It shot out of the pond. Leon thrashed about for a bit and then stood up, covered in mud." Ruby doubled over with laughter at the memory. "I promise on everything I hold sacred that a frog jumped out of his shirt."

Closing her eyes, Myra imagined Leon looking like some kind of pond monster stumbling out of the muddy water. She laughed so hard that she almost knocked the bowl of cornbread batter onto the floor.

"Mrs. Harrington made him wash his own clothes."

"I bet she did." Myra eyed Ruby. "What about you?"

Ruby touched her chest. "Me? I was a perfect angel."

Myra raised her eyebrows.

"Okay, so I did get into a little bit of trouble. Mrs. Harrington didn't appreciate it when she saw me sitting in the middle of the yard holding a garter snake and petting it. I think she had a mild heart attack that day." Ruby shrugged. "It just wanted to be my friend."

"Oh, no." Myra could picture Ruby doing just that.

The baby started to fuss, so Myra made her bottle and fed her while Ruby finished making dinner.

"I also tried to cut my own hair when I was seven. My bangs were uneven, and I had a bald spot over my right ear." Ruby grinned. "Luckily, it was summertime, so I didn't have to go to school. My bonnet covered it when we went to town."

Myra tried hard to think of a story she could share, but really didn't have any. She cooked and cleaned for her adoptive parents. They did let her go to school, but Myra was so shy, she didn't make many friends. After school, she did her lessons and then did her chores. When she had free time, she drew.

They ate dinner and discussed some of the unusual cases that Adam had treated, ranging from a child who had stuck a bug up his nose to a man who had managed to hammer his hand into a board.

Myra told Ruby about her love for drawing and painting, explaining that it came naturally to her. "Some things are just so beautiful, and I want to capture them forever."

"I've seen your work. It is absolutely beautiful. I'll have you paint the curtains in my sitting room. Once people see them, everyone in town will want you to do theirs, too. It'll be a great way for you to earn a little money for your own."

Ruby was so enthusiastic that Myra got excited.

It was starting to get late, and Myra was exhausted. The baby had been fed and had her diaper changed. She lay down in the spare room, but despite being tired, she couldn't sleep.

She got back up and went to the kitchen for a drink of water. Ruby was doing the same.

"I can give you some tonic the doctor prescribes to help people sleep," Ruby offered, holding up a bottle of laudanum. "I brought this out of his office in case you needed help getting some rest."

"No, thank you. That stuff is dangerous." Myra finished the water. "Besides, I really want to be able to wake up and be alert in case something happens."

"We're safe here," Ruby said. "You're right about the laudanum. A lot of people get addicted to it, although I doubt if you would."

"Thanks anyway," Myra said, giving Ruby a quick hug.

She tried to lie back down, but she struggled to sleep in the unfamiliar bed. The sounds of a wagon rolling through town, people talking, and a dog barking in the distance were comforting because they let her know that help was close by, should Paul or one of his gang members show up.

An image of Leon came to her mind. She pictured his handsome face and warm brown eyes. Myra looked forward to the end of the day when they could spend time together. They sometimes played chess, and at other times, he watched her paint.

When she was with him, she knew everything in the world was right. Every time he touched her, warmth spread through her veins.

She closed her eyes and sighed.

A bolt of lightning had exploded inside her when they kissed. The kisses were gentle and brief, not like the ones she read about in her adopted mom's romance novels that she sneaked into her room. But she felt everything those women did.

Myra knew that she loved Leon. She wanted a family with him. Closing her eyes, she pictured them being together with a few more kids, with Kitten being the happy big sister, probably bossing everyone around.

She sighed and opened her eyes, staring at the ceiling. She was certain that Leon felt something for her, too. He wouldn't have kissed her if he hadn't.

Does he love me the way a man loves a wife? He acts like he does, sometimes. Other times, he withdraws into himself and puts up a wall between us. He can be hard to understand.

Unable to lie there any longer, she pulled her pencils and some paper out of the bag she'd brought with her. She tried to draw Kitten lying in her crib with her thumb in her mouth, but for once in her life, even that couldn't soothe her.

What if they get attacked by the entire gang? What if Leon gets hurt or killed?

Her heart lurched, and she mentally shook herself. Her adoptive mother always scolded her for having an overactive imagination.

He, Adam, and Sheriff Stabler will be fine.

Myra bowed her head. "Dear Lord God who art in heaven, please watch over the men as they try to capture Paul, who killed his wife and has been stealing from everyone. Kitten really needs her father, and I…well, God, you know that I need Leon, too. Adam and the sheriff need your protection as well.

THE COLORADO RANCHER'S DOORSTEP BRIDE

Thank you, God, for all you are and all you do. In Jesus' name, I pray, Amen."

Taking a deep breath, Myra felt a little better. She always counted her blessings and knew that the Good Lord always watched over her. The Bible said that if someone asked God for assistance, then they would receive help.

Still feeling restless, knowing she couldn't sleep, she quietly walked to the window, trying not to wake the baby.

She stared out into the darkness, hoping to see the three men riding up the street to tell her and Ruby that they had caught the bad man. It was hard to see through the inky black of the night because the moon was just a sliver, and clouds covered most of the stars.

Myra was startled when she thought she heard a distant cry carried on the wind, almost like a woman calling for help.

She listened intently for a few seconds, thinking she must've misheard. However, about a minute later, she heard it again.

Even though she knew she should stay in the house, she couldn't let someone be hurt if she had the chance to help her.

Myra considered waking Ruby but realized she was just as tired as Myra, and if Ruby was sleeping, she wouldn't disturb her.

She undid both locks and stepped outside onto the boardwalk. "Hello? Are you hurt?"

"Over here," the faint voice called. "I think my leg is broken. I can't stand."

Myra walked toward the voice, but she didn't see anyone. "Hello!" she called out once more. "Where are you?"

There was no answer.

Her heart sank, and a wave of dread slid down her spine. Had she been tricked?

Suddenly, loud boot steps thundered behind her. Before she could spin around and face the person approaching, something hard cracked against the back of her head.

All at once, Myra collapsed in a heap, the earth rushing up to meet her.

The world went dark.

Chapter Twenty-Nine

Leon rode toward the ranch feeling like something was wrong. He hated leaving his sister, Myra, and Kitten at the doctor's office. But he was sure they'd be much safer there. They were around people who could help at a moment's notice. Plus, they were behind a locked door. If Paul tried to break in, the women had a chance to defend themselves.

Adam might be a doctor and focused on healing people and treating injuries, including gunshot wounds, but he also wasn't a fool and had the weapons to defend himself. Both Ruby and Myra knew how to use the rifle and shotgun in the house.

Sheriff Stabler and Adam cut through the prairie and approached the homestead from the back. If Paul and his gang were watching, they would think that only Leon was at the house and would attack.

Of course, if Paul's only goal is the baby, and he doesn't see any signs that Myra is there with Kitten, he might not attack the ranch.

Leon rolled his shoulders, hating to wait for anything, let alone an attack on his ranch.

I think he really wants the child, although I don't know why. It's not like he's the paternal type. Leon sighed. *It might be his pride, or it could be revenge on Elizabeth. I doubt if he knows she's dead.*

The dogs greeted him happily upon his return. He immediately checked the barn and house. It appeared that no one had visited since they left that morning.

He made sure Sampson could get a drink, grabbed one himself, and moved the sheep to the next pasture. Leon was glad to see that the north pasture hadn't been overgrazed. It would be ready for the sheep to come back in about a month.

Adam and Sheriff Stabler were already at the house when he returned. Their horses were in the corrals. Adam had started dinner.

"We need to eat," he said as he stirred the stew. "I got a rabbit on the way down here." Adam grinned. "I even know how to make biscuits. When you're a bachelor and like to eat, you become fairly decent in the kitchen."

None of the men spoke much during dinner. They were wondering when the attack would happen.

Sheriff Stabler peeked out the window for what seemed like the millionth time, looking for any signs that they had company.

The later it got, the more unsettled Leon became. It was after midnight when he shook his head. "I don't think anyone is coming."

The thought that had been bothering him in the back of his mind started screaming at him. "If Paul is after the baby, he would have been watching Myra and Kitten, not us. I bet he's going after the women." Leon jumped out of the chair and grabbed his hat. "I'm going back to town."

Sheriff Stabler and Adam joined him. They quickly saddled their horses and rode as fast as they dared back to town. The uneasy feeling in the pit of Leon's stomach continued to grow until he was certain he was about to be ill.

They rode straight to the doctor's office. Adam ran to the door and opened it. It was unlocked.

The three men hurried inside, calling for Myra and Ruby. Ruby approached them quickly. Her hair was tousled, and her face was unnaturally pale. She wore a robe over her nightgown and was barefoot.

Her mouth was bleeding from a split lip, and she had a black eye.

"I was just fixing to get dressed and come find you." She was gasping for air. "They're gone. Myra and Kitten are gone."

Adam ran over to her and looked at her face.

"I'm okay. Paul punched me twice. He was trying to get to the baby, and I tried to stop him. The second time, he hit me hard enough to knock me down. He grabbed her and ran." She glanced at Adam, her gaze frantic. "We have to find them."

Adam wrapped his arms around her, comforting her. "We'll find them. I promise."

She looked up at him and nodded, tears shining in her eyes. Adam brushed a kiss across her lips, which Leon would have found touching if he weren't so worried about Myra and the baby.

Ruby ran into the room to get dressed, while Adam, the sheriff, and he went back outside to look for any clues.

Leon walked toward the back alley. He froze in place when he heard a sound like a moan. Drawing his gun from his holster and cocking it, he carefully moved toward the noise.

There was another faint moan, followed by a knocking sound. He was confused when he saw an old wooden barrel standing next to the outer wall of the doctor's house.

A groan and a knock reached his ears. He unlatched the barrel and gasped when he saw Myra inside it.

He quickly uncocked his gun and holstered it before lifting her out. A handkerchief tied tightly around her face gagged her. Blood matted the back of her head.

She tried to fight him until he said, "It's me, Leon. You're safe."

Myra struggled to see him. Being in the dark barrel and the blow to her head probably blurred her vision. "Leon?"

"Yes, I'm here."

"Kitten? Ruby?"

"Ruby's safe. The baby is missing."

Groaning loudly, Myra's legs buckled as they walked back toward Adam's house.

Leon let out a loud, long whistle to let the other two men know that he'd found Myra.

"I feel so stupid. If anything happens to Kitten, then it's all my fault," Myra wailed once they got her back into the house.

She sat at the kitchen table while Adam cleaned her head. Ruby walked in, fully dressed, her hair hastily pulled back in a messy bun.

"I was standing at the window watching for you men to come back when I heard a woman calling for help. I didn't think; I just went out looking for her. I wanted to help her." She swallowed a sob. "I couldn't find her, so I was going back to the house. Someone hit me with something on the back of my head. I don't remember anything else until I woke up in a barrel."

Leon clenched his fists. "It was a trap. Paul used a woman to lure you outside." He walked back and forth a few times before stopping and looking at Myra. "How long were you unconscious?"

Myra sniffled. "I don't know. I know that I went outside around midnight because the grandfather clock struck twelve. I was hit soon after." She winced as Adam dabbed at her head with a wet washcloth. "I woke up right before you found me."

The sheriff quietly stepped outside to look for any signs of Paul and anyone else who might have helped him.

Adam set the bloody cloth in the basin and began applying some ointment to the wound. "So, you were out for about half an hour. You could use some stitches, but you're right there on the cusp, so we'll see if the salve helps first. It has comfrey and yarrow in it."

Myra stood up quickly, then sat back down as dizziness overwhelmed her. "I'm not worried about me. We have to find the baby."

"You're not going anywhere. You're going to sit here and let Ruby take care of you."

Myra and Ruby looked at each other.

"Not on your life," Myra said. "If you don't let us come with you, then we'll follow. Both of us know how to saddle the horses."

"Do you have to be so dad-burned stubborn?" Leon growled.

Ruby crossed her arms over her chest. "Yes," both women said at the same time.

Sheriff Stabler came back inside. "I'm guessing this was all Paul. There's only one set of fresh tracks in the area near the barrel besides Myra's. I think he tethered his horse in front of the general store and pretended to be a woman in trouble." He looked at Myra and smiled ruefully. "He knew that if you heard him, you wouldn't resist trying to help someone."

"What if I'd been asleep and hadn't heard him?" Myra asked.

The sheriff pressed his lips together and inhaled deeply. "My guess is that he would have found a way to break in. He might have even killed you to get to the baby. He's already shown that he's ruthless and won't let anything get in the way of what he wants."

"Can you tell where the tracks lead to?" Leon asked the sheriff.

"East, as best as I could tell."

"He could be going back to the Harrington Ranch." Leon scratched his head. "Although when I stopped by the other day, it didn't look like anyone was living there. It was covered in dust." He grimaced. "There was a lot of blood on one of the beds. I'm guessing that's where Elizabeth gave birth."

Sheriff Stabler groaned. "I'd asked the midwives in the area if they'd helped anyone when I was investigating Paul. All of them said they didn't even know he had a pregnant wife."

Ruby bowed her head. "That poor woman had to give birth all alone or with just Paul helping her."

Leon clenched his hands into tight, white-knuckled fists at the thought. "Paul likely wasn't much help. As a matter of fact, he probably made the situation a lot worse." He grabbed his rifle from where he'd leaned it against the wall. "We need to get going. We're wasting time talking. Every minute we stand here, the further away he gets with Kitten."

Sheriff Stabler nodded and grabbed his shotgun. "Even though you said he hadn't been to the ranch recently, that's our best starting point. I'm not sure he'd go back to where the other gang members are hiding out with a newborn."

Adam packed some supplies into his black bag. "I'd best be prepared. Paul's already proven that he'll hurt anyone who gets in his way." He picked up his rifle.

Myra stood up and steadied herself against the table. She grabbed one of the shotguns that Adam had hanging on the wall. Ruby grabbed the rifle.

"What do you two think you're doing?" Leon asked.

Ruby narrowed her eyes. "You think that just because we're women, we can't help? I can shoot every bit as good as you can, and you can get hurt just as easily as I can."

Myra stood beside her. "Do you really think I'd let you go out searching for my baby without me coming along?"

Leon's heart skipped a beat when he heard Myra call Kitten her baby.

"I told you that if you try to go without us, we'll just follow," Ruby warned. She shifted from one foot to the other. "We're wasting time."

Adam shook his head and chuckled. "I know that arguing with your sister is like arguing with a rock. We'd best be going."

"While you are saddling your horses, I'm going to grab a few men who'll ride with us. They're deputized and always ready when an emergency comes up. We'll meet you at the ranch." Sheriff Stabler walked briskly out into the cool, inky dark night.

Myra picked up the saddle they'd brought with them earlier, but didn't protest when Leon took it from her.

"You just focus on walking," Leon said.

They went outside, saddled the two horses for the women, and mounted up.

As the four of them rode as quickly as they could toward the Harrington Ranch, Leon prayed that they would get Kitten back safely. He knew that if Paul had done anything at all to hurt the baby, and if she had the smallest scratch on her, he would rip Paul into pieces so small that there wouldn't be enough left for Adam to patch back together.

Chapter Thirty

Myra held the reins firmly in one hand and the saddle horn with the other as the horse trotted toward Harrington Ranch.

The rhythm of the horse's hooves hitting the ground made her stomach roll. She tried to focus on her breathing to keep from throwing up all over herself and Jasper.

Each thud of Jasper's hooves jarred her spine and worsened the sharp pains in her head, until she feared her skull was going to burst. She grimaced as she remembered "The Legend of Sleepy Hollow" by Washington Irving.

Only instead of a Hessian soldier running around on a horse, it'll be a headless governess or a governess with a pumpkin head.

She gingerly touched the back of her head and grimaced when she felt the sticky, bloody mess. Her head throbbed where she believed the butt of a gun had slammed into her skull. The area was tender and swollen. A pulsing pain echoed behind her eyes, in sync with her heartbeat.

Her mouth was dry, as if someone had stuffed a wad of cotton into it. She could taste metal and figured she must have bitten her tongue or cheek and drawn blood.

The sky was just starting to get light, but everything swam around her. The trees and prairie blurred together like she was looking at them through a foggy window.

It doesn't matter. The only thing that matters is getting Kitten back.

The more she thought about her baby girl in the arms of that monster, the angrier she got. Her heart thundered in her chest, and she growled in the back of her throat.

We will get her back if it's the last thing I do in my life.

After half an hour, she heard the thunder of hooves pounding behind her. She turned around and saw that Sheriff Stabler had caught up with them. He had six other riders with him.

If Paul is alone, that should be enough to get Kitten back. If there's a gang determined to fight it out, at least we have a chance.

The ride to the Harrington Ranch seemed to last forever. If Paul wasn't there with Kitten, he could be anywhere.

What's he going to do to her when she starts crying because she's hungry or she has a wet diaper? Is he going to hurt her? He doesn't have any bottles or diapers. How is he going to take care of her?

Fear for Kitten's safety started to overwhelm her. She panted, trying to catch her breath. Her heart hurt in her chest, and her stomach twisted into a terrified knot.

Stop it. You don't need to borrow trouble. You don't know that he's going to hurt her. Being emotional means that you aren't thinking clearly, which means that you could get yourself or someone else hurt.

Myra was beginning to second-guess her determination to go along with the group, but realized that she would have been a knotted mess of worry if she had stayed behind.

Finally, the homestead appeared as they reached the top of a hill overlooking the area. Myra's heart sank. There didn't seem to be any movement around the house. Paul's horse was nowhere to be seen. The barn door swung open and closed in the morning breeze, making a creaking sound that pierced her mind.

Everyone slowed their horses. Sheriff Stabler flicked his wrist, and the riders split up, surrounding the house and the barn.

He stopped next to Leon. "Something's not right. Either Paul isn't here, or it's some kind of trap."

They rode up to the house. The sheriff, Leon, and Adam swung off their horses.

Leon glanced at Myra and Ruby. "Please stay here."

Myra and Ruby looked at each other and nodded. She wasn't sure she'd be able to walk anyway. The world still felt like it was spinning around her.

The three men cautiously walked up to the house as some of the deputies crept up to the barn. At the sheriff's signal, everyone entered at once.

Myra held her breath, praying with every fiber of her soul that Kitten would be found safe and sound, none the wiser of her traumatic night.

Her heart sank with disappointment when everyone stepped out of the house and barn, looking defeated.

Leon walked over to Myra. "They weren't here. The house looks like no one has been in there for a while."

"Noooo!" Myra moaned. "They have to be here."

"We'll find her, I promise," Sheriff Stabler said. "I'll notify every sheriff and lawman in the entire state. He won't be able to travel as fast with a baby."

"What if..." Myra started.

Ruby turned around and held up her hand. "Don't even go there. There are no 'what ifs.' We will find Kitten safe and sound. There's no other option."

Leon looked at the sheriff. "Where do we go from here?"

Sheriff Stabler rubbed his beard as he was wont to do when he was thinking hard about something. After a long while, he said slowly, "Well, I heard a rumor of an abandoned ranch about a three-hour ride south from here that could be a potential hideout for the gang Paul is thought to be riding with. We can ride that way."

Adam glanced at Myra. "You're not looking well. You're pale, and your eyes are glassy. Why don't you and Ruby ride over to Leon's place and wait for us there?"

Myra opened her mouth to protest, but Adam interrupted her. "I know you want to be there when we find Kitten. Notice I said 'when.' But you aren't going to do her a bit of good if you're half-dead yourself. And, if you happen to pass out, or worse, you're only going to slow us down."

Closing her eyes for a second, Myra hung her head. She looked over at Ruby, who nodded.

Ruby smiled sympathetically at her. "I want to ride with them as much as you do, but Adam's right. You look awful."

Myra was about to agree when a lone rider appeared over the hill. Everyone turned around, not aiming their guns, but prepared to fight if the rider was hostile.

As he approached, she heard everyone muttering that they didn't recognize the newcomer.

"Don't shoot," the man said, holding up his hands in the air.

"Well, I'll be a monkey's uncle," Sheriff Stabler said. "If it isn't Aaron George. You're the last person in the world I thought I'd see riding up to a posse of sheriff's deputies."

"Good to see you again, Calvin," the newcomer said. "It's always good to run into old friends."

Sheriff Stabler raised his eyebrows. "Friends?"

Aaron tilted his head to one side. "At least not enemies. Not this time. I figured I'd find you out here looking for Paul Graham. I know where he and the baby are. The Good Lord above knows that I've done some terrible things in my lifetime, and there's likely a cozy spot in hell for me when I die, but I'll not tolerate children being hurt. Even I'm not that evil." Aaron pulled his hat off and wiped his brow with his sleeve. "Paul Graham has a mean streak in him a mile wide. I heard you found his wife, Elizabeth, and I reckon he killed her. I won't stand by and see him hurt the child, which he will when he gets tired of her squawking."

Everyone stared at the outlaw in complete silence.

"There's an old trapper's cabin on Elk Mountain, about an hour from here, that Paul likes to go to. I'll take you to him as long as you let me ride away afterward."

Everyone looked at Sheriff Stabler. He just sighed. "Aaron is a son of a gun, and I wouldn't trust him near any valuables or cattle to save my life, but I've never known him to lie. He's always admitted to the dirty deeds he's done, and the only reason he hasn't been hanged for them is because he's as slippery as an eel and has managed to break out of every jail and prison he's ever been in."

"You help me find my daughter, and I'll personally escort you anywhere you want to go," Leon offered.

"Alright. Let's go then," Aaron said.

Myra shook her head at Ruby, instantly regretting the action. "I'm not going back now."

"Are you sure? You look like you're about to keel over," Ruby said.

"Not until I know Kitten is safe." Myra smiled wanly. "Then, I'll keel over."

Ruby chuckled. "Somehow, I knew you'd say that."

The horses were exhausted, and everyone else was so tired that they could barely sit on their horses. Leon, Adam, Myra, and the sheriff had been awake for more than twenty-four hours, and Ruby had only gotten a couple of hours of sleep. Still, no one was willing to stop until they found Kitten and she was safe in their arms again.

It seemed as though they rode on forever. Her eyes were heavy and felt as though someone had poured a ton of sand in them. Her body weighed a million tons. Her throat hurt, and her mouth was dry, tasting tinny. Sharp knives slammed into her brain.

Myra knew that no one would think less of her if she turned around and went back to the house to wait for everyone, but there was no way on God's green earth that she was going to do that. As tired as she was, she'd never be able to rest, and the waiting would drive her to distraction.

Finally, Aaron stopped. "He's in a cabin due north about a quarter of a mile from here."

Then, without another word, he turned his horse and disappeared into the forest.

They rode for a few more minutes until they saw the cabin. Everyone dismounted from their horses and moved as quietly as possible toward the small, log-built structure.

Myra winced when she stepped on a twig. To her, it sounded like an entire tree toppled over in the woods. However, no one else seemed to have heard it. All eyes were on the cabin ahead of them.

They approached the cabin and saw Paul walking around, holding a candle. He wasn't holding the baby. Myra got close enough to peek into the window of the single-room structure and took a look around.

There was no sign of Kitten.

She ducked as Paul began to turn around. She gazed at Leon, her eyes filled with panic. Shaking her head, she tried to hold back a cry.

Myra's heart nearly stopped until she reminded herself that he probably set her down somewhere. It was amazing how twenty pounds could feel like a thousand if you held onto it too long.

She's likely asleep. That's why we can't hear her. She's okay. She's okay. She's okay.

Myra forced herself to breathe.

The baby is okay.

She wished that she believed what she was saying, but fear gripped her heart.

Where is she?

Sheriff Stabler walked over to them. "Adam and I are going to go in and get the baby. He might hurt her if everyone rushes in on him. He might not be as confrontational if he sees Adam, since he's a doctor." The sheriff grinned wryly. "Plus, he hates Leon."

Myra swallowed hard and nodded.

Leon wrapped his arms around her and pulled him close to her. "It's going to be okay. I'm sure she's fine. The sheriff and Adam will bring her out to us," he whispered in her ear.

The sheriff and Adam approached the front door and knocked. There was no response.

Suddenly, the back door flew open, and a figure ran out, holding a bundle in his arms. Paul apparently hadn't planned on staying long, because his horse was still saddled.

Several men ran toward the man, but somehow, he managed to mount the horse with the baby in his arms and disappeared into the woods.

Chapter Thirty-One

Leon's heart nearly stopped when he saw Paul disappear into the forest with Kitten in his arms. His breath caught in his throat.

"Let's get back to the horses!" Leon yelled.

Sheriff Stabler and Adam burst out of the cabin, and everyone ran to the horses as fast as they could.

Leon tried to ignore the sharp pain in his knee as he moved as fast as he could, holding Myra's hand, practically dragging her behind him. He knew that she had to be in excruciating pain, but there was no time to worry about that now.

"Fan out," the sheriff shouted as everyone jumped on their horses. "Circle him. Remember that he has a baby. We don't want him to hurt her."

Myra urged her horse to move as fast as he could toward the direction that she'd seen Paul going. Her jaw was clenched, and her face was drawn into a tight grimace as she followed the man who had Kitten.

The sound of the pounding hooves echoed through the trees as everyone headed deeper into the woods.

She pointed ahead as they saw Paul ducking his head under a large tree branch, guiding the horse with one hand.

Leon knew his horse couldn't go faster without risking injury to himself or Sampson. There were too many branches, brambles, roots, and holes that could cause him to break a leg.

Paul can't keep going forever. Between us and the others on his tail, we'll catch him. Besides, it seems that his old gang leader doesn't want him around.

He leaned low over Sampson's neck and felt the heavy branch hit his back as he rode under it. Leon narrowed his eyes against the sharp wind that suddenly picked up.

Kitten's face popped up in his mind. He pictured her smile and could almost hear her tiny giggle. Leon adored how she looked at him, like she knew that he loved her.

If that scoundrel has hurt one hair on her head, I swear, he won't make it to jail.

He shook his head slightly.

No, I can't think like that. I don't believe that he'd kidnap her just to hurt her. He hasn't had her long enough for her to get on his nerves, although she's likely hungry by now and needs to be changed.

Myra was just ahead of him. She'd braided her long, red hair before bed. It was swinging like a loose rope against her back as she guided Jasper through the woods.

The branches and brambles grabbed at her dress, and one of her sleeves was torn.

After a minute, she pointed ahead of her. "I can see him."

Squinting, Leon saw Paul ahead. They were slowly gaining on him. Paul's horse was lathered, and it looked as though he was favoring one of his front legs.

"He's slowing down!" Myra yelled.

Paul looked back at them, his eyes wide with panic. The man kicked his horse to go faster, but the beast was exhausted and about ready to collapse.

Suddenly, Paul veered to the right, rode a short distance, and tried to get his horse through a thicket of thorned bushes.

The horse stumbled.

Paul slid off, managing to grab his rifle as he did. He ran off into the trees, holding the firearm in one hand and the baby in the other.

The horse bolted into the woods.

Leon's heart felt as though an icy hand was clutching it when he heard Kitten's piercing scream echo through the air.

She's just hungry and scared. He won't hurt her. If we catch him, she's the only leverage we have.

Leon kept his eyes on the man's figure disappearing through the brush.

He only wants the baby for control. Paul is just angry that someone took something that he thinks belongs to him. He doesn't love her and doesn't really care what happens to her as long as someone else doesn't have her.

He took a deep breath.

That kind of thinking doesn't help. Focus.

Myra pulled on the reins and jumped off as the horse came to a sudden stop. She quickly wrapped the reins around a branch and followed Paul and the baby through the thicket.

Leon dismounted and quickly tethered Sampson, going after her.

The baby's screams tore through the air, each cry stabbing his soul like a knife.

Myra paused and looked back at him nervously before pushing even harder through the bushes. Her skirts were torn from the thorns. Blood had started to seep from her head wound again, and beads of sweat made her neck glisten in the sunlight.

They managed to make their way through the brush, and the trees seemed to close in around them. The ground was mushy under their feet from the recent rains, and his bad leg slipped. His knee hit the ground, landing squarely on a rock right in the joint. A lightning bolt of pure pain shot through him.

He said a few words under his breath and quickly stood again. His bad leg throbbed and ached, but Leon refused to let it slow him down.

Looking around, Leon suddenly couldn't breathe. The world stood still as he realized where he was. The birds stopped singing, and even the wind died down. He saw the old tree that had been snapped in half by a lightning strike. Even now, nothing grew in the earth surrounding it.

He stopped dead in his tracks, unable to move on. His legs were frozen in place, and he couldn't force one leg in front of the other. Leon hadn't been in this place for fifteen years.

Memories came rushing back and hit him squarely in the chest, almost knocking him down. All of the color drained from his face.

The sounds from that night screamed in his head. He heard his mother yelling as the wagon was washed off the road. It sounded like wood against sandpaper. Then, the horses screamed as the wagon flipped.

Leon involuntarily touched his leg as he remembered the pain he'd felt as the wagon crushed it.

His mother had been thrown from the wagon once it came to a stop. She'd hit her head on a rock, and her neck sat at a

THE COLORADO RANCHER'S DOORSTEP BRIDE

weird angle. Her eyes were opened wide with fear. She wasn't breathing.

Leon pictured his father trapped under one of the wheels. It had crushed his chest. Blood poured out of his mouth as he whispered, "Take...care...of...your...sister."

Ruby had been thrown out of the wagon and was curled up on the road. She lay unconscious in the mud, covered in blood. He ran over to her and shook her. He was so relieved when her eyes fluttered open.

Miraculously, the horses hadn't been hurt. The harness had snapped when the wagon overturned. They were standing off to the side, their eyes wide and nostrils flaring. Although his entire body was in excruciating pain, he managed to grab one of them and help his sister onto the back of the bay mare. Using the old stump as a mounting post, he climbed on behind her, and they made their way into town.

Everything replayed in his mind.

He gritted his teeth as the tears formed.

"Leon." He felt a hand slip into his, and he looked at Myra. "Leon, are you okay?"

He shook his head, and suddenly, he remembered where he was.

"Yeah, I'm fine. I'm sorry. This was where my...where my parents died, and I haven't been back here since."

Myra's eyes widened, and she bit her trembling lip. Then, she tightened her grip on his hand, her warmth grounding. "I'm so sorry," she whispered.

"I should have recognized it sooner, but it looked so different then."

Myra rubbed his arm, continuing to gaze at him with that mournful yet understanding expression.

Leon's shoulders shook, and he choked out, "I should have gotten them...my parents."

"You couldn't have," Myra said, softly. "But you did save your sister's life, even with a shattered leg. That's a lot more than most ten-year-olds could have done. You were a hero that night."

He shook his head doubtfully.

She gave him a quick hug. "You saved your sister, and now we have to save our daughter. We have to keep going. We have to find Paul and get Kitten back."

Leon looked at Myra. Her hair was messy, her eyes had dark shadows underneath, and her face was an eerie shade of white. Despite all that, she had a resolute look in her eyes, and her lips were pressed together. She had Adam's rifle strapped to her back.

"I'm glad I'm going into battle against you," he said, some of the weight lifting from his chest.

She grinned and took his hand, pulling him through the woods.

They both jerked their heads when they heard a twig snapping next to them. Leon didn't know whether to be relieved or disappointed when a few deer jumped out of the trees in front of them.

Both of them stopped when the tree line ended at the narrow road that was just wide enough for a wagon to pass. It was rutted and muddy.

They looked down one side and then the other, their heads swinging almost in unison. There was no sign of Paul.

"There," Leon pointed out.

Faint, large, fresh boot prints crossed the road and began to descend the slope. It didn't look quite as steep as it had that fateful night long ago.

"It looks like he's not running."

"No, he's trying to find a hiding spot." Leon took the first step down the slope. "Be careful. There are a lot of loose rocks here. You don't want to slip on them and break your leg."

Myra nodded but didn't say anything. She was carefully watching her step as she walked down the side of the ravine.

They had taken a few more steps when Leon gasped. Pain surged through him, causing his leg to give way. Two wagon wheels from the accident still lay on the ground. One was trapped among rocks, and the other was caught on an old root.

He stopped and stared at them, the images flooding his mind again.

"Leon, come on. We have to go," Myra said gently.

A hawk circled overhead, searching for its breakfast. A rabbit scampered in front of them.

They continued to follow the faint bootprints they saw. A little further down, they saw a large rattlesnake sunning itself on a boulder. It looked at them and shook its tail as though it was already annoyed by someone or something. They gave it a wide berth.

"Where in Hades could he be taking her?" Leon muttered as frustration welled up inside of him.

"I don't know, but I'm not stopping until we find her," Myra said through gritted teeth.

The terrain became even more treacherous as they continued walking into the ravine. Fallen trees and loose shale rock made each step unsteady as though they were walking on ice.

Leon's leg throbbed, and he knew that it was swelling up like it always did when he pushed it too far. There was still no way he was going to stop.

They stopped when they heard Kitten's cry off in the distance.

"That's her *'I want to be fed right this instant'* cry," Myra said. "Hopefully, that means that she's still okay."

Leon nodded. He pointed to a faint heel depression. "This way," he whispered.

They both understood that the closer they got to Paul, the more desperate he would become. He had the advantage because he was holding the baby. Paul was armed and dangerous. Leon was terrified that Paul would prefer to kill Kitten rather than let him and Myra take her.

The two of them moved as quickly as they could without sliding down the rest of the slope. The bottom of the ravine was still a long way off, with a lot of rocks, thorny bushes, and snakes along the way.

Kitten's cries were getting louder and louder. They rounded a jut of a large rock and spotted a cabin that was more of a lean-to than a proper shack. They could barely make out Paul's head from a busted-out board.

Just then, Kitten screamed loudly—a pained, mournful yell that chilled Leon to his bones.

Chapter Thirty-Two

Fear surged inside of Myra as the baby's scream echoed against the ravine's walls. The scream didn't just pierce her ears; it wrapped around her and squeezed until she couldn't breathe.

Myra flinched, one hand on her chest, the other gripping a tree. Her knuckles whitened as she clung to the branch as if it could save her life. She bit the inside of her cheek, forcing herself not to cry out and let Paul know they were so close.

Paul was muttering to himself as he paced back and forth. She couldn't make out what he was saying, but he was clearly agitated. He stopped every so often and looked down at something.

Myra guessed that was where Kitten was lying. She began to slowly shift her position toward that side of the structure to check if the door was there.

Leon moved beside her with his rifle in hand, slowly making his way toward the small opening in the hovel.

"Leon," she hissed. "Stop."

He didn't seem to hear her. His jaw was tightly clenched. He slowly cocked the rifle's lever, trying to make as little noise as possible.

His entire body was tense. Anger rolled off of him like steam from a kettle. He took another small step toward the cabin.

Myra panicked. Leon was a great shot, but if he missed, then Paul just might kill the baby.

She grabbed his arm.

He turned and gave her a look that made her heart stop. It was a mixture of fear, rage, and desperation.

Myra knew that he was determined not to lose another person in this ravine.

"You can't, not yet. He's not hurt her. We need to wait for the sheriff, Adam, Ruby, and other men to get here."

Her heart thrummed in her ears. The air was still and heavy, pressing against her chest. She couldn't swallow.

She put her hand to her head. The world was spiraling out of control, spinning around in circles. Darkness crowded into the edge of her consciousness as she realized that they were running out of time. Paul could blow at any time.

Pushing back the darkness and taking a deep breath, she held onto Leon's arm. He hadn't moved, which was reassuring. She knew she couldn't have stopped him if she'd tried.

Where is everyone? They should have been here by now. We weren't that far ahead of them.

Every second that ticked by seemed like an eternity.

Another scream pierced the air, followed by several whimpers.

Myra held onto Leon's arm. "He's not hurting her. She's hungry, wet, and terrified. But if we rush into that shack, he'll panic. Paul will hurt her before we can get to her."

Leon opened his mouth to argue, but Kitten cried out again.

Myra shook her head. "I know. It's killing me, too. But he's armed, and he has our baby. We just can't risk it."

He stared at her, and Myra thought he was furious with her as well. Leon wanted to break down the door and fire several rounds at Paul before the man even realized it was coming.

Finally, he nodded, and they waited, crouching behind some bushes. Every sound they made sounded like thunder cracking in the sky, and she was sure that Paul would hear them.

The shack looked as though it hadn't been lived in for several decades. It leaned to one side, and part of the roof was missing. Several boards on the side were torn away, as though a bear had wandered by and ripped them off.

Tall weeds grew around the building, and Myra shivered to think about the snakes that might be hiding in them.

Hopefully, with all the noise and commotion, the snakes have been scared off.

Myra squinted, trying to keep an eye on what was happening inside. Leon was beginning to get restless.

"I can't lose her," he muttered.

"You won't. We just have to be very smart about this."

He nodded as another shriek exploded from the shack.

Myra put her fist to her mouth and bit it. Tears exploded in the back of her eyes. Her body ached with the need to go inside, scoop Kitten up, and hold the baby close to her.

"He's coming undone," Leon said as they watched Paul stop in the middle of the shack and stare at the spot where they thought he'd put Kitten. "We can't wait much longer."

"I know," Myra breathed.

Where in the world are they? What is taking them so long to get here? We have to rescue my baby.

Myra's head jerked around when she heard a rustling in the bushes behind them. Her heart leaped, hoping it was the sheriff and the others.

Ruby crouched low and walked over to them. Her face was streaked with dirt, and she had a long scratch on her right cheek, probably from a bramble. Her dress was shredded. She dropped to her knees next to them. "Is he in there?"

"Yes, with Kitten. Where are the others?" Leon hissed.

"Coming. They're not far behind me."

The baby wailed again.

"Oh, that poor thing," Ruby muttered.

Paul stopped and stared at the spot on the floor, then started gesturing wildly.

"We can't wait anymore," Leon said, standing with his rifle on his shoulder and his finger ready to pull the trigger.

Just then, Adam, the sheriff, and the others come out of the bushes and trees.

"He's in the shack?" the sheriff asked unnecessarily.

"Yes. He's got the baby."

"Spread out." The sheriff waved his arms at everyone.

As quietly as they could, they started to surround the broken-down cabin.

Paul must have heard or sensed something because he burst out of the front door, holding Kitten in one hand and his pistol in the other.

His eyes were wide, darting around as if he was trying to figure out where everyone was. Then, he ran toward another big patch of bushes.

Leon instantly stood up and ran after Paul. His heart was beating a million miles an hour. He didn't even notice the pain in his swollen leg as he raced through the bushes and brambles.

"Spread out!" Sheriff Stabler yelled. "Find that man. He's tired, and he's got the baby. He can't go too far."

Kitten's cries were steady now, which helped Leon and the others track them.

Hopefully, Paul doesn't realize the same thing and shut her up...permanently.

Leon heard Myra and Ruby thrashing through the bushes behind him. They hit the tree line. That made it a lot easier to run. Of course, that meant that Paul could run faster, too.

"Paul, you may as well stop. You're cornered. You're not going to get away," the sheriff called out.

"They stole my child," Paul said. "I'm not the bad man here."

"Then, stop running and let me handle this." The sheriff's voice was coming from the left of them.

Leon glanced over and saw Adam heading toward Paul from the right. The rest of the men were fanned out behind them.

A thick branch whipped across Leon's face, cutting his cheek. Blood poured out of the wound as he continued to run.

Kitten's cries were just ahead of them.

Suddenly, they stopped.

Icy fear coursed through his veins. The silence was more terrifying than her screaming had been.

Leon froze, straining to hear what direction Paul and the baby might have taken. Myra and Ruby almost ran into his back.

Instinct took over, and he veered right with Myra and Ruby on his heels. Suddenly, he slowed and put his finger to his lips.

He heard a soft whimper just ahead of them. They looked through the trees and saw Paul standing beside a huge old oak, leaning against it as if he couldn't stand upright on his own.

The three of them crept softly toward him, trying not to make a sound. They were ten yards away, then eight, and then six.

Leon stepped on a twig, which snapped loudly.

Paul's head jerked toward them, and he raised his pistol, pointing it at Leon.

Leon's rifle was on his shoulder, and his finger was on the trigger, ready to squeeze if he could get a shot off without endangering Kitten.

"Back off, Sanders," Paul called out.

"That's not going to happen. You aren't making it out of this forest. You're surrounded." Leon's voice was loud, and he hoped the other men in the forest could track them. "Put the baby down. This is over."

"She's my daughter. You have no right to try to take her from me!" Paul's voice was high-pitched.

"The sheriff said he would sort that all out as soon as this ended. If she is your daughter, then the only thing you've done is attack Myra." Leon shifted so he could try to get a bead on

Paul. "We'll let that go as long as you don't do anything stupid. You kill someone...well, that's a hanging offense."

Myra stepped up next to Leon. She put her hands out imploringly. "Paul, wait. Please, put the pistol down so Leon can put the rifle down. We don't want anyone getting hurt, especially the innocent baby."

Paul's eyes darted back and forth between Leon and Myra. The baby whimpered softly in his arms.

Leon took another step toward Paul.

Myra put her hands together, almost praying. "Just give us the baby, Paul. Please."

Sweat poured off Paul's face. The sun was high in the sky, and the hot August air was suffocating. Paul's eyes were wide. He squeezed the baby tighter and pointed his pistol at Leon's chest.

Myra took another step toward Paul. He swung his arm over toward her and pulled the trigger. The bullet lodged into the tree between Myra and Ruby.

Paul's arm swung again, taking aim at Leon, who was rushing toward him. Leon dropped his rifle, leaped, and tackled Paul.

They both crashed to the ground. Paul lost his grip on the baby, who rolled out of Paul's arms.

Myra ran forward and grabbed her. She stepped back from the men fighting on the ground. Paul was desperately trying to aim the pistol at Leon.

Kitten wailed loudly as Myra clutched her tightly to her chest. "I've got you, baby. You're safe. I promise you're safe."

Myra's voice seemed to calm Kitten, who wrapped her tiny fist around Myra's collar and popped a thumb into her mouth.

Ruby stood off to one side, trying to find an angle where she could kick the gun out of Paul's hands.

Paul's face was burning red with rage. "You stole my baby," he yelled, spit flying from his mouth.

Leon wasn't going to waste his energy arguing with Paul. The other man managed to get his leg up and cracked Leon on the side of his bad knee.

Howling in excruciating pain, Leon saw stars. Paul jumped up and pointed his pistol at Leon.

"I'm going to kill you, you—" Paul started.

He pulled the trigger just as Adam jerked his arm up and disrupted Paul's aim, sending the bullet into the air.

Then, Adam slammed Paul's wrist down on his knee, making the man drop his gun.

Sheriff Stabler ran over to Paul and jerked his arms behind his back, slapping handcuffs on him. "You're under arrest for kidnapping, murder, attempted murder, assault, and anything else I can think of." The sheriff pulled Paul to his feet, making the man yelp in pain as his wrists were jammed between his shoulder blades.

Leon felt all of the tension rush out of him at once, and he fell to the ground, his leg unable to hold him up any longer.

One of the men volunteered to bring Leon's and Myra's horses to them. Ruby hurried off to get her and Adam's horses.

A couple of men helped Leon get onto his horse. Ruby held Kitten while Myra mounted and then handed the baby up to her.

"Thanks, everyone, for helping us get the baby back," Leon called out. "We appreciate that more than you could ever possibly know."

One of them returned, "We're fathers, too. We understand."

They rode off as Myra, Ruby, Leon, and Adam slowly made their way back to Leon's ranch. The ride doesn't seem so far away now that they have a very hungry baby with them.

They didn't mind her cries because they knew that Kitten was safe. She was hungry and had a soiled diaper, but that would soon be taken care of. Kitten would never remember the trauma of being kidnapped, scared, wet, and uncomfortable.

When they finally arrived, Adam helped Leon off the horse and into the house. Ruby volunteered to unsaddle all the horses, brush them down, and make sure they had snacks so Myra could take care of Kitten.

They made it upstairs to Leon's room, and he slipped off his trousers. His leg was three times its normal size.

Adam smiled. "I don't feel a lot of excessive heat, so that's a good sign. I think you just overdid it today. Let's prop it up. I'll go down and get some poultices made from comfrey, yarrow, and mixed with cold creek water."

Leon leaned back in the bed and smiled. His leg was in a lot of pain, but it was well worth it. They had their baby back, and Paul was likely going to be put in prison for a long time.

Adam returned with the poultice and some willow bark tea for the pain.

"You'll stay off your leg for at least seventy-two hours," Adam ordered. He held up his hand when Leon tried to speak. "I'll ask some of the men in town to help you out. You caught the man who's been stealing from all the ranches around here, so they'll be grateful to you."

Leon nodded. His pride didn't like having to rely on other people to take care of his ranch, but he knew that if he aggravated his leg too much, he'd be using a cane before he was thirty.

Ruby stayed on to help Myra, and the two women made sure that he stayed in bed until Adam cleared him. Finally, after five extremely long days, the doctor said he could get up and move around some, as long as he sat down at the first twinge.

That evening, Ruby went back to town with the doctor.

After Myra put the baby to bed, Leon and she sat on the porch.

He knew now was the time.

Leon took Myra's hand in his. "I don't know how to put what I want to say in a bunch of fancy words, so I'll just spit them out. I love you. Together, you, me, and Kitten—we're a family. I can't get down on one knee, and I haven't had the chance to get a ring yet. Myra, will you do me the honor of being my wife?"

For a moment, Myra was frozen. Leon's stomach twisted at the pause, but before he could worry if he'd said something wrong, her lips stretched into the brightest grin he'd ever seen.

His heart skipped a beat at that smile, and warmth rushed through his veins.

At last, with tears brimming in her eyes and her cheeks flushed pink, she said, "Yes."

Chapter Thirty-Three

The sunny sky was a bright blue, with a few white, fluffy clouds floating lazily by. It was a beautiful, warm day for the first of September.

After Leon proposed, he and Myra decided not to waste any time, and they set the wedding date for just two weeks later.

Leon stood in front of the church, his hands slightly sweaty. He wasn't nervous about marrying Myra. He was positive that she was his soulmate. He just didn't like standing up in front of so many people.

The organist started playing music, and everyone stood.

Leon looked at Myra as she slowly walked down the aisle, a simple bouquet of wildflowers in her hands.

Myra was dressed in a forest-green dress that brought out the color in her eyes. Red curls framed her face while the rest of her hair was braided and wrapped around her head like a crown. A wreath of wildflowers was woven into her hair.

The only jewelry she wore was a string of pearls that had belonged to his mother, which Ruby had given her, and the small gold ring with an emerald embedded in it that he'd bought her as an engagement ring.

She smiled at him, and it took his breath away. When their eyes met, everyone and everything else in the world disappeared for a moment.

When she reached him, she slipped her hand into his, and they faced Pastor Frank.

The pastor smiled at them and began speaking. "We are gathered here in the presence of God, and of these witnesses, to join this man and this woman in holy matrimony. Marriage is an honorable estate, instituted of God, and is not to be entered into unadvisedly or lightly—but reverently, discreetly, and in the fear of God."

Myra squeezed his hand a little, and he felt her tremble with the same excitement that he felt.

Turning to Leon, the pastor asked, "Do you, Leon Sanders, take this woman, Myra Barnes, to be your wedded wife, to live together after God's ordinance, in the holy estate of matrimony? Will you love her, comfort her, honor and keep her, in sickness and in health, and forsaking all others, so long as you both shall live?"

Leon nodded. "I do."

The pastor then turned to Myra. "Do you, Myra Barnes, take this man, Leon Sanders, to be your wedded husband, to live together after God's ordinance, in the holy estate of matrimony? Will you love him, comfort him, honor and obey him, in sickness and in health, and forsaking all others, so long as you both shall live?"

Myra inhaled deeply. "I do."

Leon slipped a small gold band on her finger. "With this ring, I thee wed."

With a trembling hand, Myra slid a gold band on Leon's hand after almost dropping it. "With this ring, I thee wed."

Pastor Frank smiled. "Then, by the authority vested in me by God and the great state of Colorado, and before these witnesses, I pronounce you man and wife. Whom God hath joined together, let no man put asunder."

They turned to face the crowd.

THE COLORADO RANCHER'S DOORSTEP BRIDE

The pastor raised his hands. "May I introduce Mr. and Mrs. Leon Sanders?"

After the ceremony, everyone gathered in the small park near the church. It seemed like the entire town had come to celebrate, and they brought plenty of food. Every woman had to hug and kiss both of them. Leon wasn't sure he could raise his arm again after shaking all the men's hands.

After everyone greeted them, he went over to the oak tree where Ruby was sitting with Kitten. The baby had slept through the ceremony and was still deeply asleep.

"She's such a good baby," Leon said.

"You know, I've heard it said that good babies make mischievous teenagers," Ruby teased.

"Nah, we'll raise her better than that."

Ruby nodded. Then, she looked at him and winked. "So, big brother, are you still mad at me for finding you a mail-order bride?"

"What do you think?"

She winked at him. "I think that I should get a job finding wives for lonely men."

Leon shook his head. "No, but I will tell you that finding Myra was the best gift you could have ever given me." He looked down at the sleeping baby. "Elizabeth, God rest her soul, gave me the daughter I didn't know I wanted, and you gave me a wife I didn't know I needed."

Ruby tilted her head to one side. "Hmmm, what else do you want or need that you don't know that you want or need so I can find you what you want or need?"

Tilting his head to one side, Leon grinned. "Have you been sipping the whiskey the good doctor keeps in his office?"

Opening her eyes wide, she shook her head very slowly. "Not me. Nope. Never."

He wrapped his arm around his sister's shoulders and kissed her cheek. "You're the best, baby sister."

Sheriff Stabler and Myra joined them. Myra sat next to Leon. Everyone looked up at the sheriff, who towered above them.

The sheriff grinned. "The heck with it. I'll sit in the grass, too." He sat in front of them. "As you know, Paul was sentenced to life, hard labor, in prison, and was sent to Colorado State Penitentiary in Canon City. He was sent to work in the quarry."

The three of them nodded but didn't speak, waiting for the sheriff to continue talking.

Sheriff Stabler pulled his hat off, ran his fingers through his hair, and put his hat back on. "Apparently, the day after he got there, Paul mouthed off to the wrong prisoner, and that night, Paul didn't come back from the quarry detail. His broken body was found on a large rock. No one saw anything, and the guards' backs were all turned at the time."

He looked at the baby and then back at Leon and Myra. "I would never wish evil on anyone, but if there was a man who deserved to lose his life, it's Paul Graham, especially since we all know he killed his wife, at least indirectly."

Myra smiled. "That means with both of Kitten's biological parents dead, there's no question about us raising her as though she were our own."

The sheriff nodded. "That's right."

"Thank you for letting us know." Myra brushed a small dark curl away from the baby's eyes. "We'll let her know how brave her birth mother was and that Elizabeth loved her enough to save her from the monster."

"That's nice." He looked at the food. "I'd better get some before the Johnson boys eat everything. I've never seen two young men who could eat as much as they can. I'm glad I'm not the one paying their grocery bill."

Myra took a deep breath. "I swear that I'll never be like my adoptive parents. Kitten will know that she is loved more than anything."

"You are the best mother anyone could ask for. You risked your life to save her from that monster." Leon leaned over and kissed her cheek. "You faced him down even when he had a gun and shot at you. That's bravery, and that's love."

Myra blushed. "I wasn't thinking about being brave. I just knew that I couldn't let anyone hurt her."

Leon looked at her and smiled. He leaned in and pressed his lips to hers. A fire erupted from deep inside him, and he knew that this woman completed him.

Ruby stood up and allowed Adam's mother to hold the baby. Mrs. Reid had been itching to hold her all day, but Ruby hadn't been ready to give her up yet.

"Everyone wants cake, and you need to open presents," Ruby declared.

Myra was delighted with everything. They'd been gifted with a couple of quilts, a hand-woven rug, a knitted shawl, fruit jars, and a set of paints for Myra.

Ruby made a list of all the gifts and who they were from so Myra could write thank-you letters later.

They ate the beautiful cake Adam's mother had made for them, and then the band started playing.

"Let's dance," Ruby said, pulling Myra and Leon to the grassy area in front of the band.

The first tune was slow. Leon put one hand on Myra's waist and held her hand with his other, placing them close to his heart.

They swayed together to the music.

Leon looked into Myra's green eyes and smiled. "Mrs. Sanders," he whispered into her ear.

"I love the sound of that," she said.

She rested her head on his shoulder as they moved together in perfect harmony. Once again, Leon thanked God for his sister's impulsive act of placing the ad for a mail-order bride in the paper—even if he had wanted to choke her when Myra arrived on his doorstep expecting a wedding ring.

After a couple of dances, Leon needed to sit down. Ruby and Adam joined them.

Ruby's eyes sparkled, and Leon knew she was excited.

Adam cleared his throat. "Leon. I've fallen in love with your sister, and I would like your blessing to ask for her hand."

Leon grinned widely. "It's about time. You two have been making eyes at each other for at least a year now. I thought I was going to have to intervene."

Ruby hugged her brother and kissed his cheek. "Thank you."

A couple of weeks later, everyone was back in the same church, going through the same wedding ceremony.

When it was over, Leon shook Adam's hand. "I'm pleased to call you my brother."

And, from the bottom of his heart, he meant it. No one else could deserve his sister.

Epilogue

Five years later

The kitchen smelled like vanilla cake and burning wood. Myra stood over a large bowl, mixing butter, powdered sugar, cream, and vanilla to make the frosting. Once all the ingredients were whipped together, she set some aside and squeezed strawberry juice to give the icing a pink tint.

She carefully spread the frosting over the yellow cake she'd made for Kitten's fifth birthday, decorating it with flowers she "painted" on using the pink frosting.

Kitten had chosen the type of cake she wanted this year. She specifically asked for two yellow cakes with strawberry jam spread between the layers and the special frosting Myra made.

Ruby sat at the table shelling peas, her belly round with her and Adam's second child. A bowl of rising dough, covered in a tea towel, was on the table next to Ruby.

Myra grinned, walked over to her sister-in-law, and wiped the smudge of flour off her cheek.

"Hey, I was saving that for later," Ruby said. "You know how those painted ladies in town do. I thought I'd try that."

Myra looked out the window at Adam, who was minding the spit. "I wonder what the esteemed doctor would say about that?"

Ruby laughed. "Honestly, I don't think he'd say anything if he thought it would make me happy. He spoils me."

Smiling, Myra nodded. "He loves you. You can see it in his eyes every time he looks at you."

"Leon is the same with you. He was so afraid of losing another person he loved that I was afraid he'd never marry anyone. Plus, he thought that he wasn't man enough for everyone because of his leg." Ruby squeezed Myra's arm. "I'm so thankful you came into our lives."

"That was all your doing," Myra laughed. "I just answered the advertisement."

A small sound from the corner of the kitchen made Myra turn around. A tiny baby boy was sleeping in the same small basket that Kitten had slept in.

His little fists were tightly holding onto the blanket. One of his feet poked out from under the blanket, and Myra gently tucked it back in.

They named him Benjamin, after Leon's and Ruby's father. Myra quickly shortened it to Benny. Ruby and Leon both protested, saying that their father hated it whenever anyone called him that.

She knelt beside him and brushed a small curl out of his face. Benny made cooing sounds but never woke up.

"I can still remember seeing Kitten sleeping in that basket. It's amazing how quickly five years have gone by, and she's so big." Myra glanced outside. "Ellen and Nathan, too," she said, referring to her and Leon's three-year-old daughter and Ruby and Adam's four-year-old son.

"I know. I still remember the first day you showed up. I wasn't sure whether Leon was going to shoot you or me first." Ruby laughed. "He should know that little sister knows best."

Myra sat in one of the kitchen chairs. "You know, growing up, I never thought I'd be here."

Ruby raised her eyebrows. "In the kitchen, or in life?"

Playfully swatting at Ruby, Myra chuckled. "Life, you silly goose. I always knew my adoptive parents never loved me. I was useful for cleaning house, cooking, and other chores, but that was it." She sighed and rested her chin in her hands. "I always dreamed of marrying for love, but I honestly never thought I'd find someone who actually would love me."

"Then along came your matchmaker. You got pulled into a life with a baby who suddenly appeared on a doorstep and a cranky man with a limp." Ruby waved her hand at the window. "Now you have a five-year-old arguing with her father about whether red and pink do go together for a party and a ton of diapers hanging on the clothesline."

Myra glanced out the window and smiled at the pink and red fabric hearts that hung on the fence from bits of twine. "Guess who won that argument?"

Ruby shook her head. "The same person who always wins arguments against her father."

Laughter floated in from the yard. Leon and Adam, pretending to be monsters, were chasing Kitten, Ellen, and Nathan around. Ellen squealed when Leon picked her up and blew little puffs on her belly.

"Kitten might be a little spoiled, but she's such a sweet girl. She always wants to take care of her brother and sister and do chores around the house. She's in charge of the chickens and gathering eggs, as well as a few other things, but I'd never treat her like I was treated." Myra watched the little girl chase after Nathan and tickle him. "She loves to read and paint, too."

"You and Leon are doing a great job with her," Ruby said. "She's a good girl." She pointed to the baby. "He's going to be the one getting into all kinds of trouble, just like his dad."

The two women laughed.

A few minutes later, Kitten ran into the house. "Are you done with the cake, Ma?"

"I am."

The little girl pressed her hands together and looked at Myra beseechingly. "Can I please, pretty please, lick the bowl?"

"What about Ellen and Nathan?" Myra asked.

Kitten held her fingers up to her mouth. "They're playing outside, so they'll never know. Please."

Nodding, Myra handed over the bowl. "Only because it's your birthday. When it's their birthday, they get the bowl."

Kitten smiled, took the bowl, and sat next to her brother. She doted on Benny, even helping change his diapers.

"He looks just like me," she announced. "But she has Pa's nose."

Ruby and Myra laughed. Leon and Myra hadn't told her about Elizabeth and Paul yet. They wanted to wait until she was just a little bit older so she'd understand.

Myra watched Kitten scrape up every bit of frosting with her fingers, carefully licking them off.

She handed the bowl back to Myra and smiled. "All done. Thank you."

"Wow, you got this cleaner than the dogs do when they lick out the bowls."

Kitten put her hands on her hips, tilted her head to one side, and said, "Who do you think taught me? Only Brigid does a better job than me." Then, she skipped outside.

Ruby and Myra looked out the window. The first wagon was pulling up into the yard.

"Are you ready for the entire town to descend upon you?" Ruby asked. "You know people around here love a party, and they don't care about the reason."

Myra nodded. "I just hope one pig will be enough."

"It should be since everyone will bring a side dish, bread, or dessert." Ruby grimaced. "You know Mrs. Johnson is going to bring her pickled beet, onion, and boiled egg salad doused in plenty of sweet and sour dressing."

Biting her bottom lip, Myra bowed her head and sighed. Mrs. Johnson was one of the sweetest women Myra had ever met. She was always the first person to lend a hand whenever anyone needed it.

Mrs. Johnson was also particularly proud of her salad and brought it for every occasion. Of course, everyone took some and found some way of getting rid of it without her knowing.

"The problem is, she always makes enough for an army." Myra sighed. "Last time, Leon and Adam had to sneak it out to the pigs when no one was looking."

"Do you think her sons eat it?" Ruby asked, looking at Myra out of the corner of her eye.

"Judging by the fact that they're both over six feet five inches tall and are built like gristmill mules, I'd say they don't turn down any food."

Leon came in a minute later. Myra looked at her husband, and her heart skipped a beat. He was so incredibly handsome, and he took her breath away when he smiled at her in that certain way he had.

He walked over and hugged her. "I suppose Kitten came in and licked the bowl, huh?"

"She did, but I saved you the spoon." Myra held up the spoon for him.

He popped it into his mouth. "You make the best frosting." Leon nodded out the window. "The Hendersons have arrived, and I'm pretty sure the Millers' wagon is coming up behind them." Leon caught Myra around the waist and brushed a kiss across her lips. "Are you ready?"

"As ready as I'll ever be," Myra said. She picked up the basket by the handle and followed her husband out the door.

Kitten was a sweet hostess. She greeted every single person who came with a smile. She shared her toys with everyone and made sure that no child was left out of the games. The Jergenson's son was very shy, but Kitten soon had him running around with everyone else.

The afternoon wore on. Everyone ate dinner—even Mrs. Johnson's salad disappeared, although Myra wasn't sure where to. Kitten opened her gifts and thanked each person prettily.

Then, as the sun began to set, Adam and Leon lit the lanterns. The band started playing.

Leon walked over to Myra, smiled, and bowed. "May I have this dance, Mrs. Sanders?"

She slipped her hand in his. "I'd be honored, Mr. Sanders."

As the full moon slowly peeked its head over the mountains and one by one the stars lit the sky, Myra and Leon swayed together in time with the music.

She looked into his eyes and smiled. "I love you."

He put his fingers under her chin. "I love you."

And not caring who saw, he lowered his lips to hers, making the world disappear around them.

THE END

Also by Nora J. Callaway

Thank you for reading "**The Colorado Rancher's Doorstep Bride**"!

I hope you enjoyed it! If you did, here are some of my other books!

My latest Best-Selling Books

#1 An Unexpected Family in Montana

#2 A Governess at His Door

#3 Sheltered by the Mountain Man's Love

#4 The Rancher's Bride

#5 Faking Their Hearts on the Trail

You can also check out **my full Amazon Book Catalogue at:**

https://go.norajcallaway.com/bc-authorpage

Thank you for allowing me to keep doing what I love! ♥

Printed in Dunstable, United Kingdom